EMILY'S
next chapter

A NOVEL

EMILY'S
next chapter

A NOVEL

ANN
SCHREIBER

www.foxpointepublishing.com/author-ann-schreiber

Library of Congress Cataloging-in-Publication Data
SCHREIBER, ANN, author.
TOWN, SCOTTY, designer.
EMILY'S NEXT CHAPTER/ ANN SCHREIBER. – First edition.
Summary: A heartfelt romance about second chances,
blending families, and finding love later in life.
Hardcover ISBN 978-1-955743-86-0 / Softcover ISBN 978-1-955743-85-3
[1. General – Fiction. 2. Family – Fiction. 3. Relationships – Fiction.]
Library of Congress Control Number: 2 0 2 5 93 5 8 3 5

First printing May 2025

Prologue

Emily

IT WAS A WINTER EVENING when I met Lily for the first time. Her father and I had only been dating for a few months, and he had decided just that afternoon that today was the day. As with any parent with a young child, Lucas had been hesitant to make the introduction. He worried about what it would mean and how it would impact Lily. He worried about Jessica's reaction, and, if I am being honest, he worried about me, too.

I remember countless late-night discussions on the phone. How would Lily react to Daddy's new friend? How would Jessica react to finding out that a new woman was in Lily's life? How would Jessica deal with learning about Lucas progressing in a potentially serious relationship?

There were so many things to consider. And for all those fears that Lucas had, I had my own. Was my heart big enough to love another child? As an empty nester with two grown children, did I want to explore a relationship involving a young child? Did I have the energy? Would she like me? Would my kids like her? How would my parents react?

The questions I asked myself were endless. It was frustrating because I had no answers. I had no crystal ball to help me look ahead at what would happen, not just at that first meeting but in the days and weeks to follow.

But as we explored these feelings and emotions, one thing was clear—talking and thinking about Lily was doing something to me. It opened my heart, not necessarily to love another child but to Lucas. Seeing his love and concern for his child was something extraordinary. And I was feeling it so deeply. Here was a man who carried so much love for the people in his life despite all his past and present responsibilities. His fears were not just about his happiness but about everyone around him. But mainly about Lily, his only child.

Coming out of a marriage where my own children's father had betrayed me—and, ultimately, betrayed them—I was nervous. I'd lived through a relationship that had felt like a promise broken. And here I was, even though it was still quite early, contemplating the beginning of a new one, with a man whose commitment to his daughter was front and center in every word and every hesitation. In a way, that frightened me more than any question about Lily or Jessica, or even about my own readiness. Because in Lucas, I saw a love I hadn't had in years, maybe ever.

I tried to tell myself that I was prepared for the worst—that I could go into this introduction with low expectations, treating it as just another casual evening in case things fell apart. But the truth was, my heart was already cracking open in ways I hadn't expected. Part of me was terrified that Lily wouldn't like me, that she would feel my presence as an intrusion into her precious, small world. That she would feel threatened, still far too young to understand the relationship between a man and a woman—especially a relationship where that woman was not her own mother.

In the days leading up to that evening, I found myself reflecting on my own children, Sarah and Jake, and the earlier days of raising them. The ache of those memories surprised me; I hadn't realized how much I missed having children in the house until Lucas and I began discussing Lily. My days with Sarah and Jake had been filled with small routines and big dreams, but more than anything, with a sense of purpose that was comforting and steady, if not always easy. They were my life's work, my heart walking around outside my body. They were my biggest source of joy. My biggest source of fear. My biggest source of worry. And yet, the most prized relationships in my world.

And now they were grown, with lives and dreams of their own. But that purpose had stayed with me, buried under the daily routines of life, waiting for something—or someone—to awaken it.

And then there was Jessica. Although I had yet to meet her, she had become a presence in my life. I wondered what kind of mother she was and how she and Lucas had handled their separation and, ultimately, their divorce. Despite their differences, Lucas spoke of her with respect and gratitude in most cases, though I always suspected a layer of hurt lying not too far below the surface. To be honest, that vulnerability that he displayed from time to time only made my affection for him grow stronger. It showed his humanity and his ability to show his true feelings.

That said, I admired that he took the high road and did all he could to portray the mother of his child in such a good light despite what might have happened between them. It would have been easy for him to criticize and frame her in a way that made him look like the hero. But that wasn't Lucas. He was the kind of man who took his share of the responsibility and saw co-parenting as a partnership rather than a competition.

But even with all his assurances, I couldn't help feeling uneasy. I knew enough about mothers to know that Jessica would be watching, assessing, and looking for signs of threat or instability. And I wanted, so deeply, for her to see me as safe. Not as a replacement or competition, but someone who might make her daughter's life a little brighter, someone she could trust. I felt that desire, which only made the upcoming meeting more worrisome. It kept me awake at night—a cruel gift to my already lingering insomnia.

But on that winter evening, when Lucas called and asked me if I was ready to meet Lily, I stared at Lucas's name on my screen for a long moment before picking up the call. It wasn't like I knew why he was calling. How could I? We hadn't planned to see each other that night because I knew it was his week with Lily. And I knew he'd call after he'd put her to bed—a ritual that had become one I could count on, night after night on those evenings that we would not spend together.

That evening, my house was quiet, the stillness that settles in during winter. And with no one home but me, what sound or energy could there be? That stillness and quiet seemed to amplify the anticipation and the uncertainty swirling in my chest. But deep down, there was a warmth—a small but growing confidence. And I answered the phone. It was as though my subconscious knew what the call would entail. It was his invitation. It was time to meet Lily. And my answer came without hesitation—yes. I knew I wanted this for reasons I couldn't quite articulate. And so, despite the questions and nerves, I said goodbye for now, put on my shoes, turned off the lights, grabbed my coat and handbag, and headed out the door.

When I arrived at Lucas's home, I felt my heart racing, a nervous thrill mingling with the quiet sounds of his neighborhood. The front door opened before I reached it, and there he stood, grinning that familiar, gentle grin. He leaned in for a light kiss and then stepped aside so I could come in from the cold.

Lily was playing on the floor with a dozen or so stuffed animals. She had them lined up in rows, clearly playing teacher. Her stuffies were the students. It took my mind back, so many years to when Jake used to line all his toys up in a row. I shook my head, pushing that memory away. Tonight was about Lily.

I knelt to her level, introducing myself as "Daddy's friend, Emily." She looked at me for a long moment as if trying to gauge my intentions. It struck me how perceptive children are, how their intuition often surpasses ours. Lily didn't say much, only nodded slightly and continued to watch me. Slowly, she reached out and grabbed her father's hand—was it a lifeline? Was this going to be over before it started? I worried that this was a bad sign, and I took a step backward, my eyes quickly searching out Lucas's face.

But before his eyes could meet mine, I noticed him give her a gentle tug. She had reached out to stand, clearly something made easier by her father's strength. Once standing, she seemed to relax a bit. And after looking me up and down, I noticed the corners of her lips turn up just a bit. Was it a smile? I wasn't sure, but I quickly assured myself it was not a frown, and what happened next was not what I expected. "Do you like Candyland?" she asked me.

We spent the evening together, just the three of us, sharing stories and laughter. And, of course, Lily won every round of this beloved childhood game. At one point, Lily looked at me and asked, "Will you be coming back again?" It was a simple question, but it felt monumental. But was it monumental good or monumental bad? I couldn't be sure. I could feel Lucas's gaze on me, waiting as if he, too, wanted to know my answer. It was then that I realized this was definitely a 'monumental good.' At that moment, I realized that saying yes to Lily wasn't just about being with Lucas. It was about accepting a role I hadn't anticipated but one that had the potential to be extraordinary.

"Yes," I replied softly.

That night, as I left Lucas's house and stepped into the cold, crisp air, I felt a strange mix of fear and elation. I knew I had crossed a threshold that didn't just lead to Lucas but to a future that would be filled with uncertainties and, hopefully, with love. As I drove home, the questions in my mind seemed quieter, replaced by a sense of calm determination. I didn't know where this path would lead, but I knew I was willing to walk it one step at a time.

Looking back, I realize that was the night everything changed. That was the night I met Lily, not just as Lucas's daughter but as a child who would soon claim a place in my heart. And it was the night I allowed myself to hope again, to imagine a life where trust and love could coexist without fear.

1

Emily

IT'S BEEN A FEW DAYS since I met Lily for the first time, but her image had become ingrained in my mind. Her red sweatpants with a matching hoodie. Her wide, curious eyes. The soft way she clung to Lucas's hand, half-shielding herself from me while still leaning in just enough to make me hope she liked what she saw.

I hadn't expected her to stay with me the way she had, to occupy my thoughts so completely. I kept replaying the evening in my head, searching for hidden meanings in her small, simple gestures. The way she studied me, her eyes staying there a little longer each time I spoke. The quiet but determined question: "Will you be coming back again?" That question had struck something deep within me, leaving a small but profound ache behind.

The truth was, I wasn't sure how to answer her—at least not the answer I gave myself. My heart had been torn apart before, and while I'd stitched it back together over the years, it felt fragile still. That first meeting with Lily had been beautiful, yes, but it had also cracked something open in me, exposing fears I thought I'd buried long ago.

In the last few days, I've done more thinking than writing, which was a problem. My manuscript was due in six weeks, and the cursor blinking at the top of my laptop screen seemed almost accusatory. I'd spent hours sitting at my desk, staring at my latest story—a book about a young boy named Caleb who was trying to figure out life after surviving a cancer diagnosis. It was a story I had loved crafting with both tears of joy and tears of hope. One I'd poured months of energy into. But now, my connection to Caleb felt strained and distant. I couldn't help but think about Lily instead.

Whenever I tried to write Caleb's next chapter, I saw Lily's little hand reaching out to Lucas, her absolute trust in him. I imagined what it might feel like to be the mother in my story, desperately trying to fill the void left by her husband, knowing she would never be able to replace, fully, what had been lost. The parallels unsettled me and made me feel exposed. Meeting Lily had stirred something in me that I hadn't expected—a longing, not just to love but to be loved in return.

My ex-husband's voice surfaced in my mind, sharp and uninvited. "You'll never be enough for anyone else," he said during our final arguments. Back then, I believed him. I'd spent years trying to be enough—enough as a wife, enough as a mother, enough as a woman. I had built a life around him, our marriage, and our children, only to discover that he had built a second life without me. All of this had been like a cold, hard slap to the face, leaving me gasping for breath and questioning everything I had thought was solid in my world.

I left him not long after that fight, packing his bags for him with shaking hands and a heart that felt too heavy to carry. I still remember when he walked in the door that last night and saw all of his things laid out, ready for him to take. He was irate, for sure. But without looking at me, he took his things, loaded them into his truck, and then he was gone.

The decision hadn't come easily. I remember sitting in the quiet of the house we had built together, the memories pressing in from every corner. The laughter of our children. The late-night conversations over cups of coffee—decaf for me, but fully loaded for him—the caffeine never seemed to keep him from sleeping. The promises we'd made when we were young and naive had seemed enough to carry us on through forever.

Walking away from all of it had felt like walking away from myself. But staying in a loveless marriage would have meant losing even more. In the end, I chose to end things because I had to. For my own well-being, for my own survival. And though it took years, I'd learned to find pieces of myself again, rebuilding who I was outside of him.

Now, years later, I had Lucas. And perhaps Lily, too. They were a package deal. And the quiet, growing hope that maybe, just maybe, I could be part of something good again. But the scars from my first marriage hadn't faded. They whispered warnings to me now, reminding me of what it felt like to give your whole heart to something only to have it shattered.

I leaned back in my chair, running my fingers over the keyboard without pressing any keys. My home office was quiet, save for the occasional rattle of the furnace kicking on. My desk, usually a place that inspired the best in my creativity, felt cluttered and oppressive. My manuscript was open on the screen with Caleb frozen in a moment of uncertainty. I sighed, shutting the laptop gently and picking up the mug of lavender tea that had long since gone cold.

Maybe I just needed time—time to process everything, time to figure out where this road with Lucas and Lily was leading me. I was used to writing about young people finding themselves, overcoming obstacles, and working through life's messy realities. But when it came to my own story, I felt as lost as Caleb.

A soft knock on the door broke my thoughts. I turned to see Sarah poking her head in, her warm smile a welcome sight.

"Hey, Mom. Thought I'd see if you wanted to grab lunch," she said, stepping inside and glancing at my desk. Her brow furrowed. "You're not writing?"

"I'm... thinking," I replied, offering her a weak smile. "What are you doing here?"

"I was in the area and wanted to surprise you, " she said, then crossed her arms, tilting her head in that way she always did when she knew I wasn't being entirely honest. "Thinking about Lucas and Lily?"

I laughed softly. "You know me too well."

"Of course I do," she said, leaning on the edge of my desk. "And I know that meeting Lily probably stirred up a lot for you. But, Mom... you don't have to have all the answers right now."

I nodded, grateful for her words, though they didn't erase the questions swirling in my mind. "I just... I want to do this right. For Lucas. For Lily. For all of us."

Sarah reached out, squeezing my hand. "You will. I know you will."

Her confidence in me was so solid, so unquestioned, but it also made me wonder: Could I really trust myself to step into this new role, to be the partner and stepmother they needed should the relationship get that far? And more importantly, could I trust myself to let them in?

As Sarah and I headed out for lunch, something we tried to do together at least once a month, the cold winter air nipping at our faces, I couldn't help but feel that my story with Lucas and Lily was just beginning. And I simply had more questions than I had answers.

2

Lucas

A FEW DAYS HAD PASSED since Emily came to the house to meet Lily, but the memory of the evening seemed like the aftertaste of a strong drink—warm and comforting, yet stirring something deep inside me I couldn't quite name. I couldn't stop replaying it in my head: the way Emily had knelt to Lily's level, speaking softly, carefully, like she had a delicate secret to share. The way Lily had stared at her, her wide eyes filled with curiosity and maybe just a hint of uncertainty. Then, Lily asked the question after they had finished several rounds of Candyland and when it was time for Emily to head back home. It was a question that had struck me straight in the chest: "Will you be coming back again?"

It was such a simple question, but its weight wasn't lost on me. For Lily, the people who came into her life and those who left were everything. I'd seen her excitement when a new teacher joined her school and her tears when a beloved babysitter moved away. At seven years old, her world was small but intensely meaningful. If someone made it in, they became a part of her foundation. And Emily? I wasn't sure if she'd realized it yet, but Lily had already let her in.

That realization had brought a tangle of emotions. On one hand, I felt relief that Emily had handled the meeting gracefully and that Lily had warmed to her as much as she had. But on the other hand, there was a gnawing doubt. What if I was wrong? What if this was all moving too fast? What if, after everything Lily had already been through, I was making a mistake by letting someone new into her life?

I hadn't felt this conflicted since Jessica and I split. Even now, nearly two years later, I wasn't sure if I'd made peace with it. I'd held on to the idea of reconciliation for so long after our separation. I had been hopeful that we could somehow find our way back to being a family again for Lily's sake, if not our own. I'd imagined us sitting at the dinner table together, laughing about something Lily had said at school—she had started second grade this year—putting her to bed and watching a movie like we used to in the early days. I wanted that for her so badly—a sense of normalcy and stability. I wanted Lily to have that nuclear family.

But wanting something and making it work were two very different things. The last few years with Jessica had been hard, not because we didn't care about each other, but because we seemed to have lost something between us. The spark, the connection—whatever made two people more than great co-parents—was gone. And the more I thought about it, the more I wondered if it had ever truly been there.

I sighed, running a hand through my short hair as I sat at my drafting table, surrounded by the chaos of my latest project. The blueprints for a new boutique restaurant lay before me, half-finished sketches and notes scattered across the surface. I loved this part of the process—the brainstorming, the creativity, and the challenge of designing spaces that felt unique and personal. It was what drew me to architecture in the first place: the idea that a building could tell a story and bring on a feeling. I'd built a career working with mom-and-pop businesses, the kind of places that needed to stand out in a sea of big-box chains. Each project felt like a puzzle, and I thoroughly enjoyed finding the perfect solution to set the owners-to-be up for success.

But today, my focus was shot. I leaned back in my chair, staring at the ceiling, my thoughts drifting back to Emily. Meeting her had changed something in me, too. She wasn't just kind and thoughtful—though she was definitely both of those things. She was steady in a way I hadn't realized I needed. She listened, really listened, and when she talked about her own kids, there was a warmth and pride in her voice that just felt so good to hear. After years of feeling like something was missing, Emily had walked into my life and filled the space so effortlessly that it scared me.

"Daddy?"

Lily's voice pulled me from my thoughts. I turned to see her standing in the doorway, holding a stuffed bunny by one ear. She was wearing her favorite pajamas, the ones with tiny polar bears on them, and her hair was a tangle of curls from her bath.

"What's up, sweetheart?" I asked, gesturing for her to come closer.

"Can we call Olivia before bedtime?" she asked, climbing onto my lap without waiting for an answer.

I laughed. "You just saw Olivia yesterday."

"I know, but I forgot to tell her about the new book Miss Harper read to us at school." Her eyes lit up as she launched into a description of the story, and all my worries faded for a moment. This was what mattered. This was what I was fighting for.

Lily and I had ended up at Cole's house the previous night after dinner. He'd invited me over for drinks, and I needed the distraction. We'd been best friends since middle school, when his family moved to Minnesota from Oregon, and over the years, our friendship had been one of the few constants in my life. Cole's wife, Rebecca, greeted us at the door with a warm smile before retreating to the living room, where Olivia was waiting to play school with Lily and their stuffed animals. I could hear their giggles start up immediately as I joined Cole in the kitchen, grabbing a beer from the fridge and settling onto one of the barstools.

"So," Cole began, leaning against the counter with a knowing look. "How'd it go with Emily?"

"Straight to the point, huh?" I asked, rolling my eyes. But that was Cole. He didn't waste time, and I appreciated that about him.

"Come on, man. I've been waiting all week to hear about this. And Rebecca keeps pushing me to have her come over the next time with you and Lily. She won't let up about it."

I laughed. That sounded just like Rebecca. "The evening went... well. Better than I expected. Lily liked her. Asked if she was coming back."

Cole raised an eyebrow. "That's a big deal."

"Yeah," I said, taking a sip of my beer. "It is."

"And you're freaked out."

I sighed. "I'm not freaked out. I'm... cautious."

"Dude, you're freaked out," Cole said, laughing. "Look, I get it. You're worried about Lily. And Emily. And yourself. But you've been walking on eggshells for the last two years, trying to make everything perfect for Lily. At some point, you have to trust yourself, man. You're a good dad. You'll figure this out."

His words stuck with me as the night went on, even as we shifted the conversation to hockey scores and summer fishing plans. I couldn't deny that he was right. I'd spent so much time second-guessing myself, trying to be everything for Lily, that I'd forgotten how to take risks for my own happiness. But Emily? She was worth the risk. I just had to figure out how to let myself believe it.

3

Emily

THE PAST WEEK HAD BEEN A BLUR of words—though not nearly enough of them had made it into my manuscript. Since meeting Lily, my focus had been fractured - my thoughts tugged in too many directions at once. Poor Caleb still sat frozen in the middle of a scene I couldn't seem to finish. I'd been staring at that blank space between paragraphs for days, unsure how to guide him forward. It wasn't Caleb's fault. It was mine. My mind kept wandering back to Lily and how she'd asked if I'd be coming back.

I hadn't seen Lucas since that night, either. Between his work projects and my desperate attempts to catch up on my book, we'd been limited to a few texts and our regular evening phone calls. I had missed him, more than I cared to admit. It was still such a new feeling to be missing a man. In fact, I couldn't remember the last time I had missed Andrew, my now ex-husband. But tonight was date night, and I was determined to put everything else aside and enjoy it.

As I slipped on my favorite earrings, I couldn't help but smile at my reflection. These nights were our little ritual, a way to carve out time for each other even though life seemed to keep throwing hurdles and roadblocks, preventing time with one another. But as I smoothed the front of my dress and added a spritz of perfume, my mind wandered to the very first time I met him.

It still made me laugh. That night, I had been at a dive bar, of all places—a spur-of-the-moment decision after weeks of chatting on the dating app, endless texts, and nightly phone calls that often lasted far too late. I'd been cautious, of course. You can't be too careful these days. I'd done my homework—thoroughly. I'd even run a quick background check on him, which Lucas had found both amusing and perfectly understandable when I confessed it later.

But we'd both been so busy that scheduling an actual meeting felt impossible until that one Friday. Out of nowhere, I suggested we just stop overthinking it and meet. Right then. That night. To my surprise, Lucas agreed immediately.

"Why not?" he'd responded.

I pulled up Yelp on my phone and started scrolling for a spot between where we lived. I saw the name and description of a classic-style American bar and grill. It sounded casual and unpretentious—perfect for a first meeting. I texted him, "How about this place?"

"Works for me. Let's do it," he replied.

The Yelp description had been far too generous. The place was dimly lit, sticky in that way only old bars can be, and smelled faintly of stale beer and fried food that should have been thrown out hours ago. My chicken was overcooked, Lucas's burger was limp and uninspiring, and the server barely remembered we existed. But none of it mattered - not even a little.

I remember the moment he walked in, and I realized how handsome he was in person. He had this calm confidence about him that immediately put me at ease. He spotted me right away and smiled—a real smile that reached his eyes.

"Emily?" he asked, his voice familiar from all our phone calls.

"Lucas," I replied, standing to shake his hand. What else was I to do? A kiss seemed a bit too forward, even though I felt as if I already knew him.

From the moment we started talking, everything else faded away. It was effortless, the way the conversation flowed. We talked about everything—work, kids, food, travel, even the little things, like our mutual dislike of cilantro. I laughed so much that night. I hadn't realized how much I needed to laugh like that again.

Before we knew it, the server came over, clearing his throat awkwardly. "Sorry to bother you, but we're closing up."

Lucas looked at his watch, his eyes wide. "It's midnight? Really?"

I laughed, shaking my head. "I guess we lost track of time."

Outside, as we walked to our cars, he stopped and gently touched my arm. "I'd really like to see you again," he said, his voice quiet but sure.

I'd felt my heart flutter in a way it hadn't in years. "I'd like that too," I'd said.

Now, as I adjusted my necklace and grabbed my purse, I thought about how far we'd come since that dive bar. Thankfully, we were now a bit more cautious about what restaurants we picked for our nights out.

Lucas had picked an Italian restaurant a few towns over, one I had been wanting to try ever since I read about their famous wine pairings. I loved trying new places, and though Lucas was perfectly content with a sports bar and a burger, he always indulged me. He always laughed when he saw my face light up when we walked into a new spot.

The hostess led us to a cozy table near the back when we arrived. The dim lighting and conversation around us created a warm, intimate atmosphere. I took a moment to absorb the surroundings— the flickering candlelight, the clink of wine glasses, the rich scent of garlic and fresh basil hanging in the air. Lucas watched me with a small smile, the kind that made me feel like I was the only person in the room.

"You're already in love with this place, aren't you?" he teased as I picked up the menu.

"Maybe," I admitted, grinning. "But the night is young."

He laughed, unfolding his napkin and leaning back in his chair. "Well, let's hope they live up to your high expectations."

The waiter arrived to take our drink orders, and as Lucas asked for a beer—no surprise there—I ordered a glass of their house Chardonnay. Once we were alone again, I found myself leaning forward, eager to talk about the one thing lingering in both of our minds: That first meeting with Lily.

"So," I began, swirling my glass of water, "How's Lily been? Has she mentioned anything about... You know?"

"You mean you?" he asked, raising an eyebrow. "Only about a dozen times. She keeps asking when you'll be back."

I felt a warmth spread through me, a mix of relief and something more profound. "Really?"

"Really," he said, his expression softening. "She liked you, Emily. I could see it that night. And honestly, it was a huge weight off my shoulders."

"That's good to hear," I said, taking a sip of water. "I just... I don't want to rush anything. I know how important this is—for both of you."

Lucas nodded, his fingers drumming lightly on the edge of the table. "I've been thinking about that, too. I want to give you more time to get to know her, but I also want it to feel natural, not forced. Jessica and I have an every-other-week arrangement, starting Sunday nights. Maybe we can plan something for next week while she's with me."

"An outing?" I suggested. "Something where she's not just at home?"

"Exactly," he said, smiling. "And Sarah had mentioned she'd love to join us if we plan something. Maybe we can have her join us? She seems excited about all of this."

I couldn't help but smile at the mention of my daughter. Sarah had been so supportive ever since Lucas and I started dating four months ago. From the moment I told her about him, she'd been supportive. She'd met Lucas a few times already, and she had put him at ease each time.

"Sarah's been amazing," I said, my voice soft. "I don't know what I'd do without her."

"She's great," Lucas agreed. "She's so put together—and she's so open and welcoming. I think Lily's going to adore her."

I nodded. "Jake's a little more reserved," I added, the thought of my son bringing a different type of emotion to the surface. "He likes you, don't get me wrong. But he's... protective. Always has been."

Lucas smiled knowingly. "That's not a bad thing. I get it. He wants to make sure you're okay."

"And I think he's still adjusting to the idea of me being in a relationship," I admitted. "Before you came along, I was pretty set on being an empty nester. I was excited to pick up some new hobbies and spend more time with my friends. I think he's worried that I'm giving all of that up."

"Are you?" Lucas asked, his tone a bit wary.

"No," I said quickly. "At least, I don't think so. My life feels… fuller now since I met you. But I can see where he's coming from. I just need to show him that this doesn't mean I'm losing myself. If anything, I think I'm finding parts of myself I didn't even know were missing."

Lucas reached across the table and placed his hand over mine. "I think you're doing an incredible job, Emily. With your kids. Your books. With everything."

I squeezed his hand, feeling the meaning of his words settle into me. "Thank you," I said, my voice barely above a whisper.

The waiter arrived with our drinks, and we spent the next few minutes perusing the menu, the conversation shifting to lighter topics. Lucas told me about a particularly challenging project he was working on—a boutique bakery that wanted a design as unique as its pastries. I loved listening to him talk about these projects and how he wanted to do his part in helping set these small businesses up to be successful.

As the evening went on, I felt calm. This was what I'd been missing during those long, quiet years after my divorce—connection, laughter, the unpretentious joy of sharing a meal with someone who cared. Lucas had a way of making everything feel lighter. Easier.

By the time we left the restaurant, I knew one thing for sure: I wanted to be part of this. I wanted to be part of his life, of Lily's life, of the future we were starting to imagine together. I knew it was early, and I had only met Lily once. However, the way I felt when I was

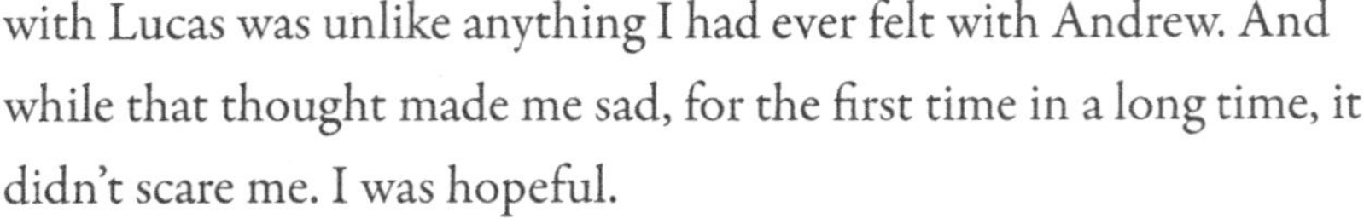

with Lucas was unlike anything I had ever felt with Andrew. And while that thought made me sad, for the first time in a long time, it didn't scare me. I was hopeful.

4

Lucas

SATURDAY MORNINGS were usually slow and easy around our house, a chance to truly savor breakfast and enjoy the quietness of the weekend. But today, the air felt charged with anticipation—at least for one of us.

Lily sat at the table, swinging her legs back and forth as she munched on a piece of toast spread with butter—her favorite breakfast. She was already dressed in her favorite overalls, a polka-dot long-sleeved T-shirt peeking out beneath the straps, and a pair of pink rain boots that were completely unnecessary indoors but perfect for our plans this afternoon.

"Daddy," she said between bites, "do you think I'll get to hold more than one baby goat? What if they're really wiggly?" She paused for a second, mid-bite. "Do baby goats bite?"

I chuckled, leaning against the counter with my coffee in hand. "I think you'll do just fine, kiddo. You've got a knack for animals. And yes, baby goats bite. But if you are gentle, they won't feel the need to."

"Like when we fed the ducks at the lake?" she asked, her eyes lighting up at the memory.

"Exactly," I said. "You were the duck whisperer that day. I'm sure the goats will love you just as much."

Her excitement was bubbling over in the way it always did when she was looking forward to something new. And honestly, I couldn't blame her. A nearby goat farm with baby goats, goat-milking demonstrations, and an afternoon with Emily and Sarah? It sounded like the kind of day I wished I could have had at her age.

As Lily finished her toast and milk, I let my thoughts drift back to the past week. It had been good—really good. After our dinner at the Italian restaurant on Friday night, Emily and I spent Sunday at the Mall of America, exploring Nickelodeon Universe like a couple of kids ourselves. We screamed through the roller coasters, tried our luck at midway games, and shared a massive funnel cake that we absolutely did not need but enjoyed anyway.

It had felt easy with her, as though we could shed the burden of responsibility and just be. That's what I loved about being with Emily—she brought out a version of me that I hadn't seen in years.

The rest of the week had been quieter. Late-night phone calls after Lily went to bed had become the norm; our conversations ranged from her book-in-progress to my latest project and where things were with the bakery. I told her how I'd recently received a call from a small business owner looking to design a tree-house experience for their bed-and-breakfast, and Emily was fascinated. I had a feeling we would be one of the first couples to book a night.

No matter what I had to say, she listened with a genuine interest that made me feel seen and understood.

She had told me how Caleb, the boy in her story, was finally starting to feel more real again, though she admitted it was still slow going. She had recently connected with an oncologist who had agreed to review the book as a beta reader to ensure she had everything accurate. It interested me how much thought and care she put into her storytelling. I wasn't much of a reader and had not thought about what went into writing a book. I quickly learned that there was far more to it than I thought.

"Do you think Emily's going to like the goats?" she asked, turning to face me with a purple scrunchie in one hand and a pink one in the other. I jolted a bit at the sound of Lily's voice, having found myself lost in memories of my recent time with Emily.

"I think she's going to love them," I said. "And I bet Sarah will, too."

Lily nodded, satisfied, before holding up the scrunchies. "Which one should I wear?"

I pretended to study them carefully, as if the decision were of monumental importance. "Hmm. Tough call. But I think the purple one's got goat-farm vibes."

She laughed, rolling her eyes in that exaggerated way only kids can pull off. "Goat-farm vibes. You're so silly, Daddy."

"Hey, I'm just trying to keep up with the trends," I said, ruffling her curls as she tied her hair back. I then noticed the confused look on her face, and my mistake became obvious—what seven-year-old knows what a trend is? But she didn't ask for any clarification, so I left it to her imagination.

As we got ready, I couldn't help but feel my nerves start to twitch. Today was the first time Lily would spend extended time with Emily outside of our home, and it was the first time Sarah would be part of the mix. I knew Sarah adored her mom and had been nothing but supportive about our relationship, but there was always that little voice in my mind, wondering if today's outing would go as well as I hoped.

On the other hand, Lily seemed fine and ready to go. She chattered away about the goats as we packed her backpack with the things she would need for the day—water, snacks, and her little sketchpad. She loved to draw animals, and I had no doubt the goats would inspire a masterpiece or two.

"Do you think we'll see a goat that's black and white? Like the ones in my picture?" she asked, holding up a drawing she'd done earlier that week.

"Could be," I said. "But you never know. There might be some brown ones, maybe even some with spots."

"Spots would be cool," she said thoughtfully. "I bet Emily would like a spotted goat. And the goat would match my shirt," she said, looking down at her polka dots.

"I bet you're right," I said, smiling. "She's going to have a great time with you, you know."

"You think so?"

"Absolutely," I said. "She told me she's really excited about today. And Sarah, too. They both can't wait to spend time with you."

Her face lit up at that, and the twitching in my nerves subsided just a bit for a moment. This was what mattered—making sure Lily felt loved, supported, and surrounded by people who cared about her. And Emily was part of that now, whether I'd fully wrapped my head around it or not.

By the time we headed out the door, Lily was practically bouncing with excitement, her backpack slung over her shoulders and her rain boots squeaking against the porch steps. As we got into the car, she turned to me with a grin that was equal parts mischief and joy.

"Do you think the goats will try to eat my hair?"

I laughed, shaking my head as I started the engine. "Only if it smells like hay."

"Daddy!" she squealed, dissolving into giggles.

5

Sarah

THE SMELL OF LAVENDER filled the air as I wiped down the counter, tidying up before heading out for the afternoon. Eunice, one of my clients, loved lavender—her diffuser was always on, filling her small kitchen at the assisted living center with a scent that was somehow calming and invigorating. It reminded me of my mom, who had a penchant for lavender tea while working on her books. I'd spent the morning helping Eunice sort through family photos, listening as she reminisced about her younger years with a sparkle in her eye that reminded me why I loved this work.

There was something about being with older adults, about hearing their stories and feeling the perspectives of their lives in the spaces they occupied, that filled me with purpose. Mom always said I had the patience of a saint, but I didn't think of it that way. For me, it was just... right. Helping people feel seen and valued in a world that often overlooked them felt like the least I could do.

I glanced at the clock and realized I needed to get going. Today wasn't just about work—it was about family. I'd been looking forward to this outing all week since Mom called to tell me about her and Lucas's plan to take Lily to a nearby goat farm. I was still adjusting to the idea of Mom dating someone with a young child, but I couldn't deny how happy she seemed these days. And if Lily was part of that happiness, then I wanted to be part of it, too.

As I headed home to change, my thoughts wandered back to the last five years and how much had changed for all of us.

When my parents separated, I was starting college. I'd known their marriage wasn't perfect, of course. I'd seen the silences that stretched too long, the arguments that simmered just below the surface. But knowing something is coming doesn't make it hurt any less when it finally arrives.

Jake and I handled the divorce differently. He retreated, throwing himself into his last few years of high school and his friends, barely speaking about what had happened. I took the opposite approach. I became Mom's shadow, calling her every day and driving home on weekends to make sure she was okay whenever I could get away. It wasn't just about her—it was about me, too. Watching her pick up the pieces and start over taught me more about strength than I ever expected.

When I got married last year, I carried those lessons with me. Mom's resilience inspired me to build a marriage based on honesty, communication, and refusing to let the small stuff fester. Michael and I weren't perfect, but we were a team, and I loved the life we were creating together.

Still, I hadn't expected Mom to find someone like Lucas. It wasn't that I didn't want her to date again—far from it. I'd spent years hoping she'd find someone who made her feel as cherished as she deserved. But I'd always pictured her with someone whose kids were grown, someone who would join her in exploring the freedom she'd talked about so often after Jake and I moved out.

When she told me about Lucas and Lily, I was surprised, to say the least. A seven-year-old? It was a big change from the empty-nest plans she'd mentioned—book clubs, art classes, becoming part of a Bookstagram group, and weekend trips with her friends. I worried she might lose herself in this new role and that she'd let go of the things she'd wanted for herself. But then I saw her with Lucas, and it was impossible to ignore how happy she looked.

And Lily... Well, I hadn't met her yet, but from everything Mom had told me, she sounded like a sweet, curious kid. I couldn't wait to get to know her, to see her and Mom together.

Mom was already outside when I pulled into the driveway that afternoon, chatting with Lucas while Lily hopped up and down in her rain boots. Seeing them made me smile, reminding me of the winter boots that Jake used to wear when he was little. He had re-fused to wear shoes that he couldn't put on himself. Mom and Dad nick-named him 'Boots' because he'd wear them even during the hottest summer days.

Mom waved me over, her face lighting up the way it always did when we saw each other. "There she is!" she said, wrapping me in a hug.

"Hey, Mom," I said, squeezing her back before turning to Lucas. "And hey, you. Long time no see."

Lucas grinned. "What's it been, a whole two weeks?" Mom and Lucas had come over to have dinner with Michael and me at our new house. We finally finished unpacking boxes and wedding gifts and were excited to show off our new place. The house was small— really small—but it was ours, and I loved it.

I laughed, shaking my head. "You know what I mean. It's good to see you."

"Hi, Sarah!" Lily's voice piped up, and I turned to see her looking at me, excitement and curiosity spreading throughout her expression.

"That's me," I said, crouching down to her level. "And you must be Lily. I hear you're the expert on all things goats today."

Her face lit up. "I'm going to milk one! And hold the babies! As long as I am gentle, and they don't bite."

"That sounds amazing," I said. "I hope you'll teach me everything you learn."

She nodded enthusiastically and launched into a description of the baby goats she hoped to see. I glanced back at Mom and Lucas, catching how they exchanged a quiet smile. It was one of those small moments that said more than words ever could. I couldn't remember the last time I had seen Mom and Dad look at each other like that. Had they ever?

As we loaded into Lucas's car and headed to the farm, I found myself watching them, noticing the ease between them. It wasn't just how they looked at each other—it was the way they worked together, the way they both instinctively included Lily in the conversation, making her feel like the center of their little world.

It was unexpected, sure. But I realized something as I sat there, listening to Lily chatter about goats, rain boots, and her favorite books. Maybe this wasn't the life Mom had planned for herself. But I sure hoped it was a life that would bring her happiness. She deserved it so much.

6

Jake

IT WASN'T THAT I DIDN'T like Lucas—I did. He was easy to talk to, quick with a joke, and always seemed genuinely interested in whatever I had to say. Over the last four months, we'd gotten on pretty well in those brief encounters we'd had, mostly over video games. It turned out he had a soft spot for retro consoles, and our first conversation had gone pretty deep on the best games from the Nintendo 64 era. I liked that about him—his ability to connect, his easy-going nature. And he had found it amusing that I would be into those old games, especially when I hadn't been alive when they were first released.

But liking Lucas didn't mean I wasn't skeptical. My protectiveness over Mom had always been a part of who I was, even before the divorce. I remembered those last few years with Dad all too well— how tense things had gotten, how the silences stretched longer, and how the arguments grew louder. Watching Mom work through the fallout of their marriage was one of the hardest things I'd ever seen.

And while she came out of it stronger, more resilient, I knew the scars were still there. Mine were, too. They always would be.

Now, here she was, jumping headfirst into a relationship with a man who had a young daughter. It wasn't what I'd expected for her, not by a long shot. I'd always imagined her finding someone with a similar lifestyle, whose kids were grown, or maybe someone without kids altogether. I guess I'd just assumed she'd want that freedom to explore new hobbies, travel, and spend time with her friends now that Sarah and I were out of the house.

Instead, she was venturing into this whole new world, and while I was happy to see her smiling again, I couldn't help but worry. Did she really have the energy for this? For a seven-year-old? For co-parenting, in a sense, with Lucas and his ex-wife? It wasn't that I doubted her ability to love Lily—it was more that I wondered if she'd end up giving so much of herself that she'd forget about her own dreams.

I leaned back in the worn leather chair in my apartment, staring at the stack of case files I was supposed to be reviewing for my internship. Moving closer to home to finish my degree online was a practical decision, but it was also hectic. Between my work interning at the law firm and my coursework, I barely had time to think, let alone sit down and really talk to Mom about everything that was happening.

I picked up one of the files, flipping through it without really absorbing the information. My mind kept drifting back to Lucas and Mom, to the handful of times I'd spent with him and how I'd gotten to know him in bits and pieces. He was an architect, the kind who cared about the little details, designing spaces for small businesses that wanted to stand out. I respected that about him. It wasn't about prestige or big-name clients but about creating something meaningful.

He seemed solid. Grounded. And most importantly, he seemed to care about Mom genuinely. But then there was Lily. I hadn't met her yet, though not for lack of trying on Mom's part. Between my packed schedule and the every-other-week custody arrangement regarding Lily, the timing just hadn't worked out. Part of me wondered if that was a blessing in disguise. Meeting Lucas was one thing—meeting his daughter was something else entirely.

What if she didn't like me? Or worse, what if I didn't like her? It wasn't like I had a ton of experience with kids. I'd spent most of my life as the youngest in the room, with Sarah always taking on the role of the nurturer. My patience for seven-year-olds wasn't exactly well-developed, and the thought of Mom pouring so much of her energy into a child who wasn't hers made me uneasy.

I set the file down and rubbed my temples, feeling the weight of my thoughts pressing in. It wasn't like I didn't want Mom to be happy. I did—more than anything. But I needed to know that Lucas and Lily were the right people to bring into her life. I needed to see it for myself, to feel it, to know that this wasn't just another risk that could end in heartache.

My phone buzzed on the table, and I glanced at the screen to see Mom's name pop up.

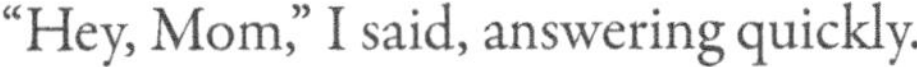

"Hey, Mom," I said, answering quickly.

"Hi, sweetheart. I hope I'm not interrupting anything."

"Just pretending to be productive," I joked. "What's up?"

"Well, I was wondering if you'd like to come over for dinner tomorrow," she said. "Lucas and Lily will be here, and I thought it might be a good time for you to meet her."

There it was. The invitation I'd been waiting for—and dreading.

"Yeah," I said after a moment because I knew Mom wouldn't accept a noncommittal answer. "Yeah, I can do that."

"Are you sure?" she asked, her tone careful. "I know you're busy."

"I'm sure," I said, meaning it. "It's time, right?"

She laughed softly. "I think so. I know it's a lot, Jake, but I really think you'll like her. She's... Well, she's something special."

I could hear the hope in her voice, the cautious excitement that had been there since the day she told me about Lucas. And as much as I wanted to protect her, to shield her from the possibility of pain, I knew I couldn't hold her back.

"Alright," I said, leaning back in my chair. "Tomorrow, it is."

As I hung up the phone, I felt a flicker of something I couldn't quite name. Anticipation, maybe. Or curiosity. Whatever it was, I knew one thing for sure—I needed to see this for myself. Because if Mom was willing to take this leap, then the least I could do was be there to catch her if she fell.

7

Lucas

SUNDAY AFTERNOONS ALWAYS FELT like the calm before the storm—a pocket of quiet before the week started its relentless march forward. But today, my thoughts were anything but calm. As I packed a small bag for Lily—just in case she wanted to bring her sketchpad or a book to dinner—I couldn't stop running through all the scenarios in my head.

No question, the trip to the goat farm the day before had been a hit. Lily was still buzzing from the experience, chattering on and on about how she got to milk a goat and how soft the baby goats were. At one point, she started asking me so many questions about goats that I feared she would want to bring one home with us. Thankfully, that specific question never surfaced.

Sarah had been fantastic, too, easing into the role of honorary big sister—dare I say that? Watching them together had been a relief, even better than I'd hoped.

But tonight was different. Tonight, we'd be having dinner with Emily and Jake.

Jake was the wildcard in all of this, and I couldn't help feeling a bit of heartburn as I thought about him. Sure, he was polite, and I did not doubt that he cared deeply about his mom. But something under the surface—something hesitant, guarded—made me wonder if he'd ever fully accept me being in Emily's life. Or his mom in Lily's.

It wasn't that I blamed him. The guy had watched his mom go through hell with her divorce, and here I was, bringing a kid into the mix when Emily had probably been looking forward to a simpler chapter in her life. I got it. Really, I did. But that didn't make it any easier.

I glanced over at Lily, who was carefully choosing which crayons to bring with her. She'd been so excited when I told her we were going to Emily's for dinner. Meeting Sarah had gone so well that she didn't seem the least bit nervous about meeting Jake. But I was.

Meeting Sarah had been one thing. Sarah had this easygoingness about her. Jake, though? Jake was different. He wasn't just another sibling figure—he was Emily's son. And I had a feeling he wasn't thrilled about the idea of his mom's life taking a detour that included a seven-year-old.

"Daddy, do you think Jake likes to draw?" Lily asked, looking up at me with wide eyes.

"I'm not sure," I admitted, crouching down to help her zip up her bag. "But you can always ask Jake when we get there."

She nodded, slinging the bag over her shoulder. "Do you think he'll like me?"

The question hit me square in the chest. "Of course, he will," I said, running my hand across the soft curls on the top of her head. "What's not to like? You're pretty great, kiddo."

She grinned, and I stood up, trying to ignore my own nerves.

As we drove to Emily's, my thoughts drifted, not just to tonight but to the week ahead. Tomorrow, I'd be meeting with the owners of the bed and breakfast who wanted to design a treehouse experience for their guests. It was the kind of project I lived for—creative, unconventional, full of possibilities. But to really get a sense of what was possible, I needed to see the space for myself, walk the property, and start dreaming up plans. While the project would be fun, there were many engineering things to work through since the space couldn't simply be designed to rest in the trees. I need to make it look like that, of course, but creating that truly magical experience would be complicated.

Still, no matter how much I tried to focus on work, my mind kept circling back to tonight. I was exhausted over all the thoughts trying to compete for residence in my mind.

Yet, when we arrived at Emily's house, Lily bounded out of the car, her excitement bubbling over. I gave my shoulders a quick roll

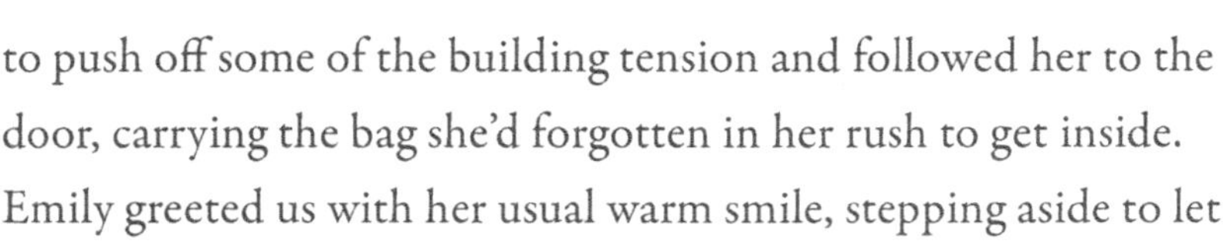

to push off some of the building tension and followed her to the door, carrying the bag she'd forgotten in her rush to get inside. Emily greeted us with her usual warm smile, stepping aside to let us in.

"Hi, Lily," she said, crouching down to give her a hug. "I'm so glad you're here."

"Me too!" Lily said, her voice bright. "I brought my crayons. Do you think Jake will want to draw with me?"

Emily laughed softly, glancing up at me. "Let's ask him."

As we walked into the living room, Jake was already there, standing by the window with his hands in his pockets. He turned when he heard us, a faint smile on his face.

"Hey," he said, his voice even. "Good to see you again, Lucas."

"You too," I said, extending a hand. He shook it firmly, his grip firm but not overly so.

"This is Lily," I said, placing a hand on her shoulder.

Lily tilted her head back to look at him, her expression curious. "Hi, Jake," she said. "Do you like to draw?"

Jake blinked, clearly caught off guard by the question. But to his credit, he didn't miss a beat. "I'm not very good at it," he said. "But maybe you can teach me."

Lily's face lit up, and more of that tension rolled off my shoulders. "Okay! I brought crayons!"

As the evening unfolded, I kept an eye on Jake, watching how he interacted with Lily. He wasn't as openly warm as Sarah, but he wasn't standoffish, either. He asked her questions, listened to her answers, and even sat down with her to draw while we waited for dinner to be ready.

It wasn't until later, after Lily had gone to the kitchen with Emily to help set the table—she had been assigned fork and napkin duty—that Jake and I had a moment alone.

"She's a good kid," he said, breaking the silence.

"Thanks," I said, glancing at him.

He nodded, his gaze thoughtful. "Look, I like you, Lucas. I do. But this... All of this? It's not what I expected for my mom."

I paused for a moment, trying to think of the right words. His honesty caught me off guard. Jake was anything but discreet in his feelings. He would definitely make a good lawyer one day. "I get that," I said after a moment. "And I know it's a lot. But I care about her, Jake. And I care about making sure this works for everyone— not just for me and Emily, but for Lily, too."

He studied me, his expression unreadable. Then he nodded again. "Alright," he said. "Let's see how it goes."

It wasn't a glowing endorsement, but it was something. And as we sat down for dinner a few minutes later, I couldn't help but feel like tonight was a step in the right direction: a small step, maybe, but an important one.

8

Emily

THE STEADY CLACKETY-CLACK of my fingers on the keyboard was a sound I hadn't heard in weeks. It was like welcoming an old friend, and the words seemed to pour out of me again. Caleb's story flowed, and his world was piecing together—his struggles and quiet resilience.

In the chapter I'd just finished, Caleb had started building a treehouse in his backyard, a project that felt like a metaphor for the fragile connections he was rebuilding with his mom. It wasn't lost on me how much my writing mirrored my own life, though I hadn't planned it that way. Lucas's recent project had simply sparked something in me. And Caleb's story was about working through fear and pain and finding strength in unexpected places. While my life was far from tragic, there was something about his journey that felt personal.

I leaned back in my chair, stretching my arms overhead as I let the scene settle in my mind. The goat farm from last week drifted into my thoughts.

Lily had been full of energy, darting from one pen to the next with a mix of awe and determination. She'd charmed the farm staff, patiently waiting her turn to milk a goat and asking a dozen questions about the baby goats she got to hold. Watching her interact with Sarah had been a joy. My daughter had such a natural warmth about her, the kind of energy that made people feel at home. Seeing her laugh with Lily and helping her draw a picture of the goats later that afternoon were some of those moments that felt right.

And then there was Lucas. He'd been the perfect balance of present and laid-back, letting Lily take the lead while staying close enough to support her. There was something so steady about him, a kind of quiet confidence that made everything feel simpler.

I thought back to the phone conversation I'd had with Sarah earlier in the week.

"So, how are things going with Lucas?" she'd asked, her tone laced with curiosity.

"They're good," I'd said, a little too quickly.

"Good? That's all you've got?"

I laughed, shaking my head even though she couldn't see me. "Okay, fine. They're... really good."

There was a pause on the other end, the kind that only lasted long enough to let me know she was waiting for more. My daughter knew me so well. She was wise beyond her years.

"I think I might be falling in love with him," I admitted. I said the words so fast they surprised even me.

Sarah let out a soft, happy gasp without any hesitation. "Mom! That's amazing. Are you sure?"

"Sure? No," I'd said honestly. "But I feel it. When I'm with him, when I'm not with him, it's like he's always in my thoughts, but not in a bad way. It's... nice. He makes me feel happy, Sarah. And safe."

She'd been over the moon, of course, telling me how proud she was of me for opening my heart again. And while her enthusiasm made me smile, it also left me a little exposed. Falling in love wasn't something I'd planned on, not after everything I'd been through with her father, Andrew. But here I was, wading through the uncharted territory of a new relationship and finding that it wasn't quite as scary as I'd expected.

And Lucas? He wasn't making it any easier to guard my heart.

During our evening phone calls that week, he told me all about his progress on the bakery. I could hear the excitement in his voice as he talked about the little details he was working on—the custom light fixtures, the playful tile patterns, and the cozy built-in seating nooks.

But the treehouse project had truly captured his time and attention.

"They said yes," he'd said one night, his voice excited like that of a child.

"To the treehouse?" I'd asked, already smiling.

"Yep. They want me to design it. And not just any treehouse—they want it to be an experience. A place where guests can stay overnight, like a little retreat in the trees. Well, a big retreat with three elevated treehouses built around a cluster of old oak trees."

I'd laughed, hearing this boy-like wonder in the tone of his voice. "You sound like a kid who just got the best toy for Christmas."

"Because I feel like one. What kid wouldn't like to design a treehouse?" he'd responded with a laugh, his voice increasing a few octaves. "I've already started sketching ideas, now that I've seen the space in person and they've hired me. It's going to be incredible, Emily."

And just like that, he'd drawn me into his world, his passion infectious.

Now, as I sit in my quiet office, the memory of those conversations makes me smile. I saved my progress on Caleb's story and stood, stretching my legs as I wandered into the kitchen for another cup of lavender tea.

The house was quiet, but it didn't feel empty. Not in the way it had in those first few months after Sarah and Jake moved out. These days, it felt like the quiet was holding space for something new, something I was still figuring out but was excited to explore.

I glanced at the clock, realizing it would be time to call Lucas soon. Our nightly check-ins had become something I looked forward to more than I cared to admit. As I poured my tea and leaned against the counter, I felt the edges of my world softening, expanding.

9

Lucas

WINTER HAD A WAY of holding on in Minnesota, but the weeks were ticking by, and spring was getting closer. I was enjoying the longer days and less of the dreariness that comes during those dark nights that come so early. Though snow still blanketed the ground, there was a softness to the air.

Change has been the theme of my life lately, but for once, it wasn't something to fear.

Emily and I had been dating for seven months now, though it felt both longer and shorter at the same time. In February, we'd escaped the grind for a weekend trip to Lutsen, a small mountain town that felt like it had been plucked straight from a postcard. Neither of us were skiers—our idea of winter sports was more about watching hockey on television than participating—but we'd signed up for a snowshoeing day trip and had an absolute blast.

By the end of the day, we were sore in places we didn't even know could get sore, but we couldn't stop laughing about it. Emily

had face-planted in a snowbank at one point, and the memory of her brushing herself off, red-faced but laughing, still made me grin. My laughs only got bigger as I remembered trying to help her right herself with those bulky snow-shoes still attached to her feet. She'd practically pulled me down with her.

The rest of the weekend had been equally perfect. We visited a local brewery and sampled flights of beer—okay, I sampled as she watched and sipped a hot chocolate. Emily is more of a wine girl than a beer girl, but she had clearly enjoyed the time with me.

We spent hours poking around shops that smelled of pine and leather, buying little things for Lily and laughing at the quirky souvenirs. At one point, we found a little polar bear figurine, and Emily was convinced that Lily had to have it. I couldn't agree more and was delighted she put so much thought into choosing something reflective of one of Lily's favorite animals.

At the end of the weekend, we'd shared our first "I love yous." It had been over a bottle of wine after dinner at a cozy little winery with fairy lights strung across the ceiling. She'd been telling me about Caleb and how much he'd grown as a character.

"It's strange," she'd said, her voice soft and thoughtful. "I feel like I know him, like he's a real person. But at the same time, it's like I'm saying goodbye to him as I finish the story."

I'd been watching her as she spoke, her cheeks flushed from the wine and the warmth of the room. She was beautiful, and I couldn't stop looking at her. She had this light about her, this energy that made everything feel a little more alive.

"I love you," I'd said, the words slipping out before I'd even fully realized I was saying them.

She'd blinked, startled, but then her face softened into a smile that made my heart feel like it was too big for my chest. "I love you, too," she'd replied, and just like that, everything had changed. We'd returned to the cozy chateau that night and made love for hours. We fit together so perfectly that I wondered if we could just stay in that cocoon for the rest of our lives.

Now, weeks later, the memory of that moment still warmed me, even as I tried to focus on the plans spread out on my desk. The bakery design was nearly finalized, and the treehouse project was coming along, though the logistics of building something up in an old oak tree was proving to be a challenge. But my mind kept drifting back to Emily.

She'd become a fixture at my home on the weekends, and it felt so natural, so easy. She'd camp out in my office, her laptop open and her brow furrowed in concentration as she worked through the final edits on her book. Her publisher was already buzzing about it, and I couldn't have been more proud of her.

She had a way of fitting into the rhythm of my life without disrupting it, instinctively understanding when I needed time with Lily and when I wanted to share those moments with her. And there had been plenty of those moments.

We'd taken Lily ice skating a few weeks ago—well, I'd taken Lily ice skating while Emily cheered us on from the sidelines with hot cocoa. We'd built snow forts in the yard and taken long walks through the woods behind my house, the three of us talking about everything and nothing.

I glanced at the clock and realized it was almost time for Emily to arrive. Lily has spent the morning making a "welcome banner" out of construction paper and glitter glue. It was a mess, but it was pure Lily, and I loved it. I knew Emily would, too.

As I tidied up the living room, my thoughts turned to the future. Emily and I hadn't talked about specifics yet, but I couldn't help but wonder what it would look like for the three of us together. I'd never been the kind of guy to rush things, but with Emily, it felt different. It felt... right.

The sound of the doorbell pulled me from my thoughts, and I opened the door to find her standing there, a soft smile on her face and a bag slung over her shoulder.

"Hey," she said, stepping inside and letting the warmth of the house envelop her.

"Hey," I replied, leaning in to kiss her, my hand on the back of her neck.

Lily came barreling into the room, her banner held high above her head. "Surprise!" she yelled, grinning from ear to ear. "And, gross!"

Emily backed away from our kiss, crouching down to hug her. "Wow, this is amazing, Lily. Did you make this all by yourself?"

"Daddy helped a little," she admitted.

As the two of them chatted, I felt a wave of contentment wash over me. This was my life now—a life that was fuller, richer, and more joyful than I ever could have imagined. And as I watched them together, I couldn't help but think that maybe, just maybe, the future I was starting to picture wasn't so far away after all.

10

Jessica

THE SOUND OF LILY'S LAUGHTER floated in from the living room, where she was busy coloring at the coffee table. I paused mid-stir of the spaghetti sauce, watching her through the kitchen doorway as she leaned over her paper, a small pile of crayons scattered around her. She was drawing a scene from the goat farm—one she hadn't stopped talking about since she got home from Lucas's the week before.

"And then Emily showed me how to pet the baby goat really gently!" Lily had exclaimed when she first came back. "She said I was so good with them, Mommy!"

I smiled and nodded, letting her excitement wash over me. It was hard not to. Lily had always been a storyteller, her words spilling out in bursts of color and light, and hearing about her time with Lucas—and now Emily—had become a regular part of her routine when she was with me.

At first, I had listened with a sense of detachment and trepidation, treating Emily as just another name in Lily's stories. However, as the weeks passed, it became clear that Emily wasn't just "Daddy's friend" anymore. How Lily talked about her—how she helped with school projects, joined them on outings, and even made her laugh during movie nights—was different.

It didn't surprise me when my phone rang a few days ago, Lucas's name flashing on the screen.

"Hey," he'd said, his tone measured. "I wanted to talk to you about something."

That something, of course, was Emily. He'd told me that she wanted to meet me, to talk about Lily and the role she was beginning to play in her life. It was the kind of conversation I'd known would come eventually, but it still caught me off guard.

I'd agreed, of course. Not because I wanted to, but because I needed to. I needed to know this woman who was playing such a big role in my daughter's life. And while the devil on my shoulder told me I needed to stake my claim, the stronger part of me seemed to imply it wasn't something I needed to worry about.

Leaving Lucas had been one of the hardest decisions I'd ever made. For a long time, I'd held on to the idea that we could fix things and find our way back to being the family we once were. But the truth was, we hadn't been happy for years—not really. We were great as parents, but as partners? There was just no spark, and sometimes, I wondered how we came together in the first place.

Walking away meant starting over and facing the harsh reality of what that choice would mean for Lily. I'd built a life for the two of us since then, one that I was proud of. I'd learned to be independent, to provide for her on my own terms. Lucas had always been so financially generous in our marriage that I hadn't known what it felt like to live within my means and take pride in what I could provide.

My devotion to Lily was fierce, and I wasn't going to let anyone—no matter how well-intentioned—disrupt that. And I wanted to teach Lily the value of working hard.

But then there was Emily.

I hadn't met her yet, but through Lily's stories, I'd started to get a picture of who she was. And I'd heard of her, of course, as an author. I loved to read and had read one of her books about a child named Cindy who had lost her father when she was young.

But now I would be meeting the real Emily, not just seeing a face on the back cover of a book. She sounded kind, intelligent, and patient—the kind of person who didn't rush or push but simply showed up. And maybe that's what scared me the most. Because Lily wasn't just talking about Emily anymore. She was talking about someone she clearly adored.

"Mommy?" Lily's voice broke through my thoughts.

"Yeah, sweetheart?" I said, setting the spoon down, covering the pot with a lid, and walking into the living room.

She held up her drawing proudly. "Do you think Emily would like this? It's the goats!"

I crouched down beside her, taking in the colorful scene she'd created. "I think she'll love it," I said honestly.

"Can I bring it to Daddy's house next time?" she asked, her eyes bright.

"Of course," I said, ruffling her curls.

She grinned, leaning into my side for a brief moment before returning to her crayons.

The meeting with Emily was scheduled for later this week, and I still wasn't sure how I felt about it. Part of me wanted to keep my guard up, to protect the life I'd built with Lily. But another part of me—smaller, quieter—recognized that this was about more than me.

It was about Lily.

If Emily was going to be a part of her life, then I needed to know who she was, not just through Lucas's words or through her books or Lily's stories, but face-to-face.

As I watched Lily color, singing softly to herself, I felt a pang of something I couldn't quite name. Hope, maybe. Or acceptance. Perhaps a bit of jealousy? Whatever it was, I knew one thing for sure: I'd do whatever it took to make sure Lily felt safe and loved, even if that meant opening a door I wasn't entirely sure I wanted to walk through.

11

Emily

THE COFFEE SHOP WAS WARMER than I expected, the scent of roasted beans and cinnamon swirling in the air as I stepped inside. My nerves were on edge; my palms were sweaty despite the chill in the air outside. I scanned the room and spotted Jessica almost immediately, seated at a small table near the window. She was nursing a latte, her eyes flicking toward the door when she noticed me.

Jessica didn't get up as I approached, but she offered a shy smile that felt more polite than warm. I tightened my grip on the cup in my hand, forcing my legs to move forward.

"Jessica?" I asked, stopping just short of the table.

"That's me," she said, gesturing to the empty chair across from her. "Emily, right?"

"Yes," I said, setting my coffee down and sliding into the seat. My heart was pounding, and for a moment, I wasn't sure what to say.

Jessica broke the silence first. "Thanks for meeting with me. Lucas mentioned you wanted to… talk."

I nodded, fiddling with the cardboard sleeve on my cup. "I thought it was important. For Lily, and for all of us, really."

She tilted her head slightly, her expression neutral. "Alright. I'm listening."

I took a deep breath, watching her heavy gaze. "First, I just want to say that I know how much you mean to Lily. She always talks about you, and it's clear how much she adores you. I would never try to replace the role you have in her life. That's not what this is about."

Jessica's lips pressed into a thin line, and she nodded slowly but didn't respond.

I continued. "I care about Lucas. And I care about Lily. More than I expected to, honestly. When Lucas and I started dating, I didn't know what it would mean to be in a relationship with someone with a young child. It wasn't something I'd ever pictured for myself. But now… Now I can't imagine my life without them."

Jessica's shoulders stiffened slightly, and the tension between us sharpened.

"I'm not trying to disrupt anything," I said quickly. "I just want to be someone Lily can trust. Someone who can add to the love and stability she already has with you and Lucas."

Jessica let out a slow breath, her gaze dropping to her cup. "It's not that simple," she said, her voice low. "You're asking me to accept someone else stepping into my daughter's life. To trust you with her. That's not something I take lightly."

"I wouldn't expect you to," I said. "And I know I have to earn that trust."

She looked up then, her eyes sharper. "Lucas has a good heart, but he can be... idealistic. He sees the best in people, sometimes to a fault. And I can't afford to make that mistake. Not when it comes to Lily."

Her words stung, but I understood where they came from.

"I get it," I said softly. "I know what it's like to be protective of someone you love."

Jessica's brows furrowed slightly, and I hesitated before continuing.

"Years ago, before my divorce, I found out my ex-husband was having an affair," I said, my voice quieter now. "With one of my closest friends."

Jessica blinked, her expression shifting.

"The betrayal... It shattered something in me," I admitted. "Not just my trust in him, but my trust in myself. I questioned who I could rely on and whether I could ever truly let someone in again. I wondered what was so wrong with me and why I was unlovable. It's taken me years to rebuild that part of myself. And honestly, it's still a work in progress."

Jessica's gaze softened, the tension in her posture easing just a little.

"I never thought I'd be here," I continued. "Falling in love with a man who has a young child. It's not what I planned for my life. But life doesn't always follow a plan, does it?"

She gave a faint, rueful smile. "No, it doesn't."

I took a sip of my coffee, the silence between us growing heavy but not unbearable.

"Lily is an amazing kid," I said after a moment. "She's smart, kind, and so full of curiosity. I love spending time with her and getting to know her. And I want to do right by her, Jessica. I want her to feel safe, to know she's surrounded by people who care about her. That's why I wanted to meet with you. Because I think we're on the same team here."

Jessica studied me for a long moment, her eyes searching mine. "You're asking for my support," she said finally.

"Yes," I said, my voice steady. "I'm asking for your support in building something good for Lily. For all of us."

She leaned back in her chair, letting out a slow breath. "This isn't easy for me, Emily," she said. "Letting someone else into Lily's life, into this new world we've built... It's hard. She's my only child. The only one I will ever have, and I am her mom."

"I know," I said, meeting her gaze. "And I know how much you love her. And I love her, too. And you will always be her mom."

For the first time, Jessica's face softened into something resembling a genuine smile. It was small, tentative, but it was there.

"I'll think about it," she said finally. "About how we can make this work."

"That's all I'm asking," I said.

As we finished our coffee, the tension that had been so thick when I walked in seemed to fade, replaced by something quieter. It wasn't perfect, but perhaps it was a start.

12

Lucas

HOPE WAS A TRICKY THING. It could lift you up and give you direction, but it also had a way of leaving you feeling exposed, like a tightrope walker teetering without a net. That's how I felt about Jessica's meeting with Emily. She hadn't been immediately open to the idea, but she hadn't shut it down, either. I knew Jessica well enough to understand that this was as much about protecting herself as it was about protecting Lily.

I had been replaying our history a lot lately, thinking about how we got here.

Jessica and I had met almost by accident. She was working as a receptionist at an architectural firm in St. Paul, and I'd come in to interview for a position. She was the first face I saw when I walked through the door, and I remember thinking she had a warmth about her, something that made you feel at home right away. But, considering I was young and fresh out of college, I can't deny that she was hot and there was some physical chemistry. That long blonde hair that hung down to the middle of her back in gentle waves and those piercing blue eyes. I was practically a goner.

After the interview, I worked up the nerve to ask her to coffee, and to my surprise, she said yes. Those first few dates were fun, full of easy laughter and casual conversation, but things fizzled before they really started. Life had a way of getting in the way. I took a job at a different firm, and Jessica decided to return to school to pursue physical therapy. We lost touch, and I didn't think much about it at the time.

Years later, I found myself back in her orbit, thanks to an old baseball injury from high school that refused to stay healed. My doctor had prescribed physical therapy, and as luck would have it, Jessica was the therapist who walked into the room at my first session.

We reconnected slowly, first through the sessions, and then through a shared sense of familiarity that made it easy to fall back into step with each other. Before long, we were dating again, and this time, it stuck. We dated for nearly eight years before I finally asked her to marry me. She said yes, and we got married a year later. Lily arrived just three years after that. Getting pregnant had been a struggle, and we had almost given up when finally, Jessica showed me the test results—positive.

But the things that drew us together—familiarity, shared goals—weren't enough to keep us together. We worked well together as parents, but as a couple, not so much. Our conversations became more about logistics than connection, even before Lily was born. And that spark and physical attraction? Even that was starting to flicker and fade. I had always wondered if those two years of struggling to get pregnant had pulled us apart. Intimacy had become more of a chore, something intended to make a baby and not bring us closer. But deep down, I knew that there was far more to it than that.

Letting go of the dream of a nuclear family for Lily had been the hardest part. But even now, as I sat thinking about it, I knew we'd made the right decision. We were both better off, and so was Lily.

Later that evening, I met up with Cole at a local bar. It had been a while since we'd had a proper catch-up, and as soon as I slid onto the stool next to him, I could tell he was in a good mood.

"What's got you grinning like that?" I asked, signaling the bartender for a beer.

Cole leaned back, his grin widening. "Rebecca's pregnant."

"Seriously?" I said, my eyebrows shooting up. "That's amazing, man. Congrats!"

"Thanks," he said, his voice softer now. "It's been a long road, you know? Two miscarriages after Olivia... We weren't sure if it was going to happen. And we're not getting any younger. But everything's looking good this time. Four more months to go."

I clapped him on the back, feeling genuinely happy for him. "That's incredible. I'm really happy for you guys."

Cole nodded, his eyes shining with a mix of excitement and relief. "It's a blessing, for sure. We always wanted two kids, but now that Rebecca is 40, we just felt it wasn't in the cards. But enough about me—what's new with you?"

I hesitated, taking a sip of my beer before answering. "Actually... I've been thinking about asking Emily to marry me. Or at least to move in with me first."

Cole's eyes widened, and then he broke into a huge smile. "No way. Are you serious?"

"Yeah," I said, the words feeling both terrifying and exhilarating. "I've been thinking about it for a while now. She's amazing, Cole. And Lily... She loves her."

"That's big," he said, his tone turning thoughtful. "But you're ready for it, aren't you?"

"I think so," I said. "It feels right. I just... I want to make sure it's the right thing for Lily, too."

Cole nodded. "You'll figure it out. You're a good dad, Lucas. And Emily seems like a keeper."

I smiled, my confidence stronger after hearing those words.

As we talked, I noticed someone had slid onto the stool next to me. Turning slightly, I did a double take—it was Jake, Emily's son, with a buddy in tow.

"Jake," I said, surprised.

His head jerked toward me, and his expression shifted from casual to startled. "Lucas," he said, his tone showing he was just as surprised to see me there as I was him.

"Small world," Cole said, raising his beer in greeting.

"Yeah," Jake said slowly, glancing between us. The expression on his face was odd. Something I couldn't quite place, but I pushed it aside. "What brings you here?"

I hesitated for a moment, unsure how much he'd overheard and if that was the reason for his expression. "Just catching up with a friend," I said, keeping my tone light.

Jake nodded. Was I detecting suspicion?

"I'm Cole. Join us for a beer?" Cole offered.

Jake hesitated but ultimately shook his head. "Thanks, but I'm good. Just grabbing a drink with a buddy."

"Alright," I said, offering a small smile. "Good to see you, Jake."

"Yeah," he said, his gaze taking me in for a moment longer before turning back to his friend.

As Cole and I returned to our conversation, I couldn't shake the feeling that Jake had overheard more than he let on. And while I wasn't sure what he thought about what he'd heard, I knew one thing for certain: if I was going to take this next step with Emily, I'd need to talk to Jake, too.

13

Lily

"MOMMY, ARE YOU COMING to the zoo with us?" I asked, swinging my legs under the kitchen chair as I finished my bowl of cereal.

Jessica looked up from her coffee. "The zoo? You're going with Daddy and Emily, right?"

"Uh-huh," I said, nodding so hard I almost spilled my juice. "But you can come, too! It'll be so fun! There's going to be monkeys and giraffes and—oh! Do you think we'll see polar bears or penguins?"

Mommy smiled.. "That sounds like a great time, sweetheart. But I think I'll sit this one out."

"Why?" I asked.

"Well," she said, setting her mug down and leaning closer, "It would feel like... being a third wheel."

"A third wheel?" I scrunched up my face, confused. "But cars need four wheels."

Mommy blinked, then laughed. I loved her laugh.

"Good point," she said, tucking a strand of hair behind her ear. "But when grown-ups say 'third wheel,' they mean someone who feels out of place. Like an extra part that's not really needed."

"But you wouldn't be extra!" I said, my voice rising. "You'd be the fourth wheel, and cars need four wheels anyway!"

She laughed again, shaking her head. "You've got me there, kiddo."

"So, you'll come?" I asked hopefully.

Mommy's smile softened, and she reached out to brush a crumb off my cheek. "No, sweetie. This trip is for you, Daddy, and Emily. And it sounds like you're really excited to spend time with them."

"I do like Emily," I admitted. "She's really nice. She showed me how to pet the goats at the farm, and she said I was really good at being gentle."

Mommy nodded. "She sounds like she's good at spending time with you."

"She is," I said, kicking my legs again. "But I still wish you and Daddy could all go together. Like we used to."

Mommy's face changed then—not sad exactly, but something close. "I know, Lily," she said, her voice soft. "I know it's hard to understand why things aren't like they used to be."

"Why can't you and Daddy just live in the same house?" I asked, looking at her.

She sighed, sitting down in the chair next to me. "Sometimes grown-ups stop being good partners for each other," my mom said. "But that doesn't mean we stop loving you. You know that, right?"

I nodded. "But you still like Daddy, don't you?"

Mommy smiled again, but she looked tired. "I'll always care about your dad because he's your dad. But sometimes, adults have relationships that aren't meant to last forever. And that's okay. What matters is that we both love you so, so much."

I thought about that for a moment, trying to make sense of it. "So, you and Daddy aren't partners anymore?"

"No," she said, her voice steady. "But we're still a team when it comes to you."

I smiled a little at that. "Like co-captains on my soccer team?"

"Exactly," she said, her smile returning.

I swung my legs again, feeling a little better. "And Emily's nice, too," I said. "I think she likes Daddy."

Mommy tilted her head, watching me. "What do you think about that?"

I shrugged. "I think it's okay. She's nice, and she likes doing fun stuff. And she's really good at drawing. She said she's going to show me how to draw animals better next time."

She smiled, and this time it looked real—not tired, not forced. "I'm glad you like her," she said.

I grinned. "And you'd like her too if you came to the zoo."

Mommy laughed, shaking her head. "You're not going to let that go, are you?"

"Nope!" I said, jumping up from the table.

"Go get ready, fourth wheel," she teased, ruffling my hair as I ran off.

I didn't know if Mommy would ever go to the zoo with us, but as I pulled on my sneakers, I thought about what she had said. Even if she and Daddy weren't partners anymore, they were still my team. And if Emily wanted to be part of that team, too, maybe that wasn't such a bad thing.

Besides, someone had to help me draw some polar bears better because right now, they looked more like hippos.

14

Emily

THE MORNING LIGHT CREPT through the blinds on my bedroom window, casting soft, muted patterns on the ceiling. I lay on my back, wide awake, my thoughts circling in familiar loops—I called it spinning. The house was still, and I could barely hear the old furnace running in the background. It wasn't often I woke up before my alarm, but lately, my mind has been too full for sleep.

Lucas.

I couldn't stop thinking about him.

Over the past few months, my feelings for him had grown in ways I hadn't expected. What started as a tentative curiosity had definitely evolved into something deeper, something I couldn't quite put into words but felt deep within my core.

I rolled onto my side, staring at the faint light spilling from the crack in the door. I was in love with him. That much was clear now.

It wasn't the heady, all-consuming kind of love I'd experienced when I was younger—the kind that burned too hot and too fast. No, this was different. It was warm and grounding. If I were honest with myself, it terrified me.

I'd thought about Andrew a lot lately, more than I had in years. Not because I missed him—I didn't—but because reflecting on that relationship had given me a clearer perspective on what I wanted and what I didn't.

Andrew and I had been disconnected almost from the beginning. At the time, I hadn't realized it. I was swept up in the idea of us, of the life we were building together. On paper, we had everything—jobs, a gorgeous house that I loved, two kids that were my everything, vacations planned months in advance, even a lake home in northern Minnesota. But beneath the surface, something was missing.

When it came, the betrayal was almost anticlimactic. I was devastated, of course, but looking back, it felt inevitable. We weren't partners, not really. We were two people moving through parallel lives, never quite meeting in the middle. Even intimacy had become robotic, and I wished I could pinpoint when that had changed.

With Lucas, it was different.

Something about him made me feel seen in a way I never had before. He didn't just hear what I said—he listened. He asked thoughtful questions, remembered the little things, and seemed genuinely interested in my world, just as I was in his.

It wasn't just the way he looked at me, though if I were being honest, the physical chemistry between us was something I hadn't felt in years. Lucas had this way of making me feel desired, but it was more than that. With him, I'd rediscovered a part of myself I thought I'd lost. The part that enjoyed the closeness, the quiet intimacy of being with someone who cared.

But it wasn't just physical. That may have been what started it, but it was everything else that made me fall for him: his intelligence, drive, and quiet determination to make the world around him just a little better. I loved his devotion to helping small businesses stand out from the crowd. And I so loved the way his eyes lit up when he talked about his projects, the way he approached every problem with a mix of creativity and pragmatism.

But I loved the quiet moments, too. The way we could sit together in comfortable silence, each lost in our own thoughts, and still feel connected. There was a peace in those moments that I hadn't known I was missing until I found it with him. As an introvert, this was so refreshing and felt long overdue.

I sighed, turning onto my other side and pulling the blanket up to my chin. I couldn't help myself—I was starting to think about the future. About what it would look like to build a life with Lucas.

Would we get a place together someday? Would we blend our families in a way that felt as natural as our relationship? Could I be a stepmother to Lily, not just someone who spent time with her but someone she relied on, someone she trusted?

The thought filled me with both excitement and fear. It wasn't just about me and Lucas. There were so many other pieces to consider—Lily, Jessica, my own kids, my own heart. I didn't want to get hurt again, that was for sure. And I didn't want to be in a relationship that wouldn't go anywhere, either.

But as I laid there, the faint sound of birds chirping outside, I realized something important. I wanted to try. I wanted to see where this path led, even if it scared me.

Today was another step forward, a trip to the zoo with Lucas and Lily. I smiled at the thought of Lily's excitement, her endless energy as she talked about the animals she hoped to see. And Lucas—well, he'd be there, too. But what did it mean that I was looking forward to the time with Lily almost as much as the time with Lucas?

15

Lucas

LILY WAS IN HER ROOM, sprawled out on the rug with a pile of crayons, her sketchpad open to a fresh page. She was singing to herself, a tune I didn't recognize but had heard on repeat all morning. I'd noticed her singing more and more lately but didn't want to ask her about it for fear that she would be embarrassed. And her singing was adorable, definitely something kids do when they are happy.

I sat at the dining table, absently flipping through a set of blueprints that had been sitting there for days. The firm I worked for had asked me to take on another project—modifying an existing bed and breakfast to be handicap accessible to meet current regulations. Normally, I could lose myself in the lines and measurements, the challenge of turning an idea into something tangible. But today, my thoughts were somewhere else entirely.

Emily.

Yesterday's trip to the zoo was perfect—full of laughter, wide-eyed wonder, and moments that made my chest ache with how right everything felt. Emily and Lily were inseparable.

And me? I'd watched them, a quiet certainty settling in my chest, almost replacing this pressure I'd been feeling in recent weeks. I wanted Emily in my life, not just on weekends or for special outings but in a way that felt permanent. I wanted her to move in with us. I was tired of the thirty-minute drive to her house on the weekends I spent there, and I hated the idea of another winter approaching with her making the thirty-minute trek to my home. And as a writer, she could live anywhere, right? She no longer needed that big home that she and Andrew had lived in for all of those years—the home she had kept in her divorce when Andrew pretty much walked away from everything they had built together. Then again, she had sent him packing.

The idea of asking Emily to move in with me had been circling my mind for weeks, but now it felt urgent, like the next natural step. The thought of coming home to her, of sharing the everyday rhythms of life, was something I hadn't realized I craved until recently. And waking up in bed with her each morning? I couldn't deny how nice that would be.

But I was nervous. Emily valued her independence, her autonomy. She'd spent years rebuilding herself after her divorce, and I knew this wasn't a decision she'd take lightly. She loved doing her own thing. And I knew how she could get so absorbed in her writing, often not noticing the things going on around her. It was nice, actually, that independence. She was her own person. She could make her own decisions. She didn't need me. But I knew she wanted me. And that felt good, really good.

And then there was Lily.

"Daddy?" I looked up to see Lily standing in the doorway, her sketchpad in hand. She tilted her head, her curls bouncing just a bit, making me realize that tonight was bath night. "What are you thinking about?"

I smiled, patting the chair next to me. "Come sit, kiddo."

She climbed up onto the chair and set her sketchpad on the table. It was a drawing of the zoo, complete with giraffes, monkeys, and what I assumed were penguins, though they looked more like upside-down bowling pins.

"This is really good," I said, pointing to a particularly colorful giraffe. "What about your polar bears?"

"They still look like hippos. And besides, our zoo doesn't have polar bears," she said, swinging her legs. This kid could rarely sit still. She got it from me, I thought. "What are you thinking about?"

I hesitated, unsure how to start. "Well, I was thinking about Emily."

Her face lit up. "I like Emily. Is she coming over today?"

"Not today," I said, smiling at her enthusiasm. "But I wanted to ask you something. How would you feel if Emily... spent more time here? Like, if she lived with us?"

Lily's eyes widened, and for a moment, she looked like she was processing the idea. "She would live here all the time? Like you and me, well, except for when I am at Mommy's house?"

"Yeah," I said, watching her carefully. "It's something I've been thinking about. But I wanted to know how you feel about it first."

A slow smile spread across her face. "That would be fun! She could help me draw and read me bedtime stories."

I felt a wave of relief wash over me. "I think it would be fun, too."

"Could Mommy live here too?"

That next question hit me like a gut punch. I stared at her, unsure how to respond.

"Mommy could have her room back with you," Lily continued, her voice earnest. "And we could all be together like one big family."

I swallowed hard, trying to keep my voice steady. "Sweetheart, Mommy and I... We're not together anymore. That's why she has her own house, and I have mine."

"But why?" she asked, her eyes big and searching.

I took a deep breath, leaning closer to her. "Sometimes grownups stop being good partners for each other. But that doesn't mean we stop loving you or being a team when it comes to you."

She looked down at her sketchpad, her fingers tracing the edge of the paper. "But you and Emily are good partners, right?"

I smiled softly. "I think so, yeah."

"Then maybe Emily can be the mommy at your house, and Mommy can be the mommy at her house," she said.

I felt a lump form in my throat. "Well, Mommy will always be your mommy. But yes, Emily would be your stepmommy at our house."

She nodded, her expression thoughtful. "What's a stepmommy?"

I figured this would be the inevitable question. "A stepmommy is like having a second mom. She loves you like she is your real mom. But she isn't actually your mom. So, she is called your stepmom."

"Claire at school has a stepdad. Is it like that?"

I nodded, the thought of Lily having another man in her life being something I couldn't quite handle at the moment. "Yes, kind of like that."

"Good," she said, hopping down from the chair and grabbing her sketchpad. "I'm gonna draw Emily another picture of the penguins now."

As she ran off, her curls bouncing with each step, I leaned back in my chair, exhaling slowly.

The conversation hadn't gone the way I'd expected, but it had reminded me of just how much Lily's world was shaped by the people who loved her. Jessica would always be a part of her life, just as Emily was becoming a part of mine.

But one thing was for certain. It was time to ask Emily to take things a bit further.

16

Jake

THE MEMORY OF THAT NIGHT at the bar played over in my head like a scratchy recording on repeat. Lucas's voice, as I had saddled up to the bar, not realizing it was actually him there with his buddy, Cole.

"I've been thinking about asking Emily to move in with me." Or at least that is what I thought he said.

I hadn't meant to eavesdrop. At first, I didn't even know it was Lucas. But the words had stopped me cold. Had I heard him right? I couldn't be sure, but it was enough to plant a seed of doubt and confusion in my mind.

Sitting at my desk now, a stack of case files in front of me, I realized I'd been staring at the same paragraph for the past ten minutes. My mind was too wrapped up in what that kind of decision would mean for Mom.

She'd come so far in the years since the divorce. I'd watched her rebuild herself, piece by piece, into someone stronger and more in-

dependent than I ever thought possible. She'd told me about all the things she wanted to do now that Sarah and I were out of the house: Take up hobbies, read more (her bookshelves were already overflowing), and reconnect with her friends.

Would living with Lucas derail all of that?

I didn't dislike Lucas. He was a good guy, as far as I could tell. He treated Mom well, and Lily was adorable in the way only seven-year-olds can be. They'd attended my college graduation a couple of weeks back, and even with Dad and his new wife there, we'd all managed to get along. Obviously, Mom and Dad had kept their distance. But Lucas had openly chatted with Dad, and Lily had talked with anybody who would give her their ear. So I could definitely see that Mom and Lucas were good together. And Mom was good with Lily, too.

But I couldn't help but worry about what Mom wanted for her life—and whether she could have that while being part of Lucas's world. She had been so adamant after the divorce was final that she was going to embrace her newfound singlehood to do all the things she hadn't had time to do when we were young.

Mom had reconnected with several of her high school classmates in recent years, and they all got together once every month or so for dinners at restaurants around town. And some of them had even gone on a trip to Cabo San Lucas one winter—my mom included. Would all of that change if Mom moved in with Lucas? Would she have to check in with him when she wanted to do something on her own that didn't involve him?

There was also the practical side of things. They lived nearly thirty minutes apart. Lily was in school, and I doubted Lucas would uproot his routine. That meant Mom would likely be the one to move. She'd leave our childhood home behind.

I leaned back in my chair, rubbing my temples. The house had always been a complicated symbol for me. It was where I'd grown up, where I'd made countless memories with Sarah and Mom and Dad. It's where I kissed my first girlfriend, among other things. But it was also where their marriage had unraveled, leaving behind echoes of arguments and silences too thick with unhappiness to ignore.

Still, it was home. And the thought of Mom giving it up made my chest tighten. If she let it go, would there be anything left of the life we'd had before? If things were further into the future, I would buy the house and live there myself. But that simply wasn't in the cards right now.

I needed to talk to her. Pulling out my phone, I scrolled to her name and hit 'Call'. She picked up after the second ring.

"Hi, sweetheart," she said, her voice warm. "This is a nice surprise."

"Hey, Mom," I said, leaning forward on my desk. "Are you busy tomorrow?"

"Not really. Why?"

"Want to grab lunch? My treat."

She laughed softly. "When my son asks to go to lunch, what other option is there than to say yes? Sure, where do you want to go?"

"Anywhere's fine," I said. "I just... I want to talk about some stuff."

Her tone shifted slightly, curiosity creeping in. "Everything okay?"

"Yeah," I said quickly. "I just think it's time we caught up."

"Alright," she said, and I could hear the smile in her voice, possibly laced with a bit of trepidation. "Text me the time and place."

"Will do."

As I ended the call, I stared at my phone for a moment longer. I wasn't sure how the conversation would go or if I'd even find the right words to say. But one thing was clear: I needed to understand what Mom wanted for her life, not just for her sake, but for mine too.

17

Emily

I SET MY CELL PHONE DOWN on the kitchen counter, and my mind was racing. Jake rarely called out of the blue, and when he did, it was usually because something was wrong or he needed something. He was never the clingy type—if anything, he was fiercely independent, sometimes to a fault.

I loved my son deeply, but staying connected with him had always been more of a deliberate effort on my part—or Sarah's. We'd orchestrate family dinners, plan group outings, and check in with him regularly just to make sure he wasn't isolating himself. It wasn't that he didn't care, but Jake had a way of keeping the world at arm's length, especially after everything he'd been through.

The last five years hadn't been easy for him. Andrew and I had separated and divorced right before his senior year of high school, throwing an already challenging time into chaos. Then COVID hit, disrupting the last year of high school and first year of college, and he'd been left scrambling to adjust to virtual classes and the loss of

the typical collegiate experience. It had been heartbreaking for all of us, especially when he didn't get the opportunity to walk across the stage to receive his high school diploma. It was simply mailed to him by the high school.

Through it all, however, he'd managed to stay focused. He got through high school, and we moved him up to college. He had balanced his studies well with a part-time job at the campus newspaper. But it had been a lot, and I knew those concerns were still there, likely in ways even he didn't recognize.

Which was why his call had my hackles raised. Something was on his mind, and I couldn't shake the feeling that it had to do with Lucas.

The next day, I drove to the sandwich shop we'd agreed to meet at, a cozy little place not far from his apartment. Jake had been living there for about six months now, largely thanks to Andrew, who had agreed to help cover the rent once room and board were no longer expenses at college. It was one of the few things I could still appreciate about my ex-husband—his willingness to step up for the kids, even if our marriage had fallen apart. Andrew had even worked out a plan with Jake now that he had graduated from college and had an income from his paid internship. They would split his rent until Jake could handle it on his own.

Jake was already there when I walked in, seated at a small table near the window. He looked up as I approached, offering a small smile that didn't quite reach his eyes.

"Hey, Mom."

"Hey, sweetheart," I said, leaning over for a hug and squeezing his shoulders tightly before taking the seat across from him. "How's it going?"

"Good. Busy, but good."

I couldn't help but notice that his eyes were now locked on the menu on the table in front of him, not meeting mine. What was this all about?

So, we placed our orders, and I encouraged some small talk about his classes and his work at the law firm while we waited. But I could tell there was something else on his mind. His eyes darted to the window after the waitress took the menus. I noticed his fingers tapping lightly against the edge of the table.

"So," I said finally, leaning forward. "What's going on, Jake? You didn't call me out for sandwiches just to talk about your coursework."

He hesitated, his jaw tightening slightly before he spoke. "I wanted to talk to you about Lucas."

"What about Lucas?"

Jake glanced down at his hands, then out the window, and then back up at me. "I, uh... I was at the bar the other night with a friend and saw him there. He was talking to his buddy, and I think I overheard something."

I raised an eyebrow, waiting for him to continue.

"He said something about asking you to move in with him," Jake said, his voice careful. "I don't know if I heard it right, but... is that true? Are you guys thinking about moving in together?"

I leaned back in my chair, my heart skipping a beat. "We haven't talked about that yet," I said honestly. "But it's possible that it is on his mind. We've been seeing each other for a while now, and things are going really well."

Jake frowned, his hands still tapping against the table. "I don't know, Mom. Don't you think it's kind of fast?"

"I'm not sure, Jake. This isn't something Lucas and I have discussed yet," I said gently. "We've been together for seven months. But this is the first I am hearing that this is on his mind."

"But what will you do if he asks?"

I honestly didn't know and wasn't sure how to answer. As I said to Jake, this isn't something Lucas and I had talked about yet. And why was Jake so concerned? He was pursuing his own life and interests now. He didn't even live at home with me anymore, fiercely independent as he was. "I would need to think about it," I finally said.

But it's not just about you and Lucas," he said, his voice a little sharper now. "There's Lily. And your house. I mean, what happens if you move in with him? You'll leave the house, right? The house we grew up in?"

I sighed, reaching across the table to place a hand on his. "Jake, I understand why this is hard for you. The house holds a lot of memories, good and bad. But I'm not making any decisions lightly. Lucas hasn't even asked me yet."

Jake shook his head, his frustration clear. "I just... if you do, I feel like you're giving up everything you said you wanted. You've been so independent, doing things for yourself for the first time in years. What happens to all of that if you start building your life around him and Lily? What about all your friends and the trips you want to take? What about those art classes you wanted to sign up for at the community center?"

His words stung, but I knew they came from a place of love. "First, those art classes were a mistake. My creative talent lies in writing and nothing more. But Jake, more importantly, no matter where this goes, whether I decide to move in with him or not, being with Lucas doesn't mean I'm giving up my independence. If anything, he supports it. He encourages me to write, to pursue my interests, and to be myself. He loves his dedicated time with Lily, and I don't see how that would have to change. My going on a trip gives him time to spend with Lily one-on-one. And this isn't about losing who I am—it's about building something new, something good."

Jake was quiet for a moment, his gaze focused on the table. "I just don't want you to get hurt again," he said finally, his voice barely above a whisper.

I squeezed his hand, my chest tightening at his vulnerability. "I know, sweetheart. And I promise you, I'm being careful. But I may also have to take chances as things move forward. That's part of life."

He nodded slowly, his shoulders relaxing just a bit. "Okay," he said, though his voice was still tinged with doubt.

As we finished our lunch, I couldn't help but feel a mix of emotions—gratitude for his protectiveness, sadness at his fears, and hope that he'd come to see Lucas as someone who truly cared for me. And I honestly wasn't sure what to do with this information he had given me.

I walk to my car, and as I get in, I know what I need to do. I pull out my phone and click on my beloved daughter's face in my contacts. I need to talk to Sarah.

18

Sarah

I WAS IN THE MIDDLE of folding laundry when my phone buzzed on the counter. Glancing at the screen, I saw Mom's face light up on the caller ID. I smiled and answered quickly, balancing the phone between my shoulder and ear.

"Hey, Mom!" I chirped, shaking out one of Michael's shirts before folding it.

"Hi, sweetheart," she replied, but something about her tone made me pause. It wasn't her usual upbeat voice—it was softer, almost uncertain.

I stopped folding, frowning slightly. "Everything okay?"

There was a pause on the other end before she spoke. "I think I could use some mother-daughter time. Are you free today?"

I straightened, the shirt in my hands forgotten. "Of course," I said, lowering my voice as Michael walked into the room. "Mom's on the phone," I whispered to him, and he raised a curious eyebrow before retreating into the kitchen.

"Why don't you come over?" I suggested. "Michael and I are just hanging out, and we can chat here. I'll make coffee—or we can have some wine if you need it."

Mom let out a soft laugh, though it sounded a little strained. "Coffee's fine. I just... I need to talk, and I wasn't sure who else to call."

Her words tugged at my chest. Mom was strong and fiercely independent and rarely asked for help. If she was reaching out like this, something was definitely on her mind.

"Come over," I said again. "We're here, and we'll figure it out together."

"Okay," she said, her voice soft. "I'll be there soon."

When the call ended, I leaned against the counter, staring at the cell phone in my hand.

"What's going on?" Michael asked as he reappeared, holding out a cup of tea in my direction. This man knew me so well, and I took a brief sip of the lavender tea. My mom's favorite tea has become my own throughout recent years.

"Mom sounded... off," I said, setting the phone down. "She wants to come over and talk. I think it's about Lucas."

Michael's expression was thoughtful. "You think something's wrong?"

"I don't know," I admitted. "But if she's calling me like this, it must be important."

He walked over, pressing a kiss to my temple. "You two talk. I'll keep busy in the other room if you need privacy."

I smiled, grateful for his understanding. "Thanks, babe."

About thirty minutes later, I heard Mom's car pull into the narrow driveway of our small home. I opened the door to greet her before she even knocked. But the moment I saw her face, I knew she was carrying some worries and fears she didn't know what to do with.

"Hi, sweetheart," she said, giving me a quick hug as she stepped inside.

"Hi, Mom. Come in. Sit down." She followed me into the living room.

Michael popped his head in briefly to say hello before disappearing into the bedroom, giving us the space we needed. I appreciated him in so many ways.

I tucked my legs beneath me on the oversized couch that occupied most of the room. "Okay, spill. What's going on?"

Mom hesitated, running her hands over the knees of her jeans. "I had lunch with Jake today."

I nodded, waiting for her to continue.

"He overheard Lucas at the bar the other night," she said slowly, her gaze fixed on her hands. "He thought he heard Lucas talking about asking me to move in with him."

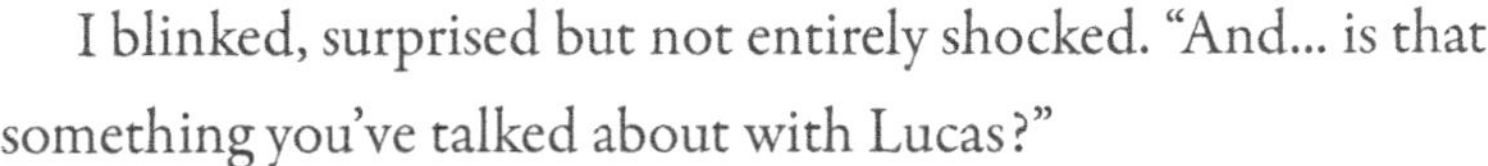

I blinked, surprised but not entirely shocked. "And... is that something you've talked about with Lucas?"

She shook her head. "No. We haven't had that conversation. But the idea doesn't feel far-fetched, given how close we've become."

"So what's the problem?"

"It's Jake," she said, her voice suggesting frustration. "He's worried. He thinks I'm moving too fast, that I'm giving up the independence I've worked so hard to build. He brought up the house, too—how much it means to the two of you and what it would mean if I left it behind."

I sighed, leaning back against the cushions. "That sounds like Jake. Always protective, always thinking ten steps ahead." I paused. "But what makes you think you can't leave the house behind if that is what you want to do?"

Mom let out a shaky laugh. "This isn't even something Lucas and I had talked about yet. For all I know, Jake misheard what Lucas said."

I reached over, taking her hand in mine. "So, what if he didn't mishear? How does that make you feel?"

She looked up at the ceiling. "I don't know, to be honest. This is all new territory for me. Your dad and I were together for decades. I never imagined myself living anywhere but in that house, in the home we had built together. Even when things fell apart, I guess I never looked that far ahead to see that my future would indeed be different."

Mom looked so confused that I wanted to take her in my arms. But I knew that wasn't what she needed. She needed me to be straight with her. "Mom, the world is your oyster. You can do whatever it is that you want to do. And it isn't up to me or Jake to tell you what you should or shouldn't do. If you want to move in with Lucas—if he asks you to—then you need to make the decision that feels right for you."

She looks at me, her eyes searching mine. "I don't know. I love Lucas, Sarah. And I love Lily. But Jake's concerns aren't completely unfounded. I've spent so much time rebuilding my life, and I'm scared of losing that—of losing myself again."

I squeezed her hand, my voice soft. "You're not the same person you were with Dad. You've grown, Mom. And if Lucas truly loves you—and it sounds like he does—then he'll support you no matter your decision."

Her eyes welled up, and she let out a soft breath. "I just want to do what's best for everyone. But sometimes, it feels like I'm being pulled in too many directions."

"Then maybe it's time to stop thinking about everyone else for a minute and focus on what you want," I said gently. "What makes you happy, Mom? What feels right for you? Forget about Jake and answer this question for you."

Mom smiled faintly, a tear slipping down her cheek. "Lucas makes me happy," she said quietly. "But I want to be sure I'm making the right choices for the right reasons."

"And you will," I said, pulling her into a hug. "You've got a good head on your shoulders, Mom. You'll figure it out."

She held me tightly for a moment before pulling back, wiping her eyes. "Thanks, sweetheart. I needed this."

"Anytime," I said, smiling. "That's what daughters are for."

We spent the rest of the afternoon talking, laughing, and sipping coffee, and by the time Mom left, she seemed lighter, more at peace.

As I watched her car pull out of the driveway, I couldn't help but feel hopeful. Whatever decisions she made, I knew she'd make them with her whole heart. And that was all I could ever ask for. But in the meantime, I had a bone to pick with my little brother.

19

Emily

I HAD LONG SINCE USED letters to help me work through complicated feelings in my mind. Often, I wrote to no one in particular. Sometimes, I wrote letters to God. Other times, I wrote letters to my kids, even though they were letters I would never give them. I even wrote a letter once to Andrew shortly after that day, in which I packed up all his stuff and told him to get out.

It wasn't that I wanted, or needed, anyone to read the letters. It was simply my way of coping, of helping myself get things out on paper, so to speak, so that I could move on. Many of those letters took up residence in a banker's box on the top shelf of the closet in my bedroom.

It had been a while since I had written one of my letters to anyone besides the people who wrote me fan letters once in a while. The few I selected to write back to always held special meaning for me, and I put my all into every word.

Today, I felt the need to write another letter. I knew that Jake was having a hard time processing everything. And though Sarah would never say it, I knew she had her own fears. But the thing is, I needed them to let me figure things out for myself. I wasn't perfect, and I would make mistakes. But I was, I am, a grown woman, and it is my life that I need to set the direction for.

And so I took out a piece of stationary from the drawer in my desk and started to write.

Dear Sarah and Jake,

As I sit here at my desk, with a fresh piece of stationery in front of me, I find myself overwhelmed with so many thoughts and emotions. Writing has always been my way of making sense of the chaos in my head, and today, I feel the need to put some of those thoughts into words for the two of you.

The last few years haven't been easy for any of us. We've all endured heartache and challenges that have tested us in ways we couldn't have imagined. I think about those early days after your dad left—the hurt, the anger, the uncertainty. It wasn't just my world that crumbled; it was yours, too. And for that, I will always carry a sense of responsibility. As your mom, I wanted to shield you from pain, but I couldn't.

Looking back, I know I made mistakes. I didn't always handle things the right way, especially in those early months. I leaned on you, Sarah, more than I should have. I relied on your maturity and your strength at a time when you should have been free to focus on your own life. And Jake, I know I wasn't always as present as I should have been for you during your senior year. I was lost in my own pain, and for that, I am deeply sorry.

Then came those first few tentative steps back into the world of dating. Oh, how awkward and messy those were. I stumbled through bad dates, learned the hard way about red flags, and felt more unsure of myself than I had since my twenties. There were times when I wondered if I was chasing something I didn't really need. But deep down, despite my desire for my independence, I knew I wanted to find someone who would love and accept not just me but all of us—the complicated, beautiful, messy life we've built together.

And then I met Lucas.

He wasn't what I expected, not at all. I don't think I even realized how much I needed someone like him until he walked into my life. He's steady, kind, and patient in a way I didn't think was possible. He doesn't just care about me; he respects me and sees me for who I am, flaws and all. And more than that, he values both of you.

Jake, I see the way Lucas looks at you, as though he admires the man you're becoming. And Sarah, I see how he listens to you, truly listens, the way every person should feel listened to. It's these little moments that make me believe he's someone worth holding on to, someone worth taking a leap of faith for.

I don't know what the future holds, but I do know this: if Lucas asks me to move in with him, I will say yes. I want to share my life with him, to create something new and beautiful in a space that isn't tied to the pain of the past. Selling this house won't be easy. I know it holds so many memories for all of us, good and bad. It's the home where you both grew up, but it's also the home where I discovered your dad had built a life without me. It's where I patched walls and packed boxes in the middle of the night, trying to figure out how to move forward.

Creating new memories in a place that isn't haunted by old ones feels like the right step for me. Lucas's home isn't tied to Jessica; it's a fresh start—a place where we can build a life together, where you both—and Lily—will always be welcome.

I know this isn't just a change for me; it's a change for all of us. And that's why I'm writing to you now. I need your support, your love, and your understanding. I need you to know that this decision isn't one I make lightly. It's one I make because I believe in the life Lucas and I can build together, a life that includes you both, always.

And I need you to be open to Lily. She's a sweet, curious, spirited little girl who has brought so much light into my life. I've fallen in love with her, not as her mom, but as someone who cares deeply for her. She's a part of Lucas, and loving her feels as natural as loving him.

Thank you for being the incredible people you are. You've both shown me more love and strength than I deserve, and I'm so proud of the adults you've become.

I hope you'll help me move forward and embrace this new chapter with me. No matter where life takes us, you'll always be my heart.

With all my love,

Mom

20

Jake

MY PHONE BUZZED on the desk, Sarah's name and picture flashing on the screen. I frowned, staring at it for a moment. Why was Sarah calling me? We didn't talk on the phone much—texting was our usual go-to unless it was a family emergency.

I picked up the call, already bracing myself. "Hey, Sarah. What's up?"

"What's up?" she repeated, her tone sharp. "Are you serious, Jake? What's up is me trying to figure out what the hell you were thinking!"

I blinked, pulling the phone away for a second to look at the screen, half-expecting to see someone else's name. Nope. It was definitely Sarah.

"What are you talking about?" I asked cautiously.

"What am I talking about?" she snapped. "I'm talking about you planting seeds of doubt in Mom's head. What were you even thinking, Jake? Telling her what you overheard when you weren't even sure if you heard it right? Why would you do that?"

I sat back in my chair, already feeling defensive. "Hold on a second, Sarah. I wasn't trying to mess with her head. I thought she had a right to know if Lucas was thinking about asking her to move in."

"You thought?" she shot back. "You didn't know, Jake. That's the problem. You took something you weren't even sure about and turned it into a big deal, and now Mom's second-guessing everything. Do you have any idea how unfair that is to her?"

Her words hit like a slap, and I took a deep breath, trying to stay calm. "Sarah, I wasn't trying to upset her. I was just... concerned, okay? I don't want her to rush into something she might regret."

"Well, congratulations," Sarah said sarcastically. "Because now she's worried about whether she's even capable of making her own decisions. She doesn't need you playing the overprotective son right now. She needs you to trust her."

"Trust her?" I repeated a little more forcefully than I intended. "Sarah, she's talking about moving in with a guy she's only been dating for a few months. That's a big deal! I'm allowed to have concerns."

"Yes, you're allowed to have concerns," she said, her voice slightly softer but still firm. "But it's not your decision to make, Jake. And the way you went about this—sharing half-baked information and making her question herself—that's not okay. Just think about everything we went through when Mom and Dad split up. Think of everything she has done to rebuild herself. She's happy. Finally! And now you have her all confused and questioning what she wants."

I ran a hand through my hair, frustration bubbling up. "I wasn't trying to manipulate her. I just—" I stopped, searching for the right words. "I've seen what happens when she gets hurt, Sarah. I don't want her to go through that again."

There was a pause on the other end, and when Sarah spoke again, her voice was calmer. "I get that, Jake. I do. But she's not the same person she was when Dad left. She's stronger now, and she's not going to let anyone walk all over her. Lucas isn't Dad."

I sighed, leaning forward on the desk. "I know he's not. But it's not just about Lucas. It's about everything—her independence, the house, how fast this feels. It's like she's giving up everything she said she wanted."

"She's not giving up anything. She can still do all those things and be in a new relationship with someone who makes her happy," Sarah countered. "And if that means moving in with Lucas, then that's her choice to make. Not yours, not mine—hers."

I was quiet for a moment, letting her words sink in.

"Jake," Sarah continued, her tone softer now, "I know you're trying to protect her. But you need to let her live her life. She's not fragile, and she's not helpless. She's Mom. And she's doing the best she can."

I rubbed my temples, feeling what felt like a thousand bricks settling on my shoulders. "You're right," I admitted reluctantly. "I shouldn't have said anything until I knew for sure. I just... I don't want to lose her, Sarah. Or the house or the memories. It feels like everything's changing so fast."

"I get that," Sarah said gently. "But change isn't always bad. Sometimes, it's just... different. And 'different' can be good." She paused before saying carefully, "And I don't want to lose the house either. But that's not our decision to make. And it might actually be better for Mom to move on from the house to somewhere that she can make new memories that don't constantly remind her of the past."

I nodded, even though she couldn't see me. "I'll stand down," I said finally. "I'll let her figure it out for herself."

"Good," Sarah said, her voice lighter now. "Because she's capable of doing that. And honestly, I think she's happier than she's been in a long time. She needs our love and support now more than ever."

"Maybe," I said, a small smile tugging at my lips. "But I'm still keeping an eye on Lucas."

Sarah laughed softly. "I'd expect nothing less."

As we hung up, I leaned back in my chair, staring at the ceiling. Sarah was right, of course. Mom was strong and deserved the chance to make her own choices. I just hoped Lucas understood how lucky he was to have her.

21

Lucas

THE LATE AFTERNOON SUN poured through my office windows, casting golden light on the sketches spread across my desk. I leaned back in my chair, stretching my arms above my head as I surveyed the progress on the treehouse project.

It was coming together better than I'd hoped. After visiting the site and brainstorming with the owners, I had nearly finalized the designs for the three interconnected treehouses. Each would be nestled in the towering oaks surrounding the property, with wooden walkways connecting them and floor-to-ceiling windows offering panoramic views of the forest.

I'd submitted the plans the week before, and the owners were thrilled. Construction was slated to begin in just a few weeks, and I couldn't wait to see the vision come to life.

On my other desk were updates from the boutique bakery project I'd wrapped up last month. Construction was already underway, and the owners had invited me to the grand opening. It was just

a few months away, and I was looking forward to seeing the space buzzing with life and smelling the smell of fresh bread and pastries.

Things were moving in the right direction professionally, but my mind wasn't on work today.

I glanced at the clock, my heart skipping a beat. In just a few hours, I'd pick up Emily for dinner, and tonight, I was planning to take the next step in our relationship.

I was going to ask her to move in with me.

The thought sent a mix of excitement and nerves coursing through me. It had been nine months since we started dating, and every moment with her had only deepened my feelings. Emily wasn't just someone I loved—she was someone I could see a future with.

She'd become such an integral part of my life—and Lily's, too. Watching the two of them together brought a sense of peace I hadn't felt in years. Emily had a way of connecting with Lily that was genuine and effortless, and I could see how much Lily looked forward to the time they spent together.

But this wasn't just about Lily. It was about us—me and Emily.

I knew asking her to move in was a big step, especially for her. Emily valued her independence, and I never wanted her to feel like she was giving up part of herself to be with me. And I knew that I wouldn't be able to move in with her. Lily loved her school, and Jessica and I lived close enough to one another that Lily could take the bus to school no matter whose house she was at. So if anyone was going to make the move, Emily would have to move in with me. She'd likely need to sell her house, and I knew how much she had loved it. As an architect, I appreciate the thought that she and Andrew had put into the designs, working with a custom builder to get exactly what they wanted. It was a one-of-a-kind home, for sure.

I knew that I would be asking a lot of Emily, and I hoped that she would see the opportunity for what it was—an opportunity to build a future together as partners, side by side.

The past few weeks had been a whirlwind of plans for Lily's upcoming birthday. She was turning eight soon, and Emily had thrown herself into helping me organize a small party at the house. Lily had insisted on a jungle theme—complete with animal-themed cupcakes and decorations. Emily had come up with the idea of setting up an "adventure trail" in the backyard, and I'd spent the better part of last weekend helping her design it. I guess that's what happens when you are an architect—the expectations are high, and who was I to let Lily or Emily down?

But tonight wasn't about Lily or the projects I'd been working on. Tonight was about Emily and me.

I stood up, pacing the room as I mentally ran through the plans. I'd made a reservation at one of her favorite restaurants—that same cozy Italian place we'd discovered a few months back. The staff knew us by now, and I'd called ahead to request a quiet table by the window. It was odd. Emily usually loved trying new places all the time, but after we had tried this quaint place, she wanted to go back on more than one occasion. And I understood why. The food was amazing. The staff seemed to know just when to stop by the table and when to stay at a respectable distance. And the ambiance—it was the perfect place for falling in love.

The conversation I wanted to have was clear in my mind, though I couldn't help but feel a twinge of uncertainty. What if she wasn't ready? What if the idea of moving in felt like too much, too fast?

I shook my head, pushing the doubts aside. Emily and I had built something real. Something worth taking a chance on.

As the clock ticked closer to six, I grabbed my jacket and keys, heading out to pick her up. I knew tonight wouldn't just be another date night—it would be a defining moment for us.

And no matter how the conversation went, I was ready to tackle head-on whatever came next.

22

Emily

THE AROMA OF FRESH BASIL and roasted garlic wafted through the air, and my taste buds started to salivate—it was like this delicious, warm hug. This thought quickly made me think of the beloved snowman from one of Sarah's favorite childhood Disney films. I smiled in delight at the memory.

I sat across from Lucas at a cozy table by the window, the soft glow of candlelight bringing a lovely light to his already handsome face. The Italian restaurant was as charming as ever—small, intimate, and simply brimming with quiet energy from the other diners.

I twirled my fork idly in my pancetta and mozzarella tagliatelle, savoring the rich flavors with every bite. Across from me, Lucas was digging into the restaurant's signature lasagna, the cheese bubbling and golden brown.

"This is so good," I said, raising my glass of white wine for another sip.

Lucas chuckled. "Better than the last place we tried?"

I thought about it for a moment, smiling. "I think so. You know me, though—I'm all about trying new places. But this one might just be worth repeating. Again."

He nodded, lifting his glass of wine—he'd foregone his usual Peroni tonight. "Cheers to that. And to your impeccable taste in wine."

I laughed, shaking my head. "Don't act like you wouldn't rather have a beer right now."

"True," he admitted, grinning. "But I'm making exceptions tonight. Besides, this isn't bad. Even for a guy who'd normally pick a red with lasagna."

"You're welcome," I teased, raising my glass in a mock toast.

The meal was everything I'd hoped for—delicious food, great company, and that familiar comfort and easiness I always felt with Lucas. The conversation flowed so well. It was simple, as it always was. Tonight's conversation started with an update on his latest projects.

"So, the treehouse plans are almost done?" I asked, twirling a strand of pasta on my fork.

"Almost," Lucas said, leaning back in his chair. "I need to make one more site visit to finalize a few things, but we're close. The owners are thrilled so far. And I've got to say, my tree-climbing skills are about to come in quite handy."

I raised an eyebrow, laughing. "Tree-climbing skills? I'm not sure I've heard about these."

"Oh, they're legendary," he said with mock seriousness. "I was practically a squirrel as a kid. I think I climbed every tree in our neighborhood."

I couldn't stop laughing, picturing a young Lucas scaling trees. "Well, let's hope those skills don't fail you now. I'd hate for your big project to end with you stuck in a tree."

"Noted," he said, grinning, absently rubbing his chest. I'd noticed him doing that recently, but the thought came and went.

The conversation shifted to plans for Lily's upcoming birthday. She'd been talking about her jungle-themed party nonstop for weeks, and I couldn't wait to see her face light up when everything came together.

"She's so excited," I said, smiling. "I think the adventure trail idea might just make her year."

Lucas nodded, his expression softening. "Yeah, she's pretty pumped. I just hope I can pull off what she's imagining. She has high expectations."

"Gee, I wonder where she gets that from," I laughed.

Lucas chuckled, then grew thoughtful. "I was thinking about inviting Jessica to the party. What do you think?"

I paused, considering his words. "I think it's a good idea. It's a big day for Lily; having her mom there would mean a lot to her."

He nodded. "That's what I was thinking, too. Plus, I know Jessica's been struggling a bit financially lately. Physical therapists don't make nearly what they should."

"That's true," I said, swirling my wine in the glass. "It's kind of you to include her. And I'm sure Lily will love having both of you there."

"She's also been talking about inviting Sarah," Lucas added, a smile tugging at his lips. "Not your Sarah. The new girl down the street. Apparently, they've already become best friends."

"Lily is good at that," I said warmly. "She has a way of making people feel welcome."

"Wonder where she gets that from?" Lucas asked, his tone soft. "I mean, I know you're not her mom. But you are definitely rubbing off on her."

I looked up, meeting his gaze. There was something different in his eyes tonight—something serious but also tender. My stomach fluttered, and I set my glass down carefully, wondering what he was about to say. Though, based on my conversation with Jake a couple of weeks back, I was pretty sure I knew where this was going. Thankfully, I had had some time to think about it and was prepared with my thoughts. And my decision.

"Emily," he began, his voice steady, "these past nine months with you have been incredible. You've become such an important part of my life—and Lily's life, too. I can't imagine things without you."

My heart was racing now, and I felt a mix of anticipation and nerves as he continued.

"I've been thinking about us a lot lately," he said, leaning forward slightly. "And I want to take the next step. I want us to be together—

not just on weekends or special nights but every day. What would you think about moving in with me?"

For a moment, I was speechless. Even though I had been right about what he was about to ask, the words still caught me off guard. His words hung in the air, filling the space between us.

"Move in with you?" I repeated softly, my mind racing. Why was my mind racing? I thought I had already worked through all of this in my head.

Lucas nodded, his eyes searching mine. "I know it's a big step. And I know how much your independence means to you. But I also know how much better life is when you're in it. I want to build a future with you, Emily. You, me, and Lily—together. And of course, Sarah and Jake can visit whenever they want. Whenever you want."

I felt a rush of emotions—joy, excitement, and, if I was honest, a little fear. I loved Lucas, and I loved Lily. But moving in together? It was more than just a practical change—it was a commitment, a merging of lives that felt exhilarating and intimidating all at once.

"I..." I began, my voice catching. "Lucas, I love you. You know that. And I love Lily. But this is... a lot to take in."

"I know," he said gently. "I don't need an answer right this second. I just want you to know how I feel."

I took a deep breath, letting his words settle. "I think... yes. Yes, I want to move in with you." He looked up at me, his eyes full of hope but filled with questions, just the same. "But... Can we wait until after the holidays? I want to take my time getting my house ready to sell, and I don't want to rush into anything."

A slow smile spread across Lucas's face, and he reached across the table to take my hand. "Of course," he said. "Whatever timeline works for you. I just want us to be together."

I squeezed his hand, feeling a warmth spread through me. "Thank you," I said softly. "For understanding."

As the night went on, the conversation shifted back to lighter topics, but my heart felt lighter, too. This wasn't just a defining moment—it was the beginning of something new, something beautiful.

And for the first time in a long time, I felt like I was exactly where I was meant to be.

23

Jessica

THE PHONE MADE A CHIRPING noise on the kitchen counter, and I glanced at the screen. Lucas. I wiped my hands on a dish towel before picking it up, already feeling a twinge of curiosity. It wasn't unusual for us to talk, but most of our communication was through quick texts about Lily's schedule or school updates.

"Hey, Lucas," I answered, balancing the phone against my shoulder as I opened the fridge to grab a bottle of water.

"Hey, Jess," he said, his tone warm. "How's it going?"

"Not bad," I said, leaning against the counter. "Just the usual. Lily's already planning what she wants to bring to show-and-tell next week. How about you?"

He chuckled. "That sounds like her. I'm good. Actually, I wanted to ask you something."

I felt a flicker of anticipation. "What's up?"

"So, you know Lily's birthday is coming up," he began, his voice taking on that careful, measured tone he used when he was trying to gauge my reaction. "We're planning a little party for her at my place, and I was wondering if you'd like to be part of it."

My heart softened immediately. "Of course, I'd like to be part of it," I said, a smile spreading across my face. "Thank you for including me."

"Lily would want you there," he said simply. "And honestly, so would I. We're trying to keep it simple—just a few friends from school, some activities in the backyard. But if you're up for it, I was hoping you could help with the cake."

"The cake?" I asked, relieved by the manageable task.

"Yeah," he said. "I figured you could order it or bake it, whatever works best for you. Lily's been talking about a jungle theme, so something with animals would be perfect."

I laughed softly, already picturing Lily's excitement. "I can handle that. It'll be nice to do something special for her."

"Thanks, Jess," he said. "I know she'll love it."

For a moment, the line was quiet, and I was about to say goodbye when Lucas cleared his throat.

"Actually," he said, his voice hesitating, "there's something else I wanted to tell you."

I froze, my grip tightening on the phone. I had a feeling I knew what was coming, and my chest tightened involuntarily.

"Okay," I said cautiously. "What's on your mind?"

He exhaled as if bracing himself. "Emily and I have been talking, and... well, I've asked her to move in with me."

I blinked, caught off guard. Moving in. Not getting engaged. Not getting married. Just moving in. Relief coursed through me, but it was quickly followed by a bittersweet pang of sadness about what could have been or should have been but never was.

"That's... a big step," I said finally, keeping my voice even.

"It is," Lucas admitted. "But we're not rushing into anything. She's not planning to sell her house until after the holidays, and we've talked through what this will mean for Lily."

"I see," I said, my throat feeling a little tight.

There was a pause on the line, and then Lucas added, "I wanted to tell you first because I thought it was important. For you to hear it from me, not Lily."

I nodded, even though he couldn't see me. "I appreciate that," I said softly.

Truthfully, I didn't know how I felt. Relieved, yes, but also... left behind. Lucas was moving forward, building a life with someone new, while I could barely keep my head above water most days.

"It sounds like you've thought this through," I said after a moment.

"We have," he said. "I want to make sure this transition is as smooth as possible for everyone. That includes you."

I swallowed hard, forcing a smile into my voice. "I'm glad you told me, Lucas. Really. And if Lily's happy, that's what matters most."

"She is," he said. "She adores Emily. And honestly, I think this is going to be good for all of us."

"I hope so," I said quietly.

After a few more pleasantries and confirming plans for our exchange at the end of the coming weekend, we ended the call, and I set the phone down on the counter, staring at it for a moment.

I should have been happy for him. And I was, in a way. But as I stood there in the quiet of my kitchen, I couldn't help but feel the heaviness of my own life pressing down on me.

Dating hadn't even been on my radar since the divorce. Between extra shifts at the clinic, heading up to Duluth every other week to help my parents with their increasing care needs, and making sure Lily had everything she needed, I barely had time to think, let alone focus on my personal life.

And yet, a small, nagging part of me wondered what it would be like to have someone to share my life with again. I want to have a partner to lean on when the days feel too long, someone to share the little joys and victories with.

But that wasn't my reality. Not now, anyway.

I took a deep breath, pushing those thoughts aside. Right now, my priority was Lily—and making sure her birthday was everything she wanted it to be.

Even if it meant facing the bittersweet reality of watching Lucas move forward while I stayed behind.

24

Lily

I TURNED EIGHT TODAY, and it's been the best day ever! Ten of my friends from school came to my birthday party, and I was so excited when I saw all of them walking up to the house. Mommy said it was because they all like me, and Daddy said it's because I'm the coolest kid in my class. I think they're both right.

The backyard looked so cool! Daddy and Emily worked all morning to set up this adventure walk. There were big red baskets for each of us, and we got to carry them on the trail to find surprises hidden all over. The trail was full of fun stuff—packages of slime, fidget spinners, stickers, colorful water bottles, animal puzzles, pop-it toys, and even Barbies! We could pick five things, but then we could trade with each other if we wanted.

I got the best stuff: a package of slime, one pop-it toy, a fidget spinner, and two Barbies. Two Barbies! My friend Sarah really wanted one of my Barbies, but I said no. She got two Barbies, too, so she didn't need mine. We laughed about it, and

she traded one of her pop-it toys for a new fidget spinner with another friend.

Mommy made my birthday cake, and it was perfect. It was chocolate—my favorite—with a polar bear on the front because I love polar bears. I think Mommy makes the best cakes in the whole world. Emily said so too, and Daddy ate two pieces, so it must be true. There was vanilla ice cream, too, and Daddy scooped it out for everyone. I told him to make mine extra big, and he laughed and gave me a big scoop.

After we ate, everyone sang 'Happy Birthday' to me, and it felt so special to have everyone I love there. Mommy, Daddy, Emily, and even Sarah, Michael, and Jake were there. Jake kept telling funny stories to the other parents, and Michael helped Daddy clean up the adventure walk when we were done. Mommy took care of the cake, and Sarah helped me open my presents. Emily was usually just smiling at me wherever I was. It felt good.

Cole and Rebecca came too, and Olivia played with me and my friends. She's one year younger than us, but she's really fun. She liked the adventure walk so much that she went on it twice!

When it was time to blow out the candles, I closed my eyes really tight and made a wish. I can't tell you what it was, but I hope it comes true. Everyone cheered when I blew out the candles, and I felt like the happiest girl in the world.

It was the best party ever. I hope every birthday is this amazing!

25

Jake

THE HOUSE WAS FULL of activity, the smell of cinnamon and pine filling the air as Mom, Sarah, and Michael worked on untangling a particularly stubborn strand of Christmas lights. I sat cross-legged on the living room floor, rifling through a box of ornaments that hadn't seen the light of day in years.

"Do we really need every decoration out this year?" I called over to Mom, holding up a ceramic Santa that had definitely seen better days. "It isn't even Thanksgiving yet."

"Yes," she replied firmly, her voice muffled from where she was digging through another box. "Every single one."

I exchanged a look with Sarah, who raised an eyebrow but said nothing. Usually, Mom was selective about her holiday decorations, carefully choosing which pieces would go up and keeping the rest packed away. But this year, it was like she was on a mission to transform the house into the North Pole itself.

"Are you sure about this, Mom?" Sarah asked, her tone light but probing. "It's going to take forever to put everything out—and even longer to pack it all up."

Mom straightened, brushing her hands on her jeans. "I'm sure," she said with a small smile. "It just feels like the kind of year where we need a little extra holiday cheer, don't you think?"

Michael, ever the peacekeeper, chimed in with a grin. "Well, at least the house will look amazing. I'm all for decking the halls."

I nodded, though I couldn't shake the feeling that there was more to this sudden burst of holiday enthusiasm. Mom had seemed a little... off lately. She was not unhappy but restless, like she was trying to fill a space she didn't quite know how to handle.

As the afternoon wore on, the living room transformed into a Christmas wonderland. The tree sparkled with twinkling white lights, silver garlands draped over the mantle, and the ceramic Santa I'd unearthed found a home on the side table. The upstairs hallway held a second tree, adorned with all the ornaments from our childhood. It was packed with oddly shaped ornaments, many of which we had no idea what they were supposed to be.

"Not bad," Sarah said, stepping back to admire the tree in the living room. "I think we outdid ourselves this year."

Mom smiled, though her eyes flicked to the clock on the wall. It was nearly 5 PM, and Lucas still wasn't here.

"He's probably just running late," I said, reassuringly.

Mom nodded, but I could tell she was worried. Lucas was never late without letting her know. And the fact that he hadn't called or texted? That wasn't like him.

"Did he say what time he'd be done at the treehouse?" Sarah asked, draping an arm over the back of the couch.

"Not exactly," Mom said, her voice quieter now. "But he said he'd be here by dinner. He's probably just caught up with something."

We all tried to brush it off, but the unease in the room grew as the minutes ticked by. Mom busied herself with rearranging a few ornaments on the tree, but her hands were trembling just slightly, and her smile didn't quite reach her eyes.

By the time 5:30 rolled around, I couldn't take the tension anymore.

"Mom," I said gently, "why don't you try calling him?"

She hesitated, glancing at her phone on the kitchen counter. "I don't want to bother him if he's busy."

"It's not bothering him," Sarah said, her voice firm. "It's just checking in. He'd do the same for you."

Mom nodded, wiping her hands on a dish towel before picking up her phone. She dialed quickly, holding it to her ear as we all watched her anxiously.

After a few moments, she frowned. "It went to voicemail," she said, lowering the phone.

"That's weird," Michael said, his brows furrowing. "Doesn't he usually pick up?"

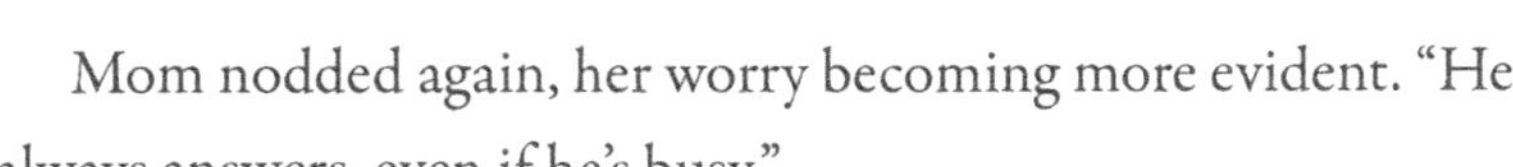

Mom nodded again, her worry becoming more evident. "He always answers, even if he's busy."

A knot tightened in my stomach. Lucas wasn't the kind of guy to leave people hanging—especially Mom. Even if he was busy, he would answer quickly to make sure all was well, then excuse himself with a promise to call back right away.

"Maybe his phone died," Sarah suggested, though her voice didn't sound entirely convinced of her own suggestion.

"Or he's still driving and didn't hear it," Michael added, trying to keep things light. I made eye contact with him, both of us knowing that Lucas drove a newer SUV and that his phone would ring through the speakers of the vehicle.

"Maybe," Mom said, but her eyes kept darting to the window, as if willing his car to pull into the driveway.

I exchanged glances with Sarah, and we both knew what the other was thinking. Something didn't feel right.

As the clock edged closer to 6 PM, the atmosphere in the house had officially shifted from festive to tense. The lights on the tree twinkled merrily, but Mom's face was fraught with worry.

"Maybe I should drive over there," I said finally. "See if he's still at the site."

Mom looked at me, her eyes filled with uncertainty. "You don't have to do that, Jake. It's a long drive, and you'd probably end up passing him heading in the opposite direction."

"I want to," I said firmly. "I'm sure it's nothing, but it'll put your mind at ease, right? And, if he arrives, all you need to do is call me, and I'll turn around and head back."

She hesitated, then nodded. "Okay. Thank you."

I grabbed my coat and keys, the knot in my stomach tightening as I stepped outside into the crisp evening air.

As I slid into the driver's seat and started the engine, I couldn't shake the feeling that something was wrong. Lucas wasn't the kind of guy to be late without a reason.

And I was determined to find out what that reason was.

26

Lucas

THE MEMORY OF LILY'S laughter filled my mind as I crouched on a thick branch, the cool bark rough beneath my hands. Her birthday party last week had been a resounding success, and the joy on her face had made all the effort worthwhile.

The weather had stayed unseasonably warm, letting the kids run wild on the adventure trail Emily and I had designed in the backyard. Watching them carry their little apple-picking baskets and discover animal-themed trinkets, with a few Barbies and other things tossed in for good measure, hidden along the way had been one of those rare moments of pure joy.

Lily had been ecstatic, her cheeks pink with excitement as she showed off each new find. Her favorite? Two new Barbie dolls. And Jessica and Emily... Well, they'd managed the day with a kind of grace I hadn't dared to hope for.

Jessica had hung close to Lily for all the big moments—the presents, the candles, the cutting of the cake—and Emily had stepped back, giving her the space to be mom. It hadn't felt forced, either. It was natural, even comfortable, and I couldn't help but marvel at how far we'd come.

The party had felt like a turning point, a glimpse into what life could be like—a life where all the pieces fit together just as they were supposed to. And tonight, Emily and I were hosting dinner at her house—well, Emily was doing all the work, really—and would tell Sarah, Michael, and Jake about our plans to put Emily's house on the market after the new year, and for her to move in with me and Lily.

But right now, my focus was on the treehouse project.

I glanced at the camera strapped around my neck, adjusting the lens as I aimed it at a particular angle of the trunk where one of the walkways would connect. The Wilsons had driven off in their truck about twenty minutes ago, leaving me alone on the property to wrap up my final measurements and photos.

The towering oak I was perched in was the centerpiece of the project. Its sprawling branches would cradle the largest of the three treehouses, and I wanted to make sure I got everything just right before handing the plans over to my graphic designer for rendering.

Shifting slightly, I carefully braced my foot against the ladder for a better view.

That's when it happened. My toe tapped the top of the ladder— just enough to throw it off balance. I froze, watching in horror as the ladder teetered momentarily before crashing to the ground below.

"Shit," I muttered, leaning my head back against the sturdy branch. For a moment, I just sat there, staring down at the fallen ladder. The Wilsons were gone, and I hadn't seen anyone else on the property all day. I was completely alone.

"Okay, Lucas," I muttered to myself. "You've been in worse situations. You just need to think this through."

The branch I was on was sturdy enough, and I could probably lower myself to the one just below it. From there, it was only about a ten-foot drop to the ground. "Easy enough," I said, trying to convince myself.

But as I adjusted my position, I felt the telltale ache in my knee—the one that had been bothering me ever since that high school baseball injury. My physical therapist, Jessica, of all people, had warned me about putting too much strain on it. And there was a pressure in my chest, one that I had felt periodically in recent days. I'm sure it was just anxiety—I was stuck in a tree, after all.

Still, I couldn't exactly stay up in the tree all night. I took a deep breath, gripping the branch tightly as I lowered myself to the one below. It creaked slightly under my weight, but it held.

"Almost there," I said, more to keep myself calm than anything else. That pressure in my chest was getting a bit worse. It was actually getting a bit uncomfortable.

I eyed the ground, gauging the distance. It wasn't that far—surely I could jump down and land on my feet, right? But as I prepared to make the leap, doubt crept in. My knee wasn't what it used to be, and the ground below was uneven. One bad landing and I could be in a world of trouble.

I hesitated, my heart pounding in my chest, and the pressure was increasing.

Then I heard it—the distant rumble of an engine.

I craned my neck, relief flooding through me as I saw the Wilsons' truck pulling back into the driveway. The pressure subsided, just a bit. I wasn't imagining it, was I?

"Thank God," I muttered, waving my arms to catch their attention. And as I lifted my arms in the air, that pressure got worse yet. It was like a vise grip was squeezing my heart.

It took a few moments, but eventually, Mr. Wilson spotted me and stepped out of the truck, looking up at me with a mix of confusion and amusement.

"Lucas, what the hell are you doing up there?" he called.

I couldn't help but laugh, despite the incredible pressure of anxiety in my chest. "Long story," I said. "But I could really use that ladder."

Mrs. Wilson appeared from the other side of the truck, taking in the scene with a raised eyebrow. "You architects sure have a funny way of working," she said, shaking her head.

Within minutes, Mr. Wilson had the ladder propped back against the tree, and I climbed down carefully, my knee protesting slightly with each step. And that pressure. "Thanks for coming back," I said as I reached the ground, shaking Mr. Wilson's hand. But my chest really ached now, and the pain was radiating around to my back and up my arms. It even seemed a bit difficult to breathe in enough air.

"Don't mention it," he said with a chuckle. "But maybe stick to the ground for the rest of the day, huh?"

"Deal." I managed to get out, but my smile faltered. Suddenly, I felt a bit faint, and a cold sweat broke out across my forehead. My face felt tingly. And my chest felt like it was exploding.

Mrs. Wilson seemed to notice and took a step toward me. "Son, are you al—" she began to ask, but it was too late. I clutched my chest and fell to the ground.

27

Jessica

THE HOUSE WAS QUIET except for the cheerful melody of a Disney song drifting from the living room. Lily was curled up on the old couch that Jessica's parents had given them when she and Lucas had split, surrounded by a sea of her new birthday toys, singing as she stacked blocks into a wobbly tower. All those new toys to play with, and she still loved building things with baby blocks. She must get that from her father. I smiled faintly, leaning against the counter as I scrolled through my phone.

Then it buzzed, a call lighting up the screen from an unfamiliar number.

Normally, I wouldn't have answered. Scam calls were all too common, and I didn't have the energy to deal with another one. But something about the number stopped me. A strange instinct, a pull in my chest, told me to pick up.

Glancing over my shoulder to make sure Lily was still engrossed in her movie and things were going well with her construction project, I pressed the green button and quickly made my way down the hall to my bedroom, shutting the door softly behind me.

"Hello?" I said cautiously.

"Hi," a woman's voice replied, hesitant but steady. "Is this Jessica?"

My stomach tightened. The voice wasn't familiar, and the uneasy tone set my nerves on edge. "Yes, this is Jessica. Who's calling?"

"My name is Janice Wilson," she said. "I... I'm not sure how to say this, but I found your phone number on a business card in Lucas's wallet."

My heart skipped a beat, and a cold knot formed in my stomach. "Excuse me?" I said, gripping the phone tighter. "Why do you have Lucas's wallet? What's going on?"

The woman hesitated, and I could hear the strain in her voice. "I'm sorry—I don't mean to alarm you. My husband and I own the property where Lucas was working today. He had an accident."

"An accident?" The word barely made it past my lips.

"Yes," Janice continued, her voice softening. "Well, he almost fell out of a tree. Thankfully, we got there—" the woman paused. "Sorry, that's not important. He was able to climb down once Richard put the ladder back in place. He seemed fine at first—but then... Well, he collapsed. We called 911 immediately, and the paramedics took him to the hospital."

I didn't realize I had stopped breathing until I felt the air rush out of my lungs. My legs wobbled, and I sat down heavily on the edge of the bed. "Where is he now?" I asked, my voice trembling.

"I think they were taking him to a hospital in St. Paul—the big one with the trauma center," Janice said, desperation in her voice. "You know, that big one along the west side of I-94? For the life of me, I can't remember the name right now. Anyway, I found your number and thought you might be someone close to him. Your business card was the only one in his wallet."

I didn't hear the rest of what she said. I knew which hospital. As soon as the woman had said trauma center, I knew. The phone slipped from my hand, clattering to the floor as my mind raced. Lucas. The hospital. Collapsed.

This couldn't be happening.

I bent down, picking up the phone with shaking hands. "I'm here," I said, my voice barely above a whisper. "Thank you for letting me know."

"We'll be here if you need anything," Janice said gently.

I ended the call, sitting frozen on the bed as the weight of her words settled over me. Lucas was in the hospital. I didn't know how serious it was or what had happened after he fell, but the thought of him lying there, hurt and alone, sent a wave of panic through me.

I pressed a hand to my chest, willing myself to stay calm. Lily. I had to think about Lily.

Standing quickly, I made my way back to the living room, my heart pounding in my ears. Lily looked up at me, her bright smile faltering when she saw my face.

"Mommy? What's wrong?"

I forced a shaky smile, crouching down in front of her. "Sweetheart, I need to go out for a little while, okay? Just for a little bit. I'm going to call Mrs. Hanson down the hall to see if she can come sit with you for a while."

Her brow furrowed. "Where are you going?"

"To check on something," I said, keeping my voice steady. I just couldn't tell her more right now, and I didn't want to worry her.

"Okay."

I returned to my room, changing out of my work scrubs and into jeans and a sweater as I placed a quick call to Mrs. Hanson. She was more than happy to help and assured me she would be right over.

Just a few minutes later, Mrs. Hanson made good on her word, arriving with a copy of The Jungle Book and her knitting bag. I kissed Lily's forehead before grabbing my phone, wondering who to call. And then I realized who I needed to call—Emily. But then another thought took over. I didn't have Emily's phone number. We had never thought to exchange phone numbers when we had had that coffee together a few months back. Not only did I not know her number—I didn't even know her last name. She used a pen name for her books.

28

Jake

AS I DROVE WEST, the headlights illuminated the dark highway, and I gripped the steering wheel a little tighter than necessary. The site of the bed and breakfast was about 45 minutes outside the Twin Cities, but my mind was already racing far ahead.

Why would Lucas just not show up? No call, no text. Nothing. It wasn't like him, at least not from what I'd seen over the past nine months. But still, this was exactly what I'd worried about.

My mom was in love, and now this guy—this guy who had seemed so perfect—was showing his true colors. Not showing up for dinner with his girlfriend's family? That was about as disrespectful as it got.

The knot in my chest tightened. My mom deserved better. She deserves someone who prioritizes her, who wouldn't leave her hanging or make her feel unimportant. Maybe Lucas wasn't that guy after all.

But as I turned onto a long gravel road, irritation gave way to something else: an unmistakable uneasiness. Something was wrong.

Lucas's sleek SUV was parked off to the side of the road, its headlights off but unmistakable in the glow of my own. I slowed to a stop, peering out the windshield.

The area was quiet, the gravel road flanked by towering oak trees. These had to be the trees Lucas had mentioned—the ones he was designing the treehouses for. A ladder was propped against the largest tree, its rungs gleaming faintly in the moonlight.

But there was no sign of Lucas.

"Where the hell is he?" I muttered under my breath.

I parked my car next to his and stepped out, the cool night air biting at my skin. The place was eerily silent, the kind of quiet that made your ears strain for any sound.

I glanced around, taking in the massive oak trees. Maybe he was still working? But it was late—too late for him to be climbing around in trees. I used the flashlight on my phone to peer up into trees, and as I suspected, he wasn't there.

I got back in my car and followed the gravel road a bit further, noticing markings for a future pool off to one side. The crunch of the gravel under my tires was the only sound breaking the silence. Ahead, a large farmhouse came into view, its lights glowing warmly against the dark.

The house was stunning, like something out of a Hallmark movie. It had a wraparound porch, neatly stacked wood near the steps, and an inviting glow from the windows. My mom would love this place, I thought to myself as I approached the front door and knocked firmly, shifting my weight from one foot to the other as I waited.

A moment later, the door creaked open, and a woman in her early 60s appeared. Her short gray hair was neat, and her eyes were kind but tired.

"Can I help you?" she asked, her voice tinged with concern.

"Where's Lucas?" I asked, my words sharper than I intended.

The woman's face fell, her worried expression deepening. "Oh, dear," she murmured, pressing a hand to her chest. "Are you family?"

"No." I paused. "Not exactly. I'm... I'm here because he was supposed to be somewhere tonight, and he didn't show up. What's going on?"

She opened the door wider, motioning for me to come in. "You'd better come inside."

I hesitated for a moment before stepping over the threshold, my boots echoing softly against the wooden floor.

The woman led me into a cozy kitchen, the faint smell of cinnamon and coffee lingering in the air. It reminded me of the cinnamon and pine scent from my mom's place. She gestured for me to sit at the small table, but I stayed standing, my nerves too wired to relax.

"My name's Janice Wilson," she said, clenching her hands in front of her. She appeared nervous. "My husband Richard and I own this property. Lucas was here earlier today, taking measurements for the treehouse project."

"Okay," I said slowly. "So where is he now?"

She sighed, her shoulders sagging and her hands gripping each other with agitation. "Lucas had an accident this afternoon. He was up in one of the trees when the ladder fell. He managed to climb down with Richard's help, but then..."

"Then what?" I pressed, my stomach twisting.

Janice's eyes filled with sympathy. "He collapsed. It seemed like he was in pain—he was clutching his chest. We called 911 right away, and the paramedics took him to that big hospital in St. Paul. Regions Hospital, I think it is. I'm so sorry."

Her words hit me like a punch to the gut. Lucas. Collapsed. Chest pain. Hospital.

"Is he... is he okay?" I asked, my voice barely above a whisper.

"I don't know," Janice said, shaking her head. "The paramedics didn't tell us much before they left. I wish I had more answers for you. Richard took our truck, but he hasn't called me with any updates."

I nodded numbly, my mind spinning. This wasn't what I'd expected. I'd been so sure Lucas was just flaking out, proving he wasn't the man my mom thought he was. But now... Now I felt sick.

"Thank you," I managed to say. "For calling 911. For letting me know."

"Of course," she said gently. "If there's anything else we can do, just let us know."

I nodded again, already moving toward the door. I needed to get to the hospital. As I stepped back outside into the cold night air, I pulled out my phone, my fingers trembling as I dialed my mom's number. She deserved to know what was going on.

The line rang twice before she picked up. "Jake?" she said, her voice tight with worry.

"Mom," I said, my voice steady despite the chaos swirling inside me. "I found out what happened to Lucas. He's at Regions. I'm heading there now."

There was a pause, and I imagined she had so many questions. But she just said, "I'll meet you there."

"Okay," I said, swallowing hard. "See you soon."

I ended the call and climbed into my car, my hands gripping the steering wheel as I pulled back onto the road. Whatever my feelings about Lucas had been before, none of that mattered now. Right now, all I cared about was getting to him—and hoping he'd be okay. And hoping my mom would be okay, too.

29

Emily

THE HOUSE WAS UNUSUALLY quiet, save for the occasional sound of Sarah and Michael murmuring in the kitchen. I sat on the edge of the couch, my phone clutched tightly in my hand. I had been staring at the screen for what felt like hours, willing it to light up with Lucas's name.

But it didn't.

I'd tried calling him again—twice, actually—but each time, it went straight to voicemail. That gnawing feeling of concern in my chest had only grown, twisting tighter with every passing minute.

Sarah peeked her head into the living room, her face lined with concern. "Mom, you need to try and relax," she said gently, walking over and sitting beside me.

"I can't," I admitted, my voice barely above a whisper. "Something doesn't feel right."

"Maybe he got caught up at the site," Sarah suggested, though her tone was more hopeful than confident. "Or maybe he stopped by his office to finish something."

"Without calling?" I asked, shaking my head. "That's not like him."

Michael appeared in the doorway, holding a steaming cup of tea. "You know, sometimes people just forget. Maybe he got sidetracked or lost track of time. Stranger things have happened."

Sarah gave Michael a dirty look. I knew they were both trying so hard to comfort me, but I knew they didn't understand. Tonight wasn't just any dinner with the family. Tonight was supposed to be special. They just didn't know how special it was supposed to be.

Lucas and I had planned to share our big news—our decision to live together and take that next step after the new year. I had been so nervous and excited, imagining how Jake, Sarah, and Michael would react. I had made lasagna in anticipation of the evening. My kids had always loved my lasagna, and Lucas and I had been surprised to find out that we both used a similar recipe.

But now, all I felt was worry.

A buzzing sound startled me out of my thoughts, and I nearly dropped my phone in my rush to answer. Seeing Jake's name on the screen sent a fresh wave of nerves through me.

"Jake?" I said, pressing the phone to my ear.

"Mom," he said, his voice steadier than I expected but tinged with urgency. "I found out what happened to Lucas. He collapsed at the site, and they've taken him to Regions Hospital in St. Paul."

I felt the air leave my lungs, and for a moment, I couldn't speak. "I'll meet you there," was all I could muster.

"The property owners said he was up in a tree when the ladder fell. He got down okay, but then he collapsed. I'm heading to the hospital now."

"We're coming too," Sarah said immediately over my shoulder.

"Okay," Jake said. "I'll meet you there."

The call ended, and I stared blankly at the phone in my hand, trying to process his words. Collapsed. Hospital. Lucas.

"Mom?" Sarah's voice was soft, but the worry in it was unmistakable.

I looked at her beside me, my vision blurring with tears. "Lucas collapsed. He's at Regions Hospital."

She was beside me instantly, wrapping an arm around my shoulders. "Oh, Mom..."

Michael appeared at my other side, his expression grim. "Do you want us to drive you?"

I nodded, too shaken to argue. "Yes. I need to get there now."

Sarah grabbed my coat from the rack while Michael fetched his car keys, and within minutes, we were on the road.

The drive from Cottage Grove felt endless, the headlights illuminating the dark highway as my mind raced with a thousand possibilities. What had happened? Was it his heart? Was it something else?

Memories of the past nine months flooded my mind—our first date, Lily's birthday party, the quiet nights we'd spent together planning for the future. All those late-night phone calls on the nights we couldn't be together. Lucas wasn't just someone I loved; he was someone I trusted, someone who had brought light and laughter back into my life after so many years of heartache.

The thought of losing him now was unbearable. It was at this moment that I knew I didn't want a future alone. I wanted a future with him. With Lily.

"Mom," Sarah said gently from the back seat, pulling me out of my spiraling thoughts. "He's strong. And he has you. Whatever's going on, we'll get through it together."

I nodded, her words a small comfort in the chaos of my emotions.

When we finally arrived at the hospital, I practically leapt out of the car, hurrying toward the entrance with Sarah and Michael close behind. The bright fluorescent lights of the emergency room lobby only heightened my anxiety. I approached the desk, my voice trembling as I gave Lucas's name.

The nurse behind the desk typed something into her computer before looking up at me with a professional but kind expression.

"He's been admitted," she said. "They're running tests right now. If you'd like to wait, someone will come out to speak with you soon."

I nodded, swallowing the lump in my throat as Sarah guided me to a row of chairs in the waiting area. Sitting there, surrounded by the sterile walls and the quiet hum of hospital machinery, I felt completely powerless. All I could do was wait—and hope. But then I looked up to see Jessica rounding the corner, a badge clipped to the waistband of her jeans. She saw me and approached quickly.

I stood. "Jessica, do you work here?"

She shook her head while shrugging her shoulders. "Kind of. I do rotations here on occasion with physical therapy patients." Then she paused and looked down at the floor. "You're here because of Lucas, right?"

My heart stopped. "How do you know?"

"He had my business card in his wallet. The people from the tree-house called me. They weren't sure who else to call. But I didn't have your number, so I didn't know how to reach you. I realized I don't even know your real last name. So I came here, hoping to find Lucas's wallet to see if I could find anything to help track you down. I'm so sorry."

I shook off the feeling of disappointment that she hadn't known how to reach me. But how could she? She didn't know my real last name, which was nothing close to my pen name, and I knew that Lucas's cell phone was locked, so she likely didn't know his password. "It's okay. Do you know anything?"

Jessica put her hand on my shoulder, her face suggesting I sit down. But I refused, imploring her with my eyes to tell me the news, whatever it was.

"The cardiologist is with him now. There is concern that Lucas suffered a heart attack," she said, and my heart skipped a beat. Jessica must have noticed the look on my face. "They have him stabilized, but he isn't awake. They're running more tests now. We should have more information soon."

At this, Sarah and Michael stood in unison, putting their arms around me. A moment later, Jake came sprinting into the room. The look on his face said it all. "Mom," he said, pulling me into his embrace.

30

Jake

THE DRIVE FROM THE WILSONS' property to Regions Hospital was a blur. The winding country roads quickly gave way to the highway, but my thoughts were so loud that I barely noticed the change in scenery.

I gripped the steering wheel tightly, my knuckles white as I replayed the past hour in my head.

When I'd first pulled up to the property and seen Lucas's SUV sitting there, irritation had been my default. Of course, he was off working late, forgetting all about dinner plans with Mom's family. Typical.

But I had been wrong. So wrong.

The Wilsons' explanation of what had happened had floored me. Lucas collapsing? Clutching his chest? It was like the plot of some medical drama, not something that happened to real people, especially not to someone like Lucas.

Now, my irritation was gone, replaced with guilt and a gnawing sense of dread.

How could I have jumped to conclusions so quickly? How could I have let my protectiveness over Mom turn into suspicion? Lucas wasn't perfect—no one was—but he wasn't some guy who didn't care about her. He'd made her happier than I'd seen her in years. And now...

Now, I didn't know what was going to happen.

The highway stretched endlessly in front of me as I tried to make sense of it all. Lucas was in his late 40s. He seemed healthy. Sure, he had joked once or twice about his knee giving him trouble after his old baseball injury, but nothing about him suggested someone who was at risk of collapsing.

Heart attack? Stroke? Something else?

I shook my head, trying to push the worst-case scenarios out of my mind, but they clung stubbornly.

And then there was Mom.

She'd fallen for Lucas hard, and I couldn't blame her. The guy had this way of making people feel like they were at home and making them feel like they mattered. He wasn't just good to Mom; he was good to Lily, too.

Oh my God. Lily. What about Lily? Her father had just collapsed. Who would tell Lily? What about Lily's mom—should we call her? I pressed my foot harder on the gas, glancing at the dashboard clock. Every minute felt like an hour. And I had so many unanswered questions.

The thought of what this could do to Mom terrified me. She'd been through so much already—Dad leaving, the loss of someone she had called a friend, the divorce, rebuilding her life from scratch. She'd finally found something good, something worth holding onto, and now...

Now, Lucas was in a hospital bed, and none of us knew why.

I clenched my jaw, shaking my head. I wouldn't let myself spiral. Not yet. I had to stay focused to be there for Mom, Sarah, and everyone. That's what the son is supposed to do, right?

Finally, the hospital loomed into view, its lights casting a pale glow against the night sky. I pulled into the parking ramp, grabbed a parking ticket, and parked in the first available spot. My heart pounded as I hurried inside.

I saw Mom right away. She stood near a row of chairs, her face pale but determined, with Sarah and Michael on either side of her. Another woman who looked strangely familiar was there, too, but I couldn't quite figure out why she looked like someone I knew. The woman had long blonde hair pulled back into a ponytail and was speaking quietly to Mom, but Mom's eyes kept darting toward the hallway as though willing someone to appear with news.

When her gaze met mine, it was as though the world's weight had settled on her shoulders.

"Mom," I said, crossing the room in a few quick strides.

She fell into my arms, and for a moment, neither of us said anything. I just held her, letting her know without words that whatever happened, we'd get through it together.

But as I closed my eyes, holding onto the only family I had ever known, I couldn't help but pray silently: Please let him be okay. For her. For Lily. For all of us.

31

Lucas

"MR. NIKOLAOU, can you hear me? Can you open your eyes?"

The voice was distant at first, muffled like it was coming through water. Then it grew louder, sharper, pulling me toward consciousness.

A bright light pierced through the fog, shining directly into my eyes. I turned my head instinctively, groaning. "Get that out of my eyes," I muttered, my throat dry and raspy.

As the fog lifted, so did the memories—the treehouse, the pain in my chest, the ladder falling.

Did I fall? Where am I now?

I forced my eyes open, squinting against the harsh light of the room. Everything was too bright, too sterile. I blinked a few times, trying to focus.

The first thing I noticed was that I wasn't wearing my shirt—or my pants, for that matter. There were wires and electrodes stuck to my chest—did they shave my chest?—and a thin gown hung loosely around my shoulders. Why was I wearing a dress?

I was in a bed, but it wasn't my bed. The sheets were stiff, the mattress firm, and the sounds around me—beeping, whirring—were foreign and unnerving. I could hear a child crying off in the distance. Lily? No, this voice was much younger than Lily's. Why didn't that child stop crying?

I let my head fall back against the pillow, squeezing my eyes shut to block out the light and sound as I tried to piece everything together. That's when I heard the unmistakable steady beeping of a heart monitor again. I opened my eyes again, this time more cautiously, and turned my head to the side.

Sure enough, a machine stood beside the bed, its screen displaying a green line that jumped rhythmically. Next to it was an IV pole, a bag of clear liquid feeding into a tube that disappeared into my arm.

I was in the hospital.

"Good, you're awake," a voice said, drawing my attention.

A woman stood at the foot of the bed, her gaze sharp but kind as she looked at me over the top of an iPad. She wore a white coat, and her ID badge identified her as Dr. Patel. "How are you feeling?" she asked, her eyes darting between me and the machines beside me.

I blinked, trying to find my voice. "I... I don't know," I said hoarsely. "What happened?"

Dr. Patel stepped closer, setting the iPad on a rolling table. "You were brought in earlier this evening after collapsing. Do you remember that?"

Collapsing. The memory came rushing back—the tightness in my chest, the cold sweat, the dizziness as I hit the ground. "Yeah," I said slowly. "I was at a job site. I... I didn't fall, but the ladder—"

She nodded. "The property owners filled us in. They said you had been up in a tree before you collapsed. Do you have any history of heart issues?"

I shook my head, wincing as a dull ache radiated through my chest. "No. Never."

She studied me for a moment before speaking again. "The symptoms you experienced—chest pain, shortness of breath, dizziness— are consistent with a cardiac event. We're running tests to determine exactly what happened, but right now, we suspect it may have been a mild heart attack."

A heart attack? The words didn't register at first. I stared at her, my mind scrambling to make sense of what she was saying. I was 48, healthy, and active. Sure, I liked my energy drinks and wasn't the best about taking breaks, but a heart attack? Was that what that tightness had been in my chest these last few weeks? I had written it off to nerves or anxiety.

"That doesn't compute," I said, my voice shaky. "I'm not... I mean, I don't have heart problems."

Dr. Patel nodded, her expression sympathetic. "I understand this is a lot to process. But heart issues can sometimes develop without obvious warning signs. Stress, diet, and genetics can all play a role. That's why we're doing a full workup to get a clearer picture."

I closed my eyes, trying to steady my breathing. This couldn't be happening. Not now. Not when everything in my life was finally falling into place. "Is… is anyone here for me?" I asked hesitantly, opening my eyes to look at her.

She glanced at her iPad. "A Jessica Nikolaou checked in earlier. I believe she's a relative?"

"Jessica," I murmured. My ex-wife. Of course, she'd be the first one called—her number was still on the business cards in my wallet. But Emily… "Did anyone else…?"

Dr. Patel shook her head. "Not that I'm aware of, but I have been in here with you and other patients since you arrived. But you're stable now; I can go check the waiting room to see."

I nodded slowly, my mind drifting to Emily. She was probably wondering where I was and why I hadn't shown up for dinner. God, what was she thinking?

"Can I see Jessica?" I asked finally.

Dr. Patel gave me a small smile. "I'll let her know you're awake."

She left the room, and I sank back against the pillow, staring up at the ceiling. A heart attack. The words echoed in my mind, each repetition heavier than the last.

I thought about Emily, about Lily, about the life I was building with them. Would this change everything? Would I be able to keep up with Lily's energy or with the demands of my work? Would Emily be turned off by a guy who had a heart attack? I was the guy. I was supposed to be strong and protect her.

Of course, I knew better. Emily didn't need someone to protect her. But it was hard not to question my manliness and my desire to keep her safe. And Lily. To keep her safe as her father.

Would Emily still want this life with me if I wasn't the man I had been?

The sound of the door opening pulled me from my thoughts. I turned my head to see Jessica step into the room, her face a mixture of worry and relief.

"Lucas," she said softly, walking over to the side of the bed.

"Hey," I said, managing a weak smile.

She perched on the bed beside me, her eyes scanning my face. "You scared the hell out of me."

"Scared myself, too," I admitted.

For a moment, neither of us spoke, the profoundness of the situation settling over us.

"Emily's here," Jessica said finally, breaking the silence. "And I met Sarah and Jake. And Michael, too. They're all here for you, Lucas."

The tightness in my chest released a bit at her words. Emily.

"Thanks," I said quietly.

Jessica nodded, her expression softening. "You're going to be okay."

"What about Lily?"

"I just checked in with her. One of my neighbors is at the apartment with her. She's fine."

"Did you tell her?" I asked.

"No. That's a lot for an eight-year-old to take in," Jessica said. "I wanted to see how you were so that I would have more information to share."

I nodded and closed my eyes. I hoped that what she said was right. That I would be okay. But as I lay there, surrounded by the monotony of the machines, I couldn't shake the fear that things were about to change in ways I wasn't ready for.

"Can I see Emily now?" I asked.

Jessica nodded, got up from her position perched on the side of the bed, and left the room.

32

Emily

I SAT IN THE HOSPITAL waiting room, trying to ignore all of the activity around me—the quiet beeping of monitors, the soft shuffle of nurses as they walked up and down the hallway, the sounds of people being given bad news, children crying, laughter. It was such a mixture of emotions in a hospital. And even with the chaos of the environment, the waiting room felt stifling, almost too still.

Sarah sat beside me, her hand resting lightly on mine, while Michael stood behind her, his presence steady and reassuring. Jake was pacing near the window, his footsteps a rhythmic backdrop to the turmoil in my mind. I reminded myself that he is only 21, about to turn 22 at the end of December. This must be a lot for him to process.

The sound of approaching footsteps pulled my attention, and I looked up to see a female doctor entering the room. The name on her white coat reads "Dr. Patel, Cardiologist." Her face was calm but serious, the kind of expression that offered little comfort.

"Lucas is stable," she began, addressing us all. "He's awake and alert, and we're continuing to monitor him closely. He asked to see Jessica."

The words hit me like a soft blow—not a punch, but a stinging reminder of my place in Lucas's life.

I forced a smile and nodded as Jessica stood, her face a mixture of relief and concern. Of course, he'd ask for Jessica. She was the mother of his child; she was family in a way I wasn't—at least, not yet. I wondered how all of that worked when you lived together and were in a committed relationship but not married. Would I not be next of kin? Surely, Lily couldn't be his emergency contact at such a young age. My head raced with these thoughts and the unanswered questions.

I watched Jessica follow Dr. Patel down the hall, my heart sinking slightly despite my efforts to be rational. This was one of the realities of loving a man with a child, of building a life within the framework of a blended family. And yet, a small part of me felt the ache of being left behind.

"Mom," Sarah said softly, pulling me out of my thoughts. "Are you okay?"

I turned to her, offering a faint smile. "I'm fine, sweetheart. It makes sense that Lucas would want to see Jessica first. They've known each other a long time, and Lily... Lily comes first."

Sarah studied me for a moment before giving my hand a reassuring squeeze. "He loves you, Mom. Don't forget that."

I nodded, but her words did little to quiet the thoughts swirling in my mind. If the roles were reversed, I would have done the same thing. Jake and Sarah would be my first thoughts if something happened to me. That didn't mean I wouldn't want Lucas by my side eventually—it just meant I would prioritize my kids. And my kids were adults. That whole first contact thing was a bit easier, and Sarah was already programmed into my phone as the person to contact in the event of an emergency.

I understood that Lucas loved me, and I appreciated Sarah's words of support, yet the sting of being second at this moment was sharp in my mind.

The minutes stretched on endlessly, the hands of the old analog clock on the wall moving far too slowly. Jake finally stopped pacing and sat down, his elbows resting on his knees as he stared at the floor. It felt like an eternity before Jessica returned to the waiting room. I looked up as she entered, my heart pounding in anticipation. Her face was calmer now, though still etched with worry.

"He's asking for you," she said, her gaze meeting mine.

For a moment, I couldn't move, couldn't speak. Relief and anxiety washed over me in equal measure, and I felt Sarah give my hand another squeeze.

"Go," she said, her voice firm but gentle.

I stood, my legs feeling like jelly as I made my way toward Jessica. "How is he?" I asked, my voice trembling. It was all I could do to hold back a sob. I needed to be strong. I couldn't let my kids see me in a moment of weakness. We'd had far too many of those already.

"He's awake and talking," Jessica replied. "He's scared, but he's okay. He wants to see you."

I nodded, swallowing hard as I followed her back toward Lucas's room.

The walk down the hall felt impossibly long, each step echoing loudly in my ears. When we reached the door, Jessica gave me a small, encouraging smile before turning to leave.

I hesitated for a moment, gathering my thoughts before pushing the door open. The room was bright; the fluorescent lights made everything feel so medicinal, so institutional. But we were in a hospital, after all. The emergency room, no less. And my handsome Lucas lay in the hospital bed, wires and monitors surrounding him. His face was pale, his eyes heavy-lidded but focused on me as I stepped inside.

"Hey," I said softly, smiling as I approached his bedside.

"Hey," he replied, his voice hoarse but steady.

I pulled the chair closer to the bed, sat down, and took his hand in mine. His grip was weak but warm, and the familiarity of his touch brought tears to my eyes.

"You scared the hell out of me," I said, my voice breaking.

Lucas managed a faint smile. "Scared myself, too."

For a moment, neither of us spoke, the quiet noise of the monitors filling the silence.

"I'm sorry I missed dinner," he said finally, his tone laced with regret.

I shook my head, brushing a stray tear from my cheek. "Lucas, don't apologize. None of that matters right now. I'm just glad you're okay."

His gaze softened, his eyes searching mine. "I'm okay," he said quietly, but I could tell something was on his mind.

"Lucas?" I asked. "Are you okay?" Realizing my error, I quickly added, "Despite the obvious?"

"I'm sorry," he said. "I know this isn't what you expected from me. And now they're saying they think I had a heart attack. You don't want to be with someone who is sick. Someone with a bad heart. You deserve to be with someone healthy and strong. Someone who can take care of you. So if this is too much, I understand."

I listened as the words tumbled out of him. He took a breath and looked like he was going to continue, but I put my hand up. He closed his mouth. "Lucas," I began. "I hate that you think so little of me to think that I would bail on you the moment you fell ill. I am in love with you. With love comes support, even in the worst of times. And if we continue the way we are doing, we're going to have some bad times. It's inevitable. But we can work through those bad times together."

Tears formed in the corner of his eyes, and he pinched them shut. I could tell he didn't want me to see the emotion. "But I'm sorry," he whispered, tugging on my hands to come in closer.

"I know. But I'm here, and we'll get through this together," I whispered, tucking my head into his neck and kissing his cheek.

And at this moment, snuggling my head against the man in that hospital bed, I knew without a doubt that my love for Lucas was stronger than ever.

33

Lucas

THE HOSPITAL ROOM was dark and quiet except for the steady beeping of the heart monitor and the occasional distant sound of footsteps in the hallway. I shifted in the bed, trying to find a position that didn't make my back ache, but it was no use. The mattress was stiff, the pillows flat, and the blood pressure cuff strapped to my arm seemed to inflate just as I was on the verge of drifting off.

The nurse had come in earlier to check on me, leaving with a kind but firm reminder: Rest is what you need most right now, Mr. Nikolaou.

Rest. Sure. Easy to say when you weren't the one hooked up to machines, your mind racing with every possibility.

The early test results had confirmed what I'd already started to suspect: it had been a heart attack. A mild one, Dr. Patel had assured me, but the words were ones I didn't want to hear. My blood pressure was high—higher than it should be, even after an event like this—and they were running more tests to assess my cholesterol levels. By morning, I'd have more answers.

For now, they said, the safest place for me to be was here.

I stared up at the ceiling, the dim glow of the monitor casting faint shadows on the walls. Everyone had gone home—Emily, her kids, Jessica. Dr. Patel had encouraged them all to get some sleep, and I'd done my best to convince them I'd be fine.

It wasn't a lie, exactly. Physically, I was stable. But emotionally? Mentally? I felt like I was holding on by a thread.

My thoughts drifted to Lily. Jessica and I had agreed not to tell her anything tonight. She was still so little, and I didn't want her to spend the night worrying. Jessica had promised to talk to her in the morning, once we had more information.

I hated it. I hated not being able to see her, to hold her, and tell her everything was okay. Lily was my anchor, my reason for pushing through even the hardest days. Even though this was Lily's week at Jessica's, I couldn't help but wish that tomorrow morning, I could be there to make her breakfast and walk her to the bus stop.

Jessica had reassured me that waiting to tell Lily was the right decision and that Lily needed her rest as much as I did mine. And she was right. But that didn't make it any easier.

And then there was Emily.

She'd been so calm tonight, so steady, even as worry etched deep lines into her face. I knew I'd scared her. The way she'd held my hand, her voice trembling as she told me I hadn't let her down—that I couldn't let her down—kept replaying in my mind.

But I had let her down.

Tonight was supposed to be special. We were supposed to share our plans with her kids, to celebrate the next step in our relationship together. Instead, I'd collapsed in a field and ended up here, my body betraying me in ways I never expected.

What did this mean for our future?

The question gnawed at me, keeping me from sleep as I shifted again, trying to ignore the persistent ache in my chest and the plastic tug of the IV in my arm. And that blood pressure cuff? How do people stand it?

Ignoring the annoying squeeze of the cuff as it took another reading, I refocused on Emily. And how could I not? She was independent, strong, and capable in ways that drew me to her from the start. She'd built a life for herself, a life she was proud of, and now I couldn't help but wonder if this would change how she saw me.

Would she see me as weaker now? Would she start to second-guess our decision to live together? Would she say yes if I asked her to marry me down the road?

And what about Lily? Could I keep up with her energy, her joy, her boundless curiosity? She deserved a dad who could climb trees and build adventure trails, not one who needed to sit on the sidelines and monitor his heart rate.

I ran a hand over my face and then through my hair, frustration and fear bubbling just beneath the surface.

The truth was, I didn't know what the future looked like anymore. The life I'd envisioned—the one with Emily and Lily and the home we were building together—felt fragile now, like it could shatter with this new reality.

But as I lay there, staring at the wall on the other side of the bed, I knew one thing for certain: I wasn't giving up.

I wasn't giving up on Emily, or Lily, or the life we'd started to build together. This heart attack was a setback, yes, but it wasn't the end. It couldn't be.

Because if there was one thing I'd learned over the years, it was that life had a way of throwing curveballs when you least expected them. And the only way to face them was head-on, one step at a time.

Closing my eyes, I took a slow, deep breath, letting the steady rhythm of the heart monitor lull me into a state of uneasy calm.

34

Sarah

AFTER DROPPING OFF MOM at her house, the drive back to our house was quiet, the kind of silence that felt too heavy to break. Michael's hand rested on my knee as he steered the car, his thumb brushing back and forth in a steady rhythm. I stared out the window at the darkened streets, the occasional streetlamp casting fleeting pools of light over the road.

Mom had insisted she'd be fine for the night. She was staying strong, though I could see the worry etched into her every movement as we left the hospital. Jake had stayed behind for now, promising to keep us updated if anything changed.

"Do you think Lucas will be okay?" I asked, my voice breaking the silence.

Michael glanced at me briefly before turning his eyes back to the road. "I think so. He's in good hands, Sarah. He's stable, and the doctors know what they're doing."

I nodded, but the tightness in my chest didn't ease. "I just—tonight felt like it came out of nowhere. One minute we were decorating for Christmas, and the next..." I trailed off, shaking my head.

Michael squeezed my knee gently. "It's been a lot. You've been through a lot tonight."

When we got home, I kicked off my shoes and sank onto that oversized couch. It was way too big for the room, but it was one of those TikTok deals, and I just had to have it. Thankfully, Michael had agreed to let me satisfy the itch. I curled my legs beneath me, and the faint scent of cinnamon still hung in the air from the candle I'd lit earlier in the day before heading over to my mom's house. But it felt out of place now, a strange juxtaposition to the swirling emotions in my chest.

"Want some tea?" Michael asked, his voice soft.

I nodded. "Lavender. Please."

As he moved into the kitchen, I let my mind wander back over the last several hours.

Decorating for Christmas at Mom's had felt like a little pocket of joy, a slice of something light and happy in the middle of a chaotic week. I'd teased her when she announced her plan to put out every single decoration she owned.

"Every decoration? Mom, seriously?" I'd laugh as she dug into the storage bins.

"Yes, every single one," she'd said with a firm nod, her eyes sparkling with determination. "Why not? This year feels like a year for everything."

Jake had rolled his eyes but dutifully handed her the next box, muttering something about how he was pretty sure she had enough garland to wrap the entire block.

It was nice, though. Watching Mom pull out ornaments that held decades of memories, telling stories about where they came from, laughing at the ones Jake and I had made in elementary school. There was something comforting about the tradition, about the way the familiar ornaments and decorations made the house feel warm and alive.

But then Lucas hadn't shown up.

During the first hour, we shrugged it off. Maybe he got held up at the site, Mom had suggested, though I'd caught the way her smile wavered. By the second hour, worry had settled over all of us like a heavy blanket.

And when Jake's call came in—when he told us what had happened—I'd felt the floor drop out from beneath me.

Mom had held it together better than I thought possible. She'd been worried, of course, but she'd stayed calm, focused. Watching her as she strode away from us to Lucas's room. I knew just how deeply she cared about him.

I sipped the tea Michael handed me, letting the warmth seep through my hands as I stared at the flickering candle on the coffee table. "It's just... a lot," I said, my voice quiet. "I've never seen Mom like this. Not since Dad."

Michael sat beside me, his arm draping over my shoulders. "She loves him," he said simply.

I nodded, swallowing the lump in my throat. "I know. And it's good—he's good for her. But tonight, I couldn't help thinking... What if he hadn't been okay? What if she lost him?"

Michael didn't respond right away; he just pulled me closer, his hand rubbing gentle circles on my arm.

"And then there's Jake," I added, letting out a soft laugh. "He was so suspicious of Lucas at first, but tonight... he was so worried. You could see it on his face when he stormed into that waiting room. I think he cares about Lucas more than he's willing to admit."

Michael chuckled softly. "Jake's protective. It's just how he is. But yeah, I think you're right. Lucas has grown on him."

I stared into my tea, my mind drifting back to the Christmas decorations again. Why had Mom been so determined to put everything out this year? Was it just excitement for the holidays, or was there something more?

Maybe it didn't matter. Perhaps it was enough that we'd had those moments together, laughing and decorating, even if the night had taken a sharp turn.

I leaned into Michael's side, closing my eyes for a moment. "We'll check in with Mom first thing in the morning," I said.

He pressed a kiss to my temple. "We will. And we'll get through this together, okay?"

35

Jessica

WALKING INTO THE HOSPITAL that night had seemed so foreign. Even though I had been here countless times as part of my job, guiding patients through their recovery, this time was different. This time, it was Lucas.

When I reached the front desk, I didn't need to explain much. The nurse recognized me immediately, her smile tight with sympathy when she recognized Lucas's last name, knowing that it was mine, too. "He's stable," she said, glancing at her screen. "You can go see him now."

My role as a physical therapist at the hospital had its perks, and tonight, it meant bypassing the usual red tape. I made my way down the hallway, the rubber soles of my shoes squeaking softly against the linoleum.

As I pushed open the door to Lucas's room, the sight of him lying there made me pause.

There he was, hooked up to monitors, wires trailing from his chest to machines that beeped softly in rhythm with his heart. His face was pale, his eyes closed, but his breathing was steady. Relief washed over me, but not in the way I'd expected.

Yes, I was glad he was okay. But as I stood there, looking at him, my thoughts didn't focus on the man I used to call my husband. They drifted to Lily.

What would this mean for her?

She adored her dad, and I knew this would shake her. Lucas was her anchor, the constant in her world. She loved her daddy so much. But seeing him like this—vulnerable, fragile—wouldn't be easy for her.

But as I watched him stir slightly, his hand twitching against the sheet, I realized something else.

The love I felt for Lucas was still there, but it was different now. It wasn't the romantic love we'd once shared as husband and wife. That part of us had been gone for years, dissolved under the mass of misunderstandings and unmet needs. What remained was a quieter kind of love—the kind you have for someone who has shared a chapter of your life, someone who is still family, even if it's in a different way.

I sat down in the chair beside his bed, my hands resting in my lap. For a moment, I just watched him breathe, the steady rise and fall of his chest reassuring in its simplicity. And then, unexpectedly, I felt something else: A shift.

For so long, I'd been focused on Lily and work, filling my days to the brim with responsibilities and routines. I hadn't let myself think about what was missing, about what I wanted beyond being a mom and a physical therapist. But seeing Lucas here, knowing how much he had moved forward with his life—with Emily, with building a new future—made me wonder if it was time for me to move forward, too.

Could I? I wasn't sure. Between the extra shifts at the clinic, the hours at the hospital, and the endless juggling act of co-parenting Lily, I barely had time to breathe, let alone think about a relationship. But maybe that was just an excuse. Perhaps I was scared.

Lucas had found someone who made him happy. Watching him with Emily, I saw a side of him that I hadn't seen in years. He was lighter, freer, more himself.

If he could find that, couldn't I? The thought was both terrifying and oddly freeing.

Lucas stirred again, his eyes fluttering open briefly before closing again. I reached out, brushing a strand of hair from his forehead.

"Get some rest," I murmured, though I wasn't sure if he could hear me.

As I sat back, I thought about the future—not just Lucas's or Lily's but mine.

I didn't have all the answers, and I didn't know if I was ready to open myself up to someone new. But for the first time in a long time, I felt like maybe, just maybe, it was something worth considering.

If Lucas could move on and find happiness, then why couldn't I?

It was a small thought, but it planted a seed.

For now, though, my focus remained on Lily and ensuring that her world stayed steady, even as everything around her seemed to shift.

I sat with Lucas a while longer, the steady rhythm of the heart monitor filling the quiet room. When I finally left, I felt a little lighter, as if a door I hadn't realized was closed had cracked open just a bit. I returned to the lobby, trying to figure out how I could reach Emily and let her know that Lucas was here.

36

Lucas

THE DAYLIGHT STREAMING through the blinds did nothing to chase away the exhaustion that clung to me. Between the uncomfortable bed, the constant beeping of machines, and the relentless blood pressure cuff squeezing my arm every fifteen minutes, sleep had been pretty much nonexistent.

My head rested against the thin hospital pillow, my eyes half-closed as the sounds of the ward drifted in from the hallway—murmured voices, the screechy wheels of carts rolling by, and the occasional distant laugh.

I wanted answers. The sooner I knew what was going on with my body, the sooner I could figure out how to move forward.

So, when Dr. Patel finally appeared in the doorway, her iPad tucked under her arm, relief swept over me. She stepped into the room with an air of calm authority, her sharp gaze scanning me as though she could read my vitals with a glance.

"How are you feeling today, Mr. Nikolaou?" she asked, pulling up the rolling stool beside the bed.

I couldn't help but smirk at the formality. The Greek roots in my name were almost laughable given how little they reflected in my life. "Lucas," I said, waving a hand. "Just Lucas."

Her lips curved into a polite smile. "Lucas, then. Well, I have some answers for you. You did indeed suffer a mild heart attack."

The words hung in the air for a moment, and I let them sink in. A heart attack. I'd heard it last night, but hearing it again, confirmed and final, felt heavier somehow.

Dr. Patel continued, her tone steady but kind. "Your cholesterol levels are far higher than we'd like to see, particularly your LDL— what we call the 'bad cholesterol.' It's a contributing factor to your heart attack, along with high blood pressure."

"Cholesterol," I repeated, running a hand over my face. "I guess I should've known. What now?"

Dr. Patel glanced at her notes on the iPad, then back at me. "The good news is that we can manage this. I'm going to prescribe medications to help lower your cholesterol and regulate your blood pressure. But medication alone isn't enough. You'll also need to make some changes to your lifestyle."

I raised an eyebrow. "Changes like...?"

She leaned back slightly, ticking off points on her fingers. "First, your diet. You'll need to cut back on saturated fats and processed foods and increase your intake of fruits, vegetables, whole grains, and lean proteins. You've heard the term 'Mediterranean diet'? It's a great model to follow."

I snorted. "The irony of my Greek name and my very un-Greek eating habits isn't lost on me."

She gave a small laugh. "Well, this might be a good time to embrace your roots."

"Fair enough," I said, trying to keep the mood light even as anxiety prickled at the edges of my mind.

"Next," she said, "exercise. You mentioned you exercise, but how regularly?"

I hesitated, thinking of the treadmill and weight bench in the basement. "Not as much as I should. I've been busy with work, and well... you know how it goes."

Dr. Patel raised an eyebrow. "I do. However, finding time for physical activity is non-negotiable moving forward. Even thirty minutes of moderate exercise most days of the week can make a significant difference."

I nodded slowly, letting her words sink in.

"And lastly," she said, her gaze narrowing slightly, "let's talk about energy drinks."

I winced. "I had a feeling you'd bring that up."

Her expression was gentle but firm. "They're loaded with caffeine and sugar, neither of which is helpful for your blood pressure or

heart health. Cutting back—or better yet, cutting them out entirely—would be wise."

"Noted," I said, though the thought of giving up my mid-afternoon pick-me-up felt like a cruel punishment.

She softened her tone. "Lucas, this isn't about depriving you of things. It's about giving your body the best chance to recover and thrive. You've got a lot to live for, and these changes will help you keep doing what you love—and be there for the people you love."

The mention of people I loved made my chest tighten, but this time, it wasn't from pain. It was Emily, Lily, and the life we were building together. That was what mattered.

"Okay," I said, meeting her gaze. "I'll do it. Whatever it takes."

Dr. Patel gave a satisfied nod. "Good. Now, I'd like to keep you here one more night for rest and observation. Your body's been through a lot, and the hospital is the safest place for you to be right now. Tomorrow morning, if everything looks good, we'll discharge you."

"Sounds good," I said, though the thought of another sleepless night in this bed didn't exactly thrill me.

"I'll also arrange for a home health care nurse to check on you the day after you're discharged," she added. "They'll monitor your vitals, make sure you're adjusting to the medications, and help answer any questions you might have."

"Thanks, Doc," I said, genuinely grateful for her thoroughness.

She smiled, stood, and tucked her iPad back under her arm. "Get some rest, Lucas. I'll see you tomorrow."

As she left, I stared up at the ceiling, my mind racing. A heart attack. High cholesterol. Lifestyle changes. It all felt like too much, too fast. But then I thought of Emily and Lily. This wasn't just about me. It was about them, too. And if this was the wake-up call I needed to make changes, so be it. But there was no way I was giving up those energy drinks.

37

Emily

THE SOUND OF QUIET conversation drifted from Lucas's living room as I leaned against the kitchen counter, sipping a cup of coffee that had long since gone cold. Lucas was home. After days of hospitals, fluorescent lights, and constant worry, he was finally home.

But the relief I felt was complicated. It wasn't the kind of simple relief you get when a storm clears, leaving behind bright blue skies. This was the kind of relief that came with tiny fibers of fear still contained deep within—a fear that contained a thousand what-ifs.

I closed my eyes, letting the memories of the past few days surface. The diagnosis—mild heart attack, high cholesterol, and elevated blood pressure—was a lot to take in. When Lucas had told me everything, sitting up in that hospital bed, his voice steady but his eyes showing the cracks in his confidence, I'd felt a wave of emotions crash over me. Relief that it wasn't worse. He worried about what it meant for his future. I was determined to support him however I could.

Lucas had handled it all with his usual quiet strength, but I could see the turmoil within him. His fears weren't just about his health. And as much as I wanted to reassure him that nothing had changed, I knew the truth. Everything had changed. But that didn't mean it was bad. It was just different. But 'different', I could do.

Yesterday, Jake and I had driven out to the Wilsons' property to pick up Lucas's SUV. It felt strange walking up to it, knowing it had sat there untouched for days. Jake had been quiet during the drive there, and I hadn't pressed him to talk. We were both processing in our own ways.

After dropping Jake off at his apartment, I'd gone straight back to Lucas's place. Using the key he'd given me, I let myself in, feeling a pang of sadness as I stepped into the quiet house. It didn't feel like Lucas—his warmth, his energy. It just felt empty.

The first thing I did was tackle the fridge. Lucas wasn't a slob by any means, but like most men living alone—especially one with an eight-year-old—his idea of "clean" and mine didn't always align. I tossed out several containers of past-its-prime leftovers and restocked the shelves with fresh groceries—fruit, vegetables, whole-grain bread, and lean proteins.

Now, as I set my coffee cup down on the counter, I could hear Sarah's voice in the other room, calm and professional as she asked Lucas how he was feeling.

Stepping into the living room, I found her seated on the edge of the couch, her home health care kit open beside her. Lucas was propped up against a pillow, his color better than it had been in the hospital but still pale.

"How's he doing?" I asked, keeping my voice light as I joined them.

Sarah glanced up with a reassuring smile. "Vitals look good. Blood pressure's a little high, but that's to be expected as it can take a bit of time for the meds to really do their magic. How are you feeling, Lucas?"

"Tired," he admitted, though there was a faint smile tugging at the corners of his mouth. "But better. It's nice to be home."

I perched on the arm of the couch, my hand resting lightly on his shoulder. "Sarah's taking good care of you?"

He chuckled. "Yeah, but she's bossy. Keeps telling me I have to cut out my energy drinks."

Sarah rolled her eyes. "Don't make me call Dr. Patel and tell her you're resisting orders."

I laughed softly, grateful for the lighthearted moment. For a brief second, it felt like everything was normal again.

After finishing her checkup, Sarah packed up her kit and stood. "You're in good shape for now, but no overexertion, okay? And if anything feels off, you call me—or the doctor."

"Yes, ma'am," Lucas said, giving her a mock salute.

Sarah turned to me. "He's all yours now. Call me if you need anything."

"Thanks, Sarah," I said, walking her to the door, giving her a quick hug, and pecking at the top of her head like I used to do when she was little.

When I returned to the living room, Lucas was leaning his head back against the couch, his eyes closed. I hesitated, not wanting to disturb him, but his eyes fluttered open as he sensed my presence.

"Hey," he said softly, his voice warm despite the exhaustion in it.

"Hey," I replied, sitting beside him and resting my head on his shoulder. He shifted, lifting his right arm to tuck me in a bit closer.

For a moment, we just sat there in comfortable silence, letting everything that had happened over the course of the last few days settle around us. "I'm sorry," he said finally, his voice barely above a whisper.

"For what?" I asked, turning to face him.

"For everything. For scaring you. For letting you down that night."

"Lucas," I said, reaching for his hand. "We've been over this. You didn't let me down. You scared me, sure, but none of this is your fault. And you're here now—that's all that matters."

He looked at me, his blue eyes searching mine. "I don't want this to change things between us. I don't want you to feel like you have to take care of me."

I smiled, squeezing his hand. "It doesn't change how I feel about you if that's what you're worried about. As for taking care of yourself, relationships are about taking care of each other, right? You've been taking care of me and Lily in so many ways. Let me do the same for you."

His lips quirked into a small, grateful smile. "You're amazing, you know that?"

"I've been told," I teased, leaning my head against his shoulder.

"Well, you know that one of the best things for a bad heart is a bit of lovin'," he quipped. I gave him a light smack on his leg but turned to face him, giving him a long, deep kiss.

"Loving goes far beyond sex," I told him, suppressing a giggle. "And today, let me just love you and take care of you."

38

Jake

THE SMELL OF TURKEY and spices filled Lucas's house, warm and inviting despite the chilly November air outside. I leaned against the arm of the couch, watching as everyone mingled. My mom was talking to Lucas's colleague, John, and his wife, Melanie, while Lucas stood by the kitchen island with Cole and Rebecca, their laughter combining with the sound of Lily and Olivia's giggles echoing from somewhere upstairs.

Thanksgiving wasn't what I expected it to be this year. It wasn't at our childhood home. The crowd was different, and there was a new energy in the air. But as I looked around, I couldn't help but admit that it felt... good. Better than I thought it would be.

Lucas looked healthier than he had since his heart attack. The color was back in his face, and while he still moved a little slower than usual, he seemed more like himself. He'd even started going back to work—lightly, as he put it—and the updates on the tree-house project had been promising. The renderings were finished, and the Wilsons were just waiting on permits to break ground. See-ing Lucas excited about his work again was a relief. I didn't realize how much I'd worried about him until I saw the difference.

I turned my attention back to the group as Lucas handed Cole a beer. He wasn't drinking much, I noticed—just sipping, really—but the sight still made me pause. Should a guy who just had a heart attack really be having a beer? I pushed the thought aside. He was an adult, and he'd earned some normalcy after the last few weeks.

Ainsley nudged me gently, her eyes sparkling as she leaned in closer. "This is nice," she said softly, her British accent still catching me off guard in the best way. I caught Sarah looking at me, and she flashed me a goofy grin.

"Yeah," I said, nodding. "It is."

We'd only been seeing each other for about a week and a half. Not long, I know. We'd actually met in person the day Lucas had come home from the hospital, though we had been texting since the end of October. She'd already started making her way into my life in ways I hadn't expected. I'd been hesitant about the dating app thing, but meeting Ainsley had made me glad I'd taken the chance. She was kind and smart and had a way of grounding me when I started to overthink, which was often the case.

Lucas stepped up to the kitchen island, tapping a spoon lightly against his beer bottle. The sound caught everyone's attention, and the conversations around the room died down.

"Hey, everyone," Lucas began, his voice steady and warm. He glanced at my mom, who sidled up beside him, her hand resting lightly on his arm. "First of all, I just want to thank you all for being here today. It means a lot to have everyone together."

There were murmurs of agreement, and I found myself leaning forward slightly, curious about where this was going.

"We have an announcement to make," Lucas said, his blue eyes meeting my mom's. She smiled at him, a kind of quiet confidence in her expression that I hadn't seen in years.

My mom took over, her voice clear but tinged with emotion. "Lucas and I have decided to take the next step in our relationship. After the holidays, I'll be selling the house and moving in with Lucas."

There was a beat of silence as her words sank in. And then, a wave of congratulations swept through the room. John clapped Lucas on the back, Melanie hugged my mom, and Cole raised his beer in a toast.

I sat frozen for a moment, my mind racing. Selling the house. Moving in with Lucas. It all made sense now—the push to put out every single Christmas decoration she owned. She was making this Christmas special because it would be the last one in our childhood home.

"Are you okay?" Ainsley whispered, leaning into me.

I turned to her, her soft eyes full of concern, and nodded slowly. "Yeah. I'm okay."

And I was. I really was.

I'd spent weeks wrestling with my emotions, trying to reconcile my protectiveness over my mom with the reality that she was moving on, building a life with someone new. And maybe I'd even spent too much time focusing on what we were losing instead of what she was gaining.

But now, seeing her standing beside Lucas, her happiness so palpable it filled the room, I felt something shift. This was good for her and for them. For all of us, really.

As I glanced around the room, my mom caught my eye and smiled. Her smile said she knew what I was feeling and appreciated my support, even if I didn't always get it right.

I smiled back, a warmth spreading through my chest. Ainsley slipped her hand into mine, her fingers lacing gently with mine. This felt good. And I realized that I really was okay with this. Christmas would be hard, but I appreciated my mom's extra attention to all those details and why she had wanted everything out so early. She wanted us to have those long-lasting memories before boxes were packed and that For Sale sign was planted into the yard. And for that, I was grateful.

39

Sarah

THE SOFT GLOW OF THE CHRISTMAS tree lights filled the living room, their reflection dancing across the TV screen where a Hallmark movie played predictably in the background. A small-town heroine was falling for a big-city executive, and despite their initial misunderstandings, they were clearly destined for a perfect holiday romance.

Michael stretched out on the couch beside me, his arm draped over my shoulders as he stared at the screen with a bemused expression. I could tell he wasn't invested, but I appreciated his willingness to indulge me tonight.

I snuggled closer, resting my head against his chest. "You hate this, don't you?" I teased, glancing up at him.

He chuckled softly, pressing a kiss to the top of my head. "It's not exactly riveting, but it's nice to just relax with you. Besides, I know you love these sappy movies."

"They're not sappy," I protested half-heartedly. "They're... comforting. Predictable in the best way."

"Right," he said with a grin, his fingers brushing lightly against my arm. "Because we'd all forgive the town baker for lying about being a millionaire while they secretly save the rec center."

"Exactly," I said, poking him in the side.

We both laughed, the sound filling the cozy room. Outside, snow fell in thick flakes, blanketing the street in white. It was the kind of night that begged for warm blankets, hot cocoa, and soft conversations. And it was so refreshing to have snow this year after last year's unseasonably warm winter.

"Speaking of predictable," I began, turning slightly to face him. "Can I ask you something?"

Michael's brow lifted slightly. "Of course. What's on your mind?"

I hesitated for a moment, gathering my thoughts. "What do you think about Mom and Lucas? About them moving in together?"

He tilted his head, perhaps a bit surprised by this question out of the blue. "I think it's great. Lucas makes her happy, and your mom seems... I don't know, lighter. More herself. I mean, I've only known her since we started dating, and I was only around for that last year that your mom and dad were together. But I can tell this is good for her."

I nodded, tracing a pattern on his sweater. "I agree. It's just... a big change, you know? Selling the house, moving in with someone. It feels so... fnal."

Michael's hand found mine, his thumb brushing over my knuckles. "It is a big step. But she's thought it through, hasn't she? She's not rushing into this."

"No, she's not," I admitted. "And you're right, she does seem happy. Really happy. I think I just needed to hear someone else say it."

"Well, consider it said," he replied with a reassuring smile.

I let out a small sigh of relief, the weight in my chest easing slightly. I turned quickly, straddling myself on his lap, entwining my hands around the back of his neck. "If Mom can take that step—move forward and build something new—maybe we can too."

Michael's brow furrowed slightly as he leaned back into the couch. His curiosity piqued, and he was clearly happy with this new position. "What do you mean?"

I sat up a little straighter, my heart suddenly pounding as I searched for the right words. "We've been married for almost two years now. And things are good—great, even. I love my job, and you're doing amazing with yours. We have this house, and the second bedroom is... well, a glorified storage closet."

Michael chuckled softly. "True."

"What if we made it something else?" I asked, my voice steady but hopeful. "What if we started thinking about... a nursery?"

His expression softened, his eyes searching mine as realization dawned. "You're talking about having a baby."

"I am," I said, a nervous smile tugging at my lips. "I know it's a big decision, and I don't want to rush into anything. But it feels like the right time to at least talk about it, you know?"

Michael was quiet for a moment, his gaze thoughtful. Then he reached for my hand, holding it firmly. "I've been thinking about it too," he admitted. "I just didn't want to bring it up until I was sure we were on the same page."

My heart swelled at his words, a mixture of relief and excitement washing over me. "So... we are?"

"I think we are," he said with a grin. "We're in a good place, Sarah. We're not millionaires, but we have what we need. And we've built something solid. If you're ready to take that next step, then so am I."

I leaned into him and gave him a long kiss. "I love you," I said as I leaned down to kiss him again.

"I love you too," he replied, his voice muffled from my kiss.

As we settled back onto the couch, the Hallmark movie continued playing in the background, the heroine and hero finally sharing their inevitable kiss. The moment felt fitting in its simplicity—life wasn't a perfectly scripted holiday movie, but sometimes, it felt just as magical.

40

Lily

THE CHRISTMAS TREE LIGHTS twinkled in the corner of the living room, casting a warm glow over the stack of presents underneath. I sat cross-legged on the carpet, carefully arranging the stuffed animals I'd brought down to help me keep watch.

Santa was coming tonight.

Last year, he came to Daddy's house. But this year, Mommy said he was coming to her house. It was so cool how Santa always knew where I'd be sleeping. He never got it wrong. Mommy said he was magic like that.

I glanced over at the plate of cookies and the tall glass of milk we'd left out on the coffee table. "You think Santa likes chocolate chip the best?" I whispered to Mr. Fluffles, my favorite stuffed bunny.

He didn't answer, but I knew he agreed. Chocolate chip was my favorite, too.

This year, I was hoping for two things: a new Barbie house—one with an elevator, if Santa could manage it—and a Nintendo Switch. Olivia had one, and we played Mario Kart at her house last week. It was the best game ever. Daddy said maybe Santa would bring me one if I'd been extra good this year.

I'd been very good.

"Lily, come on!" Mommy called from the kitchen. "Time to get ready for bed, sweetheart."

I sighed, gathering Mr. Fluffles and my other animals into my arms. Santa wouldn't come until I was asleep—that was the rule. But falling asleep was so hard when I was this excited.

After brushing my teeth and changing into my new Christmas pajamas—red with little reindeer on the pants and a big Rudolph on the shirt—I climbed into bed. Mommy tucked me in, kissing my forehead like she always did.

"Goodnight, baby girl," she said, smoothing my hair.

"Night, Mommy," I said, hugging Mr. Fluffles tightly.

As I lay there, staring at the glow-in-the-dark stars on my ceiling, I thought about what Daddy had told me yesterday.

"Emily's going to move in with us next month," he'd said while we were making pancakes.

I'd almost dropped my spatula—he always gave me my own bowl of mix so that I could pour my own baby pancakes. "Really? Like... all the time?"

He laughed. "Yes, all the time. She'll live with us, just like you and me."

"Can I give her my room?" I asked quickly. "And I can move into your room, Daddy. I don't mind."

Daddy chuckled, shaking his head. "Emily will share my room. Your room is just for you, Lily."

That part was weird. But I guessed it made sense. Emily came over for sleepovers sometimes, and she always stayed in Daddy's room. I guessed they'd just have sleepovers all the time now.

The best part, though, was when Daddy said I could have my first real sleepover at the house. He promised I could invite Olivia sometime after Christmas. I couldn't wait.

I thought about that as my eyes got heavier, the glow of the stars blurring. I imagined Olivia and me in our pajamas, playing games on the Switch that Santa was totally bringing me, and staying up late telling spooky stories—but not too spooky. I'd have to give Olivia some rules, or I wouldn't be able to sleep.

Mr. Fluffles was tucked under my arm as I drifted off, my head on my favorite polar bear pillow and the soft rhythm of Christmas music from the living room lulling me to sleep. Santa was on his way.

Tomorrow, I'd open presents at Mommy's house in the morning, then go to Daddy's house in the afternoon. After that, we'd go to Emily's for her Christmas party. It was going to be the best day ever.

And I just knew Santa was going to get it right—like he always did.

41

Lucas

THE MORNING SUNLIGHT filtered softly through the curtains, and I stretched out under the covers, unwilling to leave the cocoon of warmth that the bed offered. Beside me, Emily was curled up, her hair a messy halo against the pillow, her breathing slow and steady.

"Merry Christmas," I murmured, pressing a kiss to her temple.

Her eyes fluttered open, a sleepy smile spreading across her face. "Merry Christmas."

For a moment, neither of us moved, savoring the rare quiet of the morning. I missed having Lily for Christmas morning this year, but I couldn't say I didn't appreciate the luxury of not being dragged out of bed at 5 a.m. to see what Santa had left under the tree. I chuckled at the thought of Lily, probably already squealing with joy as she unwrapped her gifts. Looking at the clock on the bedside table and seeing that it was nearly 9 a.m., I figured that all those presents had long since been opened and Lily was playing happily.

"Thinking about Lily?" Emily asked, her voice still laced with sleep.

"Always," I said, pulling her closer. "But I have to admit, I don't mind not having to assemble Barbie furniture at dawn."

Emily laughed softly, her fingers tracing lazy patterns on my arm. "I'm sure she's having the best morning. That Barbie house is going to blow her mind." I thought back to the day before when I had assembled the house in my living room and then drove it over to Jessica's apartment complex, delivering the house to her neighbor for safe-keeping until Jessica could go retrieve it after Lily had gone to bed.

"Yeah, I'm glad Jessica and I decided to team up on that," I said. "And the Switch. We've already agreed on screen time limits, so no battles there." I paused, a small smile tugging at my lips. "It's good, you know? The way we manage things for Lily."

Emily nodded, her eyes full of understanding. "It's great, Lucas. You and Jessica do a fantastic job."

I gave her a quick squeeze, marveling at how easily she fit into my life. Her warmth, her patience—it was more than I'd ever hoped for.

"Alright," she said, stretching. "Time to get up. We have a lot to do before everyone arrives."

I groaned in mock protest. "We could stay in bed a little longer..."

She laughed, kissing me quickly before sitting up. "Tempting, but no. We've got a schedule to keep." I rolled my eyes. Emily was always on time. Me, on the other hand? The party didn't start until I walked in, or at least so I thought. The words to Kesha's well-known song TikTok now rang through my head.

Reluctantly, I let her go, watching as she headed to the shower. Once the water started running, I rolled out of bed, pulled on a hoodie, and stumbled into the kitchen. The coffee maker called to me from its place on the counter, and I set it brewing, the smell of fresh coffee filling the air.

As the machine did its work, I wandered over to the coat tree by the back door. My coat hung there, its pockets holding a secret I'd been carrying since shortly after returning from the hospital. That experience had scared me, and I still have inklings of worry about what the future will bring. But if there is anything I learned from going through that scary time, it is that Emily and I were in for the long haul. This was about more than living together. I wanted to make things officially 'official.'

I reached inside my coat pocket, my fingers brushing against the small box tucked safely inside.

Carefully, I pulled it out and opened the lid, the diamond ring catching the morning light. It was simple but elegant—two and a half carats in a round setting, perched on top of a halo of tiny diamonds, set against a simple platinum band. I knew Emily would love it.

Tonight was the night.

We'd agreed to exchange gifts before I headed over to Jessica's to pick up Lily. My plan was to arrive back just in time for everyone to arrive. I'd gone all out this year, splurging on a few other things for Emily—a silk nightgown that I hoped she'd wear to bed that night, a pair of silver hoop earrings she'd been admiring—but this was the real gift. The one that mattered most.

I closed the box and slipped it back into my coat pocket, my heart racing at the thought of what the evening would bring. I wanted her to say 'yes'—needed her to say 'yes'.

"Lucas?" Emily called from the bathroom, her voice muffled by the sound of running water.

"Yeah?" I called back, pocketing the box and heading toward the kitchen.

"Don't drink all the coffee!" she teased.

I smiled, pouring a mug for myself and leaving the rest for her. As I took a sip, the warmth spread through me, calming my nerves. Tonight was going to be perfect.

42

Jessica

LILY WAS FULL OF CHATTER as she narrated the lives of her Barbies. I lay sprawled on the couch, fighting the pull of sleep as the warmth of the room and the early hour pressed heavily against my eyelids.

Lily, on the other hand, was in full holiday mode, her excitement undiminished despite having woken me up at 5:30 that morning with a squeal of, "Santa came, Mommy! Santa came!" She had dragged me out of bed, her small hand pulling mine insistently, her feet nearly skipping as she guided me to the Christmas tree.

Now, her new Barbie house dominated the living room. Lily had set up residence for at least 20 Barbies, their outfits changing repeatedly since sunrise. Ken was sitting on the roof for some reason—likely banished for reasons only Lily understood—and the tiny plastic furniture had been carefully arranged and rearranged at least three times.

I stretched out on the couch, one arm flung over my head, the other holding my phone as I swiped idly through a dating app I'd downloaded a few weeks ago. Why did so many men think a shirtless selfie was the way to a woman's heart? Sure, some of them looked great, but flexing in front of a bathroom mirror wasn't exactly screaming "relationship material." Swipe left.

One guy's profile was all about his love for extreme sports and "living life on the edge." Hard pass. Another proudly showed off a collection of luxury cars—impressive, but not my style. Left again.

Then, there was one that caught my eye. He had kind eyes and a warm smile. His profile mentioned that he was a software engineer and loved hiking and spending time with his two kids. It felt... real. Relatable. A quick right swipe.

As I continued scrolling, I felt a strange mix of hope and hesitation. It wasn't that I didn't want to meet someone—I did. But dating as a single mom came with its own set of challenges. My time was limited, and my priorities were clear. I wasn't looking for just anyone. I wanted someone who could be a part of this life I'd built with Lily. Someone who understood that she came first.

Lily's giggles drew my attention, and I smiled as I watched her carefully position Barbie in a pink convertible parked outside the new dream house. She'd been over the moon about her gifts; the Nintendo Switch and Barbie house were definitely just what she had wanted. I had agreed with Lucas on Santa's behalf about the Nintendo Switch, but aside from assembly, which he had graciously taken care of, I handled the Barbie house on my own.

My cinnamon rolls sat on the coffee table, the remnants of a holiday tradition passed down from my mom. I'd made them from scratch while Lily played, filling the kitchen with the warm, sugary scent of cinnamon and nostalgia.

Yesterday, we'd spent the day in Duluth with my parents, watching Lily run around the same house I'd grown up in, her laughter bouncing off the walls that held my own childhood memories. It had been a long drive back, but it was worth every mile.

Now, as I lay here, I felt... content. It was a good morning. A good Christmas. But there was still something missing, wasn't there?

I sighed, swiping left on another profile. Maybe it was time. Lucas had moved on and found happiness with Emily. They were even taking that next big step, moving in together. I was happy for him—for both of them. They'd built something solid, something that worked for Lily.

And if Lucas could find that kind of connection, why couldn't I?

I swiped right on another profile, this one belonging to a teacher with a goofy grin and a bio full of dad jokes. He seemed sweet and grounded—exactly the kind of person who might fit into my world.

Lily's voice broke through my thoughts. "Mommy, can we make the Barbies have a Christmas party? They need one!"

I laughed, setting my phone aside. "Of course, sweetie. What's a Christmas morning without a Barbie party?"

She beamed, dragging her plastic friends closer to me as I sat up.

For now, this was enough. But as I helped Lily plan the Barbies' holiday festivities, a quiet hope bloomed in my chest. Maybe, just maybe, the new year would bring something—or someone—special.

43

Emily

THE KITCHEN WAS ALIVE with the smells of rosemary, garlic, and roasted vegetables. The stovetop clicked softly as I stirred the simmering mint jelly. Cooking Christmas dinner had been a rare treat for me in recent years, and I was determined to make it perfect.

A rack of lamb, generously seasoned with rosemary and olive oil, was cooking in the oven, its aroma absolutely delectable. Jake's favorite garlic potatoes were roasting alongside, while a mix of carrots and Brussels sprouts—Sarah's request—sizzled in a skillet. On the counter sat the pecan and lemon meringue pies I'd picked up from the local grocery store. After all, I wasn't a miracle worker—one oven could only handle so much.

Lucas's voice called out from the living room again, "Are you sure you don't want any help?"

"No!" I shouted back for what had to be the fifth time that morning, shaking my head with a smile.

"Okay, but the offer still stands!" His tone was teasing, and I could imagine him lounging on the couch, watching ESPN. He'd been perfectly content there all morning, a bottled water in hand, keeping himself entertained with a seemingly endless supply of holiday sports.

Every so often, he wandered into the kitchen, sneaking a kiss or wrapping his arms around me. The last time, he had come up behind me while I was chopping rosemary and whispered in my ear, "I love you."

I'd given him a quick peck on the cheek before shooing him back to the living room. "Out of my kitchen, Lucas!"

"Yes, ma'am," he'd replied with mock seriousness, backing away with his hands up in surrender.

I finally had a moment to breathe with everything either cooking or prepping. I wiped my hands on my apron, surveying my progress with pride. The meal was coming together beautifully.

Lucas popped his head into the kitchen, his blue eyes sparkling. "Are you ready to open some gifts now? You've been cooking all morning, and I think you deserve a break."

I smiled, glad for the interruption. "You know what? That sounds perfect."

I untied my apron, hanging it on a hook by the pantry, and followed him into the living room. The Christmas tree glowed softly, its lights reflecting off the shiny ornaments. Lucas had already sorted the gifts, and I saw four packages with my name on them, neatly stacked under the tree.

He grinned as he pointed them out. "Thought I'd make it easy for you."

I laughed, noticing that he'd also managed to find the four packages I'd wrapped for him. They were stacked on the coffee table, his name scrawled in my careful handwriting on each tag.

We settled onto the couch, and Lucas handed me my first gift.

The first package revealed a sexy silk nightgown in a deep emerald green. I shot him a look, and he smirked. "For you to enjoy—and for me," he said with a wink.

Next was a pair of North Face winter gloves, a thoughtful gift I needed. My hands were always cold, and Lucas, ever observant, had noticed. The third box held a beautiful pair of silver hoop earrings, elegant and understated, just my style. "They're perfect," I said, leaning over to kiss him.

Then came the final gift—a Louis Vuitton handbag. My breath caught as I pulled it from the box, its sleek design and buttery leather making my heart skip a beat. "Lucas," I whispered, running my fingers over the monogrammed surface. "This is too much."

"Nothing's too much for you," he said simply.

It was my turn to hand him his gifts. He opened the first box to find a pair of North Face gloves, and we both burst out laughing. "Great minds think alike," I laughed.

Next was a plaid jacket, perfect for his on-site work. He grinned as he held it up. "This is great. I needed a new one." The third gift was a Garmin watch, something he'd mentioned wanting during one of our walks. "This is awesome, Emily. Thank you."

Finally, he opened the laser level, his eyebrows shooting up in surprise. "I can't believe you remembered this, and you even knew the right one to get," he said, turning it over in his hands. "I was just talking to Cole about it!"

"Well, I pay attention," I said with a shrug.

We'd done pretty well for our first official Christmas together, I thought, feeling a warm glow of satisfaction. We'd barely met before last Christmas and had spent the holidays with our respective families.

But before I could savor the moment, Lucas shifted. He knelt in front of me, gently taking the Louis Vuitton bag from my lap and setting it aside.

"Lucas," I started, confused.

Then I saw it—the small velvet box in his hand.

My breath hitched as he looked up at me, his blue eyes steady and filled with emotion. He took my hands in his, the warmth of his touch grounding me.

"Emily," he began, his voice low but strong, "this year has been the best of my life because of you. You've brought love, laughter, and light into my world in ways I didn't even know I needed. You've been a friend, a partner, and a lover. You've made me a better man, and I can't imagine my future without you in it."

Tears welled in my eyes as he continued. "I love you more than words can say, and I want us to keep building this life together. So, Emily, will you do me the honor of becoming my wife?" He opened the box, revealing a stunning ring—a delicate band set with a single, brilliant round diamond perched over a diamond-studded halo. The solitaire caught the light, and sparkles leapt across the room.

All I could do for a moment was stare, my heart pounding. Then, with tears streaming down my cheeks, I nodded. "Yes, Lucas. Yes, I'll marry you."

His face broke into a wide grin as he slipped the ring onto my finger. He stood, then pulled me into his arms and kissed me deeply. The sound of the timer in the kitchen broke us apart, both of us laughing through tears. "I think dinner's ready," I said, my voice shaky but filled with joy.

"And I think this is the best Christmas ever," Lucas replied, holding me close.

I couldn't have agreed more.

44

Jake

IT WAS CHRISTMAS DAY, and Christmas on Death Row was playing from the speakers on my kitchen counter. I stood in front of the mirror, trying to adjust my tie. Eventually, I gave up. It could be crooked. Who cares? It was Christmas. Ainsley was in the bathroom, putting the finishing touches on a fresh layer of makeup.

We'd spent the earlier part of the day at her sister Bethany's house. Bethany had moved to Minnesota four years ago after marrying a local guy, and it was clear how close the sisters were as Ainsley had followed her sister to the U.S. Their bond reminded me of Sarah and me, though with a bit less playful sarcasm. Ainsley and Bethany had made me feel welcome, offering a spread of Yorkshire pudding, roasted potatoes, and plenty of laughs about the differences between Christmas in England and here in the States.

I hadn't expected to feel so comfortable so quickly. Ainsley made things easy; her easygoing nature and playful smile cut through my usual tendency to overthink. The relationship was still new, and

with my demanding schedule—law school now that graduation from my undergraduate school had come and gone, an apprenticeship at a local firm, and endless hours of studying—I wasn't looking to rush into anything.

But with Ainsley, I saw potential.

She was independent, which I appreciated. Her work as a massage therapist kept her busy, but she also had a passion for photography that she threw herself into with an infectious energy. I remembered her talking with Lucas at Thanksgiving, showing him some of her architectural shots. He'd encouraged her to reach out to local galleries, and she'd since started drafting a business plan to make that dream a reality. It wasn't something she had to do—it was something she wanted to do, and I admired that about her.

Tonight, we were heading to Mom's house for Christmas dinner. The last Christmas at the home I'd grown up in. That thought hit me with a pang of nostalgia. I hadn't fully let myself think about what it meant to say goodbye to the house. Mom had made her decision, and I was happy for her—indeed. She and Lucas planned to start the new year together, selling the house and moving into his. And while my practical side knew it was a good decision, the sentimental side was still grappling with it.

The house wasn't just a house. It was Christmas mornings with Sarah, racing down the stairs to see what Santa had left. It was summer nights on the back porch, fireflies blinking in the yard. It was the countless times I'd seen Mom curled up with a book in her favorite chair, her laughter echoing through the walls.

But I couldn't deny how happy she seemed. Lucas was good for her. He respected her independence, and she respected his. He wasn't trying to change her life—just be a part of it. That was what mattered.

Mom still had her bad days, of course. There were things about her life with Dad she missed—mostly the lake house in northern Minnesota, and I couldn't blame her. She had always told me she wrote her best words when she was up by the lake. But she wasn't stuck in the past. She'd been succeeding and venturing a path forward in her own way, balancing her love of writing with her voracious appetite for reading.

Her latest book, the one about the little boy Caleb, was now with her editor, and she'd already started working on another story—this time about a little girl named Cecelia whose parents were going through a divorce. She'd mentioned it casually at Thanksgiving, and I could see how much the story meant to her. Writing had become her way of processing her own experiences, and I admired her for that. Her books were a source of hope and inspiration for kids going through tough things.

And then there were her book reviews. Every time I scrolled through Instagram, there she was, holding up her latest read with a thoughtful caption. She was reading more books than anyone I knew, and her reviews were sharp, funny, and insightful. She was carving out her own space, building a life she was proud of, which made me proud of her, too.

Ainsley emerged from the bathroom, her dark green dress catching the light as she adjusted her earrings. "How do I look?" she asked, giving me a twirl.

"Perfect," I said honestly, stepping forward to kiss her lightly on the cheek.

She smiled, brushing a hand over my shoulder to smooth out a wrinkle in my jacket. "Are you ready?"

"Yeah," I said, grabbing the bag of gifts from the counter. "Let's go."

The drive to Mom's house was quiet but comfortable. Ainsley seemed to sense that I was deep in thought, and she didn't push for conversation. Instead, she laced her fingers through mine and rested her head against the window, watching the snow-covered landscape pass by.

When we pulled up to the house, I felt that pang again—all those memories pressing down as I looked at the twinkling lights strung along the porch. This house had been the backdrop of so much of my life. But tonight wasn't about holding onto the past. It was about celebrating the present and the new chapter Mom was starting.

As we stepped inside, the familiar warmth of the house enveloped me. The smell of pine from the tree in the corner mixed with the savory aroma of whatever Mom was cooking in the kitchen.

"Jake!" Mom called, her face lighting up as she hurried over to hug me.

"Merry Christmas, Mom," I said, holding her close.

She pulled back, her eyes shining. "Merry Christmas, sweetheart. And hello, Ainsley."

Ainsley smiled warmly. "It's so nice to see you again, Mrs.—, I mean, Emily." My mom laughed lightly and gave Ainsley another quick hug. I noticed a ring on my mom's left hand as she did. The rock was huge, but the ring seemed to fit her hand and style perfectly.

I met my mom's gaze, and she noticed I had seen the ring. She smiled lightly and gave me a look. I knew she was asking me to keep quiet for now. And what was strange to me was that had this been two or three years ago, I would have had a reaction that I wouldn't be proud of today. But now, seeing that ring actually made me smile back at her. I knew it was the right thing for Mom, and I couldn't be happier.

I nodded to her, showing her I understood her silent message. As the evening unfolded, I found myself feeling lighter than I had in weeks. How light could I get? It seemed that throughout the last two months, I had been feeling better and better about things every day. I knew that a lot of it had to do with my mom. It can be so hard to see a parent suffer heartbreak. But knowing she was happy made things different—in all the right ways.

45

Sarah

THE SMELL OF FRESHLY BAKED bread filled the kitchen as I pulled the knotted rolls from the oven, their golden tops glistening with melted butter. I set the tray on the counter, satisfied with how they had turned out. The rolls were my contribution to Christmas dinner, and while I'd wanted to bring more, Mom had insisted the rolls were enough.

"Don't argue with her," Michael had said earlier, laughing as I'd debated sneaking in a dessert or side dish. He was right, of course. When Mom had her mind set on something, it was not changing. And this Christmas was important to her.

This was her last Christmas in the house we grew up in, and she was determined to make it perfect. I could feel the weight of it in everything she did—the meticulous decorations, the carefully planned menu, the art projects she'd undoubtedly prepared for Lily and Olivia. It was her way of saying goodbye to the home with so many memories.

Michael walked into the kitchen, adjusting the cuffs of his sweater. "Are the rolls done?"

"Yep," I said, grabbing a clean dish towel to cover the tray. "And they turned out perfectly, thank you very much."

He grinned, leaning down to kiss my cheek. "I never doubted you."

That morning, we'd spent Christmas together, just the two of us. We'd agreed on it before we got married—starting our own traditions while still making time for our families. We'd exchanged gifts over coffee, with the Christmas tree lights twinkling in the background. Michael had surprised me with a pair of diamond hoop earrings I'd been eyeing, and I'd given him a set of leather-bound journals he'd been wanting for his sketching and project notes.

It had been simple and perfect, a quiet moment of connection before the whirlwind of the day ahead.

The past few days have been a blur of family gatherings. Two days ago, we spent time with my dad and his wife at their house, an informal get-together with just the four of us. Then, Christmas Eve was with Michael's family—a lively, chaotic affair that I was still recovering from.

Michael came from a huge family, the middle child of five. His older brother and sister had brought their kids, while his two younger sisters—both still in high school—alternated between helping in the kitchen and chatting about their lives. The youngest, who had just gotten her driver's license, talked my ear off about all things 'Rules of the Road'.

It was fun, though. With only one younger brother, I'd always wanted to be part of a big family, and Michael's siblings had welcomed me with open arms.

As I covered the rolls with the towel and placed them in a basket, my mind drifted to the future. Michael and I had talked about starting a family, and I'd scheduled an appointment with my OB/GYN for mid-January. I wanted to make sure I was caught up on vaccines and ready for the next chapter of our lives. The thought filled me with a mix of excitement and nervousness.

"You ready?" Michael asked, grabbing our coats from the rack.

"Ready," I said, slipping my arms into my coat and grabbing the basket of rolls.

The drive to Mom's house was short, and we arrived just after Jake and Ainsley. As we pulled into the driveway, I spotted Jake's car parked neatly in front. "Looks like Jake beat us," I said, stepping out into the crisp December air.

Michael grabbed the rolls from the backseat while I carried a small bag of gifts. We'd agreed to keep things light this year since the focus was on spending time together, but I couldn't resist picking up a few small surprises for everyone.

The door opened before we reached the porch, and Lily's voice rang out, "Auntie Sarah! Auntie Sarah!"

She came barreling toward me, her excitement bubbling over. Her cheeks were pink from running around, and her little hands clutched a piece of paper covered in glitter and glue.

"Look! Look what I made!" she said, holding up the paper.

"Wow, Lily!" I said, crouching down to admire her work. "Is this a snowflake?"

"Yes! Your Mommy said we can make as many as we want!"

Of course, Mom would have art projects ready to keep the kids entertained. It was such a her thing to do, making sure everyone had something to enjoy while the adults caught up and prepared dinner.

"Can you help me make another one?" Lily asked, her eyes wide with excitement.

"Of course," I said, taking her hand and letting her lead me toward the table where a pile of craft supplies was spread out.

Michael chuckled as he followed behind us, placing the rolls on the counter. "Looks like you've been recruited."

I grinned at him over my shoulder. "It's the price of being the cool aunt."

As Lily began explaining her snowflake-making process in great detail, I glanced around the house, taking in the warmth and laughter filling the space. Mom's last Christmas in the house was shaping up to be exactly what she'd wanted—a celebration of love, family, and new beginnings.

But then I caught Jake looking at me, as if trying to catch my gaze. The look he gave me was odd. It almost looked like his eyes were bugging out of his head, hoping to send a secret message. However, whatever he was trying to say passed me by entirely. Between Lily's chatter, happy cries for my attention, and the hustle and bustle of everyone spreading gifts under Mom's tree, it was hard to figure out what he wanted me to know. And what could it be, anyway?

46

Lucas

THE CLATTER OF DISHES and the chatter of competing voices filled Emily's kitchen as Jake, Michael, and I worked our way through the mountain of post-Christmas dinner dishes. I scrubbed a roasting pan while Jake dried a wine glass, holding it to the light before placing it on the rack. Michael was rummaging through a cabinet, muttering about how many mixing bowls one could own.

"Are we sure this goes here?" Michael asked, holding up a small stack of dessert plates.

Jake glanced over and shrugged. "Your guess is as good as mine. Just pick a spot and hope Mom doesn't notice."

I chuckled, rinsing the pan and handing it off to Jake. "I wouldn't count on her not noticing. She's got a radar for this stuff." I paused, "And how do you not know where things go? You lived here most of your life?" I asked Jake, and he just shrugged his shoulders.

Gender roles be damned, I thought to myself as I turned back to the sink. My mom would be tut-tutting me right now, shaking her head at seeing her son elbow-deep in dishwater. She'd always been old-fashioned, holding tightly to the belief that the kitchen was a woman's domain. It had been a point of contention between us when I was younger, and one I hadn't understood until I'd grown older.

She'd passed away nearly two decades ago, breast cancer taking her far too soon. She never got to meet Lily, or even Jessica, for that matter—she'd died shortly after I turned 30, before my life had indeed begun to take shape. It was a shame, really. She would have loved Jessica and Emily, too. She would have doted on Lily, spoiling her with homemade cookies and handmade scarves like she used to do for my brother and me. My brother, Peter, was off in Africa somewhere as a missionary. We only spoke once or twice a year. It wasn't that we didn't want to connect, but his calling in life kept him busy, and often without access to cell service.

I paused momentarily, the memory of Mom's laughter at Peter and my childhood antics flickering in my mind like a candle in a dark room. She would have been an incredible grandmother. She would have adored Emily, and her warmth and practicality perfectly matched my mom's spirited nature.

"Your Dad is still out deep-sea fishing, right?" Jake asked, breaking into my thoughts as he dried the last of the pans.

"Yeah," I said, shaking off the memory. "He's down in Miami with some of his buddies. Probably sitting on a boat right now with a beer in hand, waiting for a marlin to bite."

Michael laughed. "Sounds like a good gig."

"It is," I said, my voice tinged with a bit of envy mixed with disappointment. My dad had taken to the open road—and the open sea—after my mom passed, filling his days with adventure and camaraderie. It was his way of coping, of finding meaning after losing the love of his life. But he'd always been unpredictable. He hadn't been the type of father that my brother or I could count on. Nor our mother, for that matter. But she had loved him and quietly accepted his eccentricities.

Now, my dad spent his winters in warmer climates, only returning to Minnesota in the spring when the cold finally let up. As much as I admired my dad's resilience despite how tough he made our childhood, I couldn't help but wonder if I'd done the same—kept moving, kept pushing forward—as a way to outrun my own grief after Mom had died. The thought simply sat there for a moment before Michael spoke again.

"Alright, that's the last of it," he said, placing the final plate in the cabinet. "Kitchen's officially back in order."

Jake stretched, his arms brushing the low light fixture overhead. "Good timing. I think Lily and Olivia are going to bury Sarah and Mom in paper snowflakes."

I laughed, wiping my hands on a dish towel. "Sounds about right. Those two could charm anyone into glitter duty."

We stepped out of the kitchen into the living room, where the faint sound of Christmas music played in the background. Lily and Olivia were seated at a small table, their hands sticky with glue and glitter as they worked on snowflake ornaments. Sarah was helping Olivia, while Emily leaned over Lily, carefully attaching a piece of ribbon to a finished snowflake. Cole and Rebecca were watching the girls with delight, and I noticed Cole's hand resting gently on Rebecca's upper thigh as her own hand rested on her belly. They were still being relatively quiet about her pregnancy, but it was clear to me now that she was definitely very pregnant.

Emily glanced up as we entered, her eyes meeting mine with a warm smile. "Done already?"

"Kitchen's spotless," I said, crossing the room to stand behind her. I placed my hands on her shoulders, squeezing gently. "Thanks for letting us help."

"Letting you help?" Emily teased, looking over her shoulder. "I practically shoved you three in there."

"Details," I said, leaning down to kiss the top of her head.

Her laughter was soft, and for a moment, I let myself savor the scene in front of me—the laughter, the warmth, and the sense of belonging that filled the room. This was what Christmas was supposed to feel like: family, connection, love.

As Jake and Michael joined the others, I found myself thinking about the future. This would be our last—my only—Christmas in Emily's house, but it didn't feel like an ending. It felt like the start of something new, something more significant.

Emily and I planned to pack up her house in the coming weeks, preparing for her move into the home I shared with Lily. It would be an adjustment for all of us, but I looked forward to it. Having Emily by my side every day, sharing the highs and lows of life together—it felt right.

I caught Lily's eye as she held up a glitter-covered snowflake for Sarah to admire, her face glowing with pride. My heart swelled with gratitude. This was my life, my family, and I couldn't have asked for a better gift.

And it was then that I saw the look of shock on Sarah's face. Before I knew what was happening, she stood up, nearly knocking her chair over, and raced around the table to grab her mother's hand. "What is this?" she squealed with delight, clearly already understanding the ring's significance on her mom's hand.

"Oh," I said. "We have something to tell you all."

And all eyes turned my way.

47

Emily

"WHAT'S THIS?" Sarah exclaimed, grabbing my hand and staring at the ring as though it might disappear if she blinked.

I laughed softly, glancing at Lucas, who was standing a few feet away. "Well," I said, feeling a rush of warmth in my cheeks, "I suppose now's as good a time as any."

Lucas smiled and stepped forward, his calm presence grounding me. Jake had noticed the ring earlier when he and Ainsley arrived, and I'd been surprised Sarah hadn't seen it until now. Even Rebecca picked it up when she and Cole arrived earlier. The whole evening felt like a series of moments building up to this.

Lucas slipped his arm around my waist, pulling me close as he addressed the room. "We have something to tell you all," he began, his voice carrying over the quiet chatter that had filled the space moments ago.

The room grew silent, all eyes on us. I felt a flutter of nervousness but also a deep sense of contentment. This was my family now, and I couldn't imagine sharing this moment with anyone else.

Lucas glanced around the room, his gaze settling on Sarah and Jake before moving to the others. "We already shared some big news at Thanksgiving," he said, his voice warm. "Emily and I moving in together was a huge step for us, and nothing about that is changing. But…"

He paused, his arm tightening slightly around me. "But the heart attack—it made me realize just how short life can be. It was scary, not just for me but for Emily, for Lily, for all of us. And I knew—lying there in that hospital bed—that I didn't want to waste another minute."

I felt my throat tighten as he turned to me, his blue eyes filled with love and certainty. "Emily," he said, his voice dropping just slightly. I love you. I've loved you since the moment you walked into my life. You make every day brighter, and I know there's no one else I'd rather spend the rest of my life with."

My eyes filled with tears as he looked back at the room, his voice steady but filled with emotion. "I asked Emily to marry me," he said, his words soft but strong. "And she said yes."

The room erupted into cheers and applause, Sarah throwing her arms around me in a tight hug while Jake clapped Lucas on the back. Rebecca and Cole came over, offering congratulations, while Michael stood beside Sarah, beaming. Even Ainsley, who was still relatively new to the family dynamic, joined in the hugs and congratulations.

I took a deep breath, letting the moment wash over me. It felt surreal, standing there surrounded by the people we loved, sharing this incredible moment with them. Lucas caught my eye and smiled, his hand finding mine and squeezing gently.

As the excitement began to settle, Sarah pulled me aside, her eyes sparkling with mischief. "So," she said, lowering her voice, "are we talking about a big wedding or something small?"

I was about to answer when I finally noticed that Lily was looking at me strangely. Her eyes darted to her father and then to me. I hadn't seen that look on her face before, and I wasn't quite sure what to make of it.

Then she stood up, placed her hands on her hip, and said loudly, with curiosity and confusion clear in her voice, "Daddy, if you marry Emily, then who will Mommy marry? And if I get a stepmommy, will I get a stepdaddy, too?"

The room grew silent as all eyes turned to Lily. And my eyes looked to Lucas, his face full of bewilderment. He didn't know what to say. I didn't know what to say. How do you answer that question? How do you explain adult relationships to an eight-year-old? There was certainly no manual for this.

Suddenly, I felt a bit faint. I released myself from Lucas and walked across the room and down the hall to my bedroom. I could feel Lucas's eyes on me, but at that moment, I just needed space.

48

Lily

THE FLOOR AROUND US was covered in tiny scraps of paper and glitter. Olivia and I were both covered in glitter, too—it was on our hands, in our hair, even on our faces. But we didn't care. We were making the most magical snowflakes ever.

Olivia doesn't have any grandparents, so her family always comes to my daddy's house for Christmas. Daddy says it's because we're like family, even though we're not really related. I think that's nice. Olivia is my best friend, and having her here makes Christmas feel even more fun.

"Look at this one!" Olivia said, holding up a snowflake with six perfect points. She was really good at making snowflakes, better than me.

"It's pretty!" I said, trying to make my own look as good. Mine had a few crooked cuts, but Olivia said it didn't matter. "All snow-flakes are special," she told me.

I was just finishing my latest snowflake when I heard Daddy talking to everyone. His voice sounded happy, and that made me happy, too. But then he said something about loving Emily and asking her to marry him.

I paused, my scissors hovering over the paper. Daddy had talked to me about this a few days ago. He said he was going to marry Emily, and I had nodded since I was busy finishing my wish list for Santa. I didn't really know what "marry" meant, but I figured it was just like having sleepovers all the time. Emily had already been having lots of sleepovers at our house, so it didn't seem like a big deal.

But now, hearing Daddy talk about it made me think about Mommy. She was all alone at her apartment. If Daddy was going to have sleepovers with Emily forever, who was going to have sleepovers with Mommy?

I stopped cutting my snowflake and looked up. Olivia was still working on hers, but my mind was racing. This wasn't right. If I was going to get a stepmommy, then I should get a stepdaddy, too. Mommy shouldn't be alone.

I stood up, brushing the glitter off my pants. I wasn't sure if this was something I should ask, but it didn't feel fair to leave Mommy out.

"Daddy," I said. Everyone got really quiet and looked at me. I didn't mind—I was used to people looking at me when I had something important to say.

"If you marry Emily, then who will Mommy marry?" I asked, putting my hands on my hips. "And if I get a stepmommy, will I get a stepdaddy, too?"

Daddy's face looked funny, like he didn't know what to say. Emily's face looked kind of funny, too. I wasn't trying to make anyone upset, but I needed to know.

I waited, but no one answered. The grown-ups just looked at each other like they were playing a game of who's-going-to-talk-first. Finally, Emily walked away, her face looking kind of red. She went down the hall. Maybe she was going to go take a nap in her bedroom.

"Daddy?" I said, now standing closer to him and tugging on his sleeve. "What's wrong?"

He knelt in front of me, putting his hands on my shoulders. "Nothing's wrong, sweetheart," he said, his voice soft. "That's a really good question. And it's okay to ask things like that."

"But who's going to marry Mommy?" I asked, my voice smaller this time but a bit more demanding, too. I wanted an answer. Mommy needed a stepdaddy.

Daddy smiled, but it was one of those smiles that didn't quite reach his eyes. "Mommy doesn't need to get married to be happy," he said. "She has you, and that makes her very happy."

I thought about that for a second. It made sense, but it didn't feel right. If Daddy got Emily, and I got a stepmommy, it seemed like Mommy should get someone, too. "Okay," I said, even though I wasn't sure if I really understood.

Daddy hugged me tight, and I hugged him back. When he stood up, he looked at the other grown-ups and said, "Let's take a break, okay?"

I went back to the craft table and picked up my scissors, but I didn't feel like making snowflakes anymore. Instead, I watched as Daddy walked down the hall, following Emily.

Olivia leaned over and whispered, "What happened?"

"I don't know," I said quietly.

And for the first time that night, Christmas didn't feel so magical anymore.

49

Emily

I CLOSED THE BEDROOM door softly behind me, leaning against it as I let out a shaky breath. My heart pounded in my chest, a mix of guilt, fear, and an overwhelming sense of clarity coursing through me.

Lily's words echoed in my mind, those innocent questions from an eight-year-old that had somehow unraveled everything I thought I was sure about.

"If you marry Emily, then who will Mommy marry? And if I get a stepmommy, will I get a stepdaddy, too?"

They were simple questions, spoken with the purity of a child's logic, but they had cut through all my carefully constructed plans. I hadn't thought about it like that—not really.

I moved to sit on the edge of the bed, my hands trembling as I pressed them into my lap. Lily wasn't like my kids, I realized. Sarah and Jake had been through it all. They'd seen the slow unraveling of my marriage to Andrew. In fact, they'd probably known it was over long before I admitted it to myself.

But Lily? Lily's life had been turned upside down in just a few short years. Her mom moving out, and her dad left to pick up the pieces. A new bedroom in a cramped apartment, a new reality to adjust to. And then I'd come into her life, this woman from out of nowhere trying to stake a claim in her world.

It was too much. Too fast.

I'd been selfish, I realized. I'd told myself that I was thinking about everyone involved, that I was moving forward cautiously, considering what was best for Lucas, for Lily, for my kids. But had I really? Or had I just been so caught up in the idea of building this beautiful life with Lucas that I'd overlooked what Lily might be feeling?

Tears pricked at my eyes as realization settled over me. I loved Lucas deeply. I loved Lily, too. But this—this wasn't right.

I had to slow things down. For Lily's sake. For all of us.

The door creaked open behind me, and I didn't need to turn to know it was Lucas. His quiet presence filled the room as he stepped inside, closing the door softly behind him.

"Emily," he said gently, his voice laced with concern.

I couldn't hold it in any longer. The tears spilled over, and I buried my face in my hands. "I'm sorry, Lucas," I managed, my voice trembling.

He was at my side in an instant, his hand resting lightly on my back. "What's wrong?"

I lifted my head, meeting his worried gaze through tear-filled eyes. "I can't do this," I said, my voice breaking. "I can't marry you. And I can't move in with you. It's just... it's too soon."

The shock on his face was quickly replaced by confusion and hurt. "Emily, where is this coming from? What happened?"

"It's Lily," I said, wiping at my tears. "It's all too much for her, Lucas. She's only eight. Her world has already changed so much, and now we're asking her to take in even more. It's not fair to her."

He sat back, his brows furrowing as he absorbed my words. "I thought we were doing okay. She's been happy, hasn't she?"

"Yes," I said quickly. "But happy doesn't mean she's ready for this. She's still figuring it all out, and we're rushing her. Lucas, this isn't just about us. It's about her future, her stability, her sense of security. And I feel like I've been so caught up in... in us... that I haven't stopped to really think about what this means for her."

Lucas was quiet for a long moment, his eyes dropping to the floor. "I thought we were building something good here," he said finally, his voice barely above a whisper.

"We are," I said, reaching for his hand. "But we're building it too fast. And it's not just Lily—I think I need more time, too. This is a big change for all of us, and I don't want to make a mistake by pushing forward when we're not ready."

He looked up at me, his eyes searching mine. "Are you saying you don't want to be with me?"

"No," I said firmly, shaking my head. "That's not what I'm saying at all. I love you, Lucas. I love you so much. But we need to slow down. Let Lily set the pace. Let us set the pace. There's no rush, right?"

He exhaled slowly, his shoulders slumping. "I guess I just... I thought we were ready."

"I thought so, too," I admitted, my voice softening. "But tonight made me realize we need to take a step back. It's not a no, Lucas. It's just a 'not yet.'"

He turned his back to me before slowly turning back to face me. "Okay," he said, and walked out of the room.

50

Lucas

THE HOUSE WAS QUIET. Too quiet.

I leaned against the kitchen counter, staring out the window at the snow-covered yard. The mug of coffee in my hand had gone cold hours ago, but I couldn't bring myself to reheat it. It sat there. Alone.

It was New Year's Day, and I was alone.

Lily was with Jessica for the week, and for once, I was grateful for the timing. I loved my little girl, but I needed the space—time to think, time to figure out what the hell had gone so wrong.

My mind kept replaying the moment Emily told me she couldn't marry me or move in with me. The sound of her words still rang in my ears, and her reasoning pressed down on my chest.

It wasn't a no, she'd said. Just a 'not yet.'

But it sure as hell felt like a 'no.'

I hadn't seen or spoken to her since I'd walked out of her room on Christmas night. The scene played out in my mind like a movie I couldn't shut off. I had gone straight to Lily, my heart pounding in my chest as I told her it was time to leave.

"But Daddy," she'd protested, clutching the edge of her new sweater, "I didn't finish my snowflakes yet!"

I crouched down in front of her, forcing a smile that felt more like a grimace. "We'll finish them at home, sweetheart. But we need to go now, okay?"

Sarah had begged me to stay, her voice tinged with desperation. "Lucas, don't do this. Please. Just... let's talk about it."

But I couldn't. Not then. Not with everyone's eyes on me, their questions and concerns hanging in the air like a storm cloud.

Rebecca had stepped in, her hand on Sarah's shoulder. "Let him go," she'd whispered softly.

Cole had quickly gathered Lily's gifts, stacking them in the back of the SUV without a word. Then he'd turned to me, his hand resting lightly on my shoulder. "Hey man, you don't have to go," he said quietly.

I'd shaken my head, brushing past him and climbing into the driver's seat. I made sure Lily was buckled in before starting the engine, trying to avoid Cole's gaze following me as I backed out of the driveway.

The memory made my chest tighten, and I set the mug down with more force than necessary. Emily had tried calling the next day, but I couldn't bring myself to answer. What could I say? That I understood? That I didn't?

Sarah had called, too. Her voicemail was full of questions and re-assurances. Even Cole had called—a dozen times, if not more—but I ignored them all. I couldn't face anyone. Not yet.

I'd spent the rest of the week with Lily, burying my emotions under her laughter and the sound of her tiny feet running across the hardwood floors. I'd helped her build an entire Barbie village around the new house Santa had brought—Jessica and I agreed that the Barbie house would live at my house where there was more room, and the Switch at her apartment—Lily's squeals of delight a temporary reprieve from the ache in my chest.

But now, the house was empty again, and I was left with nothing but my thoughts. What had gone wrong?

I replayed the weeks leading up to Christmas, searching for signs I might have missed. Had I pushed Emily too hard? Had I been so caught up in the idea of our life together that I hadn't stopped to see what she needed?

And then there was Lily. I loved my daughter more than life itself, but I couldn't help but feel a flicker of resentment toward the power her innocent words had wielded. Emily had crumbled under the potentially misunderstood meaning behind an eight-year-old's reasoning, and I didn't know how to reconcile that.

Lily didn't mean to hurt me. Of course, she didn't. She was a child, processing the world in the only way she knew how. But her questions had planted seeds of doubt in Emily's mind, and now I was left to deal with the fallout.

I raked a hand through my hair, exhaling a shaky breath. The truth was, I didn't blame Lily. Not really. If anything, I blamed myself. For not preparing her better. For not preparing Emily better. For assuming that love alone would be enough to hold us all together.

But maybe it wasn't enough. The thought sent a chill through me, and I crossed my arms over my chest, trying to ward off the gnawing sense of doubt. For the first time in years, I felt untethered. I'd always been a man with a plan, a man who knew what he wanted and how to get it. I was the life of the party. But now? Now, I didn't know. All I knew was that I loved Emily. And I loved Lily. Somehow, I had to figure out how to make this work.

Because losing Emily wasn't an option.

Not for me. Not for Lily.

And if I had to slow down, if I had to take a step back and rebuild from the ground up, I'd do it.

For them. For us.

51

Sarah

THE SLAM OF THE FRONT DOOR echoed through the house, signaling Lucas and Lily's abrupt departure. I stood frozen in place, staring after them as if the door might magically reopen and they'd walk back in, smiles on their faces like nothing had happened.

But they didn't.

The rest of us stood in awkward silence. So, I headed down the hall and knocked softly on my mother's bedroom door, but there was no answer. I cracked it open just enough to peek inside. Mom was sitting on the edge of her bed, her hands clasped tightly in her lap, staring at the floor.

"Mom?" I said gently.

She looked up, her eyes glistening but dry. "I just need to think, sweetheart," she said, her voice thin. "Go back to the others."

I wanted to stay, to wrap her in a hug and tell her everything would be okay, but the look in her eyes stopped me. Mom needed space, and I knew better than to push her when she was like this.

Closing the door quietly, I made my way back to the kitchen. My shoulders felt heavy from the evening. Rolling up my sleeves, I began pulling out the desserts—pecan pie and lemon meringue pie—arranging them on the counter with plates and forks. I reached for the liquor cabinet, pulling out a few bottles and setting them alongside the desserts. It felt like the right move, a small offering to lighten the mood.

I poured myself a lowball of Bailey's, the creamy liquid pooling in the glass. Taking a sip, I let the warmth soothe my frayed nerves before calling softly to the others. "Dessert's ready."

The adults trickled into the kitchen, moving with a subdued air that was a far cry from the lively chatter that had filled the room just hours before. Plates were filled, drinks poured, but the energy was muted.

We sat around the dining table, picking at our desserts and exchanging the occasional comment. Michael asked Rebecca about her pregnancy, and Cole mentioned a new project he was working on. But the conversation felt forced, each of us skirting around the obvious tension.

After dessert, we gathered in the living room to watch Olivia open her gifts. The little girl's squeals of delight brought a brief reprieve, her joy cutting through the tension like sunlight through a storm.

The adults exchanged gifts next. I'd made shower steamers for everyone—small pucks of baking soda and essential oils that fizzed and released soothing scents in the shower. As each package was opened, the room began to fill with the crisp, refreshing scent of eucalyptus.

"That's nice," Rebecca said, holding her gift to her nose. "You'll have to teach me how to make these."

"Super easy," I said, managing a small smile. "I'll send you the recipe."

Despite the effort to keep things light, the evening wound down quickly. Cole and Rebecca packed up their car, bundling Olivia in her coat and carrying her out to the car, half-asleep.

And then it was just the four of us—me, Michael, Jake, and Ainsley—sitting in the living room, surrounded by the remnants of Christmas. Jake leaned back on the couch, his hands laced behind his head. He stared at the ceiling for a moment before letting out a frustrated breath. "What the fuck just happened?"

"Jake!" I snapped, scowling at him. "Language. Mom has a rule about that, remember?"

He rolled his eyes. "Come on, Sarah. After tonight, you really think Mom's worried about a little swearing?"

I sighed, sinking into the armchair and wrapping a blanket around myself. "It was a mess," I admitted. "But honestly, I'm not surprised. You saw how Lily reacted. She's confused, Jake. And Mom... I think she's overwhelmed."

Michael nodded, his voice calm and measured. "It's a big change for all of them. Maybe it's not a bad thing to slow down."

Jake shook his head, leaning forward with his elbows on his knees. "Lucas loves her. You can see it every time he looks at her. And I know Mom loves him, too. Why can't they just... figure it out?"

"Because love isn't enough sometimes," I said softly. "You know that better than anyone, Jake. Relationships take more than just love. Timing matters. Circumstances matter."

He sighed, rubbing a hand over his face. "I guess. But it still sucks."

We sat in silence for a while, the room heavy with unspoken thoughts.

Finally, Michael stood, stretching his arms over his head. "I'm going to start cleaning up. Anyone want to help?"

Jake shook his head. "I'll pass. I'm wiped." I gave him a dirty look but followed Michael into the kitchen. As we washed the dessert dishes and packed up leftovers, my mind drifted back to Mom and Lucas.

I didn't know what the future held for them, but I hoped they'd find their way back to each other. Because despite everything, they fit. I just hoped my Mom would figure that out and that Lucas could answer Lily's questions.

52

Jake

IT WAS MID-JANUARY, and I should have been fully immersed in my casework and classes. My professors at Mitchell Hamline weren't the forgiving type, and the workload at the firm was enough to make anyone's head spin. I'd been lucky to land a spot in this program—sure, the firm's generous donations might've greased the wheels, but I wasn't about to question it.

Still, none of that mattered right now. My focus was shot, my mind running circles around something far more pressing.

My mom. She was driving me insane.

I slammed my laptop shut and leaned back in my chair, rubbing my hands over my face. I'd spent the better part of the morning attempting to focus on a tort case, only to find myself obsessing over Mom and Lucas. Again. What was wrong with her? Why would she shut Lucas out like this?

A few nights ago, I'd finally broken down and called Lucas. We hadn't talked much since Christmas, but I needed to know where his head was at. It wasn't fair to him or Lily, for that matter, that everything had been left so unresolved.

Lucas had sounded tired when he answered, but his voice carried that same calm, steady tone I'd always admired. He told me how he and Lily had spent much time discussing the whole stepmom situation. Apparently, Lily was good with it now. She even understood that her mom might move forward in her own time.

"Emily called," Lucas had said during our conversation, his voice tinged with frustration. "I didn't answer at first. I needed space. But now I've been calling her back, and she's not picking up. I don't know what else to do, Jake."

Hearing him so defeated had pissed me off. Lucas wasn't the kind of guy to wallow or complain, and if he was at the point of admitting defeat, things were terrible.

And Mom? Well, she wasn't exactly helping matters. Every time I brought up Lucas, she either changed the subject or brushed it off, claiming she needed more time to think. Time to think? It had been two weeks. How much time did she need?

I stood up abruptly, pacing the small confines of my apartment. Ainsley had been supportive—her calm demeanor was a godsend— but even she was starting to lose patience with my constant venting.

"You should just talk to her," Ainsley had said the other night as she folded laundry on my couch.

"I've tried," I'd replied, throwing my hands in the air. "She doesn't listen."

"Then try harder," she'd said simply, her tone calm but firm.

Now, as I stared out the window at the streets of St. Paul—most of the December snow had since melted off—her words echoed in my mind. Maybe Ainsley was right. Perhaps it was time to stop tiptoeing around Mom's feelings and just lay it all out there.

By the end of the week, if no headway was made, I would get up in her business.

I grabbed my phone and scrolled through my contacts, hovering over Mom's name. I wanted to call her right then and there, to demand she stop ignoring Lucas and figure this out. But I knew better. If I came in guns blazing, she'd shut down completely.

Instead, I shot off a quick text to Ainsley:

Me: *Hey, wanna grab dinner tonight? Need to vent.*

Her reply came almost instantly:

Ainsley: *Of course. Your place at 7?*

Me: *Sounds good. Thanks.*

I tossed my phone on the couch and sank down beside it, staring at the ceiling.

This wasn't just about Lucas anymore. It wasn't even about Lily or Mom. It was about all of us. About the family we were trying to build together. And I wasn't going to let it fall apart because two stubborn adults couldn't figure their shit out.

<h1 style="text-align:center">53</h1>

<h1 style="text-align:center">Jessica</h1>

I SANK DEEPER into the couch, staring at my phone screen, the dating app open and ready for another round of swiping. It was practically an obsession these days. When I wasn't at work or with Lily, I found myself here, scrolling through profiles, searching for... well, I wasn't entirely sure what.

Earlier in the week, I'd gone out with Jeremy, a software engineer who worked for a local law firm. Dinner had been pleasant—good food, easy conversation about his hiking adventures, and my role as a physical therapist—but it hadn't left me with that excited tingle in my belly the way I'd hoped. He was kind, intelligent, even funny in a reserved sort of way. But a spark? Not so much.

Still, I wasn't ready to close the door on the possibility. Maybe sparks didn't always come right away. Maybe they had to grow over time. Or maybe I was just trying to convince myself that putting in the effort was worth it.

I swiped left on a shirtless gym selfie, rolling my eyes. Seriously, did these guys not realize how ridiculous they looked? Then came another profile—this one a teacher with an easy smile and an adorable golden retriever in his photo. I hovered for a moment before swiping right, thinking, Why not?

As I kept scrolling, my mind began to wander, replaying the conversation I'd had with Lucas when he dropped Lily off the week after Christmas.

He and Emily had split up. Kind of. And they weren't talking. What was that all about?

I paused mid-swipe, my thumb hovering over the screen as I thought back to how Lucas had explained it. His proposal, Emily's reaction, Lily's innocent questions—it was a lot. And while I could understand where Emily was coming from, it frustrated me to think that the words of an eight-year-old had been enough to derail everything they'd been building.

I'd only met Emily three times—once over coffee, again at Lily's birthday party, and then at the hospital. But in those moments, I'd seen enough to know she was a good match for Lucas. She was warm, practical, and grounded in a way that balanced his sometimes over-the-top enthusiasm. More importantly, she was good for Lily.

Lucas explained that Emily had said yes when he had proposed earlier in the day. Though, to be honest, I hadn't expected him to take that step so soon. Still, I supported the decision. Emily brought something to Lucas's life that he hadn't had in years: Stability and partnership.

It frustrated me to think of her refusing Lucas's calls. Yes, Lily's words might have been a catalyst, but Emily was an adult. Couldn't she see past that? Then again, maybe it wasn't that simple. I'd been co-parenting with Lucas long enough to know that nothing about blending families ever was.

I thought back to the conversations I'd had with Lily after Christmas. She'd been full of questions, her young mind working overtime to process the idea of a stepmom—and the possibility of a stepdad.

"Mommy," she'd asked one night as we were snuggled up reading a book, "if Daddy gets a stepmommy for me, will you get a stepdaddy?"

I had smiled, setting the book I'd been reading aside and pulling her closer. "Not necessarily, sweetheart," I'd said, keeping my tone simple and calm. "Right now, Mommy's been really busy with work and getting ready for Christmas. But someday, maybe I'll feel ready to talk to someone new. And even if I do, it doesn't mean you'll need a stepdaddy right away—or at all. Families come in all shapes and sizes, and ours will always be special."

She'd nodded slowly, her little brow furrowed in thought. Over the days that followed, she'd asked more questions, and we'd talked openly about her feelings. I'd watched her slowly begin to understand, a new maturity forming as she processed everything.

Now, Lily seemed to have a sense of clarity about it all. But that didn't change the fact that Emily and Lucas were stuck in limbo. And while I wanted to help, I knew it wasn't my role to play.

Now, I sighed, setting my phone down and staring at the ceiling. I hoped they'd figure it out soon—for their sake and for Lily's. Because as much as Lucas and I had worked hard to co-parent effectively, there were things I couldn't give Lily.

54

Jake

I PARKED MY CAR in front of Mom's house and took a deep breath, gripping the steering wheel as I stared at her front door. Enough was enough. She'd been wallowing for weeks, dodging Lucas's calls, and making everyone—including me—tiptoe around her. It was time to snap her out of it.

Gathering my resolve, I climbed out of the car and strode up to the front steps. I knocked firmly, not giving myself a chance to hesitate.

After a moment, the door opened, and there she was: Clad in yoga pants and an oversized sweatshirt, her hair piled into a messy bun that teetered precariously on top of her head. She blinked at me, clearly surprised to see me standing there.

"Jake?" she asked, her voice heavy with confusion.

"Hi, Mom," I said, crossing my arms and leaning against the doorframe. "Can I come in?"

She hesitated, glancing back into the house like she was debating letting me in. Finally, she stepped aside, waving me through. The living room was cluttered with notebooks, printed pages, and half-empty coffee mugs and tea cups. It didn't take a detective to figure out she was in the middle of writing—or editing. Probably one of those two books she couldn't stop talking about lately—Caleb and Cecelia, was it? All the kids she wrote about had names that started with the letter C. It was like Mom's calling card as an author.

I turned to face her as she shut the door, tucking her hands into her sweatshirt pockets. "What are you doing here?"

"I came to talk some sense into you," I said bluntly.

Her eyebrows shot up. "Excuse me?"

"You heard me," I said, dropping onto the couch and gesturing to the chaos around me. "You're hiding out here, letting your work consume you, avoiding Lucas, and for what? Because Lily said something innocent at Christmas? Because you're scared? This is ridiculous, Mom. You need to snap out of it."

Her cheeks flushed, and I saw the fire flicker in her eyes. "Jake, this is not your business—"

"It absolutely is my business," I interrupted. "You're my mom. And Lucas is a good guy. He makes you happy. Or he did until you decided to push him away because of some overblown misunderstanding."

"It's not a misunderstanding," she said, her voice rising. "It's about doing what's best for Lily. This is her life, Jake. Her family. I can't just bulldoze through that because I'm in love with her dad."

"Newsflash, Mom," I said, throwing up my hands, "kids are resilient. Yeah, Lily had questions, but that's because she's eight. She's figuring things out. And Lucas? He's already talked to her. He's reassured her. She's good now. So why aren't you?"

Her mouth opened and closed, but no words came out. She looked away, her arms crossing defensively over her chest.

"You're writing a book about Cecelia, right?" I pressed. "About a little girl dealing with her parents' divorce? Don't you think maybe that's playing into how you're handling this? Maybe you're too deep in this story, and it's clouding your judgment."

Her eyes narrowed, and I could see her body stiffen. "That's not fair, Jake."

"Isn't it?" I shot back. "You're so wrapped up in this idea of protecting Lily that you're ignoring what's right in front of you. Lucas loves you. He loves Lily. He's been calling you for weeks, trying to fix this, and you're just... what? Pretending he doesn't exist?"

Tears welled in her eyes, and for a second, I felt guilty. But she needed to hear this.

"I'm scared, Jake," she said finally, her voice breaking. "Okay? I'm scared. I've been through this before—falling in love, believing it would last forever—and look where it got me. I don't want to make a mistake. Not with Lucas. Not with Lily."

I softened, leaning forward on the couch. "Mom, I get it. But you're not the same person you were back then. And Lucas isn't Dad. You know that. He's not going anywhere unless you keep pushing him away."

She sank into the armchair across from me, burying her face in her hands. For a long moment, the room was silent.

"Do you really think I'm making a mistake?" she asked, her voice muffled.

"Yes," I said without hesitation. "You're making a mistake by not allowing him to work through this with you. By not trusting what you've built together."

She lifted her head, her eyes red but determined. "What do I do, Jake?"

I smiled faintly. "You call him. You start by calling him."

55

Emily

THE CURSOR BLINKED STEADILY on the screen, a silent rhythm that matched the thoughts swirling in my mind. I leaned back in my chair, pushing my glasses up onto my forehead as I stared at the words I'd just typed. Cecelia's story was coming along fine—better than fine, if I allowed myself a moment of pride. I'd outlined the following few chapters last night and had just wrapped up a climactic scene.

Writing has always been my solace, my escape. But lately, it had become something more—a lifeline, a way to process everything I'd been feeling since Christmas.

I hadn't called Lucas yet. Every time I picked up my phone, my hand would hover over his name, and then I'd find an excuse to put it down again. Not yet.

Instead, I'd buried myself in words—not just my own but those of others. Since Christmas, I'd devoured nearly a book every other day, pulling novels off my shelves and jumping feet-first into new ones I'd picked up online to listen to. Fiction, memoirs, thrillers, romances— stories that let me step into someone else's world for a while.

In the year or two after my divorce from Andrew, I couldn't bring myself to read anything. Books had always been my joy, my escape, but they felt too heavy back then, too full of emotions I couldn't handle. But now, they were my therapy, a way to work through feelings I didn't quite know how to voice.

Caleb's story was finished, and the manuscript was edited and sent off to the designer. I was expecting to see the layout any day now, and I couldn't help but feel a rush of excitement at the thought of holding the finished book in my hands.

But Cecelia's story—the one about the little girl navigating her parents' divorce—was hitting closer to home than I'd expected. I hoped to have the manuscript complete by the end of the month, but every word I typed seemed to tug at a thread in my own heart, bringing back memories I hadn't revisited in years.

The day Andrew left was still so front and center in my mind when I allowed it to be. It wasn't just the betrayal—the knowl- edge that he'd been sneaking around with someone I considered a friend—but the way his absence rippled through our family. I remembered the phone calls to Sarah at college, asking if she could come home for the weekend. I remembered sitting Jake down in the kitchen, telling him what had happened, and watching the disbelief and hurt flicker across his face.

They'd both admitted later that they'd suspected something was wrong. But the finality of it, the reality of their father leaving, had shattered their world. I'd seen it in the way Sarah threw herself into her studies, her determination to stay strong for everyone around her. I saw it in the way Jake pulled away, retreating into himself as he tried to process everything.

It had been years since then, and I'd rebuilt my life. I was happy now—or I had been, until Christmas shook everything loose.

I glanced at my phone, sitting on the corner of the desk. Jake's words from his visit replayed in my mind: *You're ignoring what's right in front of you.*

Was I? Or was I just being cautious?

I couldn't stop thinking about Lily's words that night. Her innocent questions had opened a floodgate of fears I hadn't even realized I was holding back. The statistics haunted me—two-thirds of second marriages ended in divorce. What if Lily and I got along now, but things changed as she got older? What if her teenage years brought tension between Lucas and me?

I didn't want to be the catalyst for another upheaval in Lily's life. She'd been through so much already. Even though I knew my relationship with Lucas was different, the questions still nagged at me. Was I doing the right thing? Could I give Lily the stability she needed? Could I give Lucas the partnership he deserved?

The doorbell rang, breaking my train of thought. I set my glasses on the desk and went to answer it, finding the mail carrier on the porch with a package in hand.

"Morning," she said with a smile.

"Morning," I replied, taking the box and thanking her before closing the door.

Back at my desk, I opened the package and found the latest draft of Caleb's book layout. I smiled, running my fingers over the crisp pages, but the satisfaction was fleeting. I knew I couldn't hide in my work forever. Sooner or later, I'd have to call Lucas. I'd have to face the questions and fears head-on, not just for Lily's sake but for my own.

But not today. Today, I needed more time. And there was something else I needed to do.

56

Emily

Dear Lily,

I'm sitting at my desk, thinking about you, and there are so many things I want to say. So, I decided to write you a letter. Maybe someday, when you're a little older, you'll read this and understand everything I've been feeling.

The first thing I want you to know is how special your daddy is to me. From the very first time we met, I could tell he was someone different, someone amazing. He has this way of making people feel seen and cared for, like they're the most important person in the world. And you, Lily, are the most important person in his world.

When I met you, I understood why he loves you so much. You're bright and funny and full of life. You have this sparkle in your eyes that makes everyone around you want to smile. I could see right away that you and your daddy have a bond that's unbreakable. And I would never, ever want to come between that.

Coming into your life wasn't easy for me, Lily. Not because of you or your daddy, but because I wanted to fit into a story that had already started long before I arrived. You and your daddy were this perfect team, and I was the new person trying to figure out where I belonged.

You see, I'm a mom, too. I have kids who are grown now, but I'll always be their mom. And I know how important it is for you to have your mom and dad in your life, loving you and supporting you. I don't want to take that away. I'm not here to replace anyone. I'm here to be someone extra—someone who can cheer you on, listen to you, and care about you in my own way.

I know it's been confusing with all the changes happening lately. Sometimes, grown-ups don't have all the answers either, and we make mistakes while we're trying to figure things out. Walking away from you and your daddy was one of the hardest things I've ever done. It broke my heart because I love you both so much. But I thought it was the right thing to do. I thought maybe I was making things too complicated for you, and I never want to make your life harder.

I hope someday you'll understand that I did it because I care about you. Because I want what's best for you and your daddy, even if it means stepping back. But, Lily, I want you to know something very important: You're not just your daddy's whole world—you've become a big part of mine, too.

No matter what happens, I will always be here for you if you need me. You're such a wonderful, special girl, and I feel so lucky to have gotten to know you.

With all my love,

Emily

57

Jessica

I STOOD IN FRONT of the bathroom mirror, smoothing a hand over my favorite green blouse. It wasn't anything fancy, but it fit just right and brought out the blue in my eyes. Tonight felt different—better, somehow—and I wanted to look my best.

Will had been a breath of fresh air. After the amicable parting with Jeremy, the software engineer, and the disastrous date with Marty, the firefighter with a knack for making every conversation about his latest gruesome injury, I wasn't sure if I'd have the energy for dating again. Marty was a walking train wreck. How had I not picked up on that in our texts? But Will? He was... different.

We'd been talking and Facetiming for over a week, and every conversation made me want to know more about him. He was a teacher, for one, and who doesn't love a guy who devotes his life to kids? And then there was Cooper, his adorable golden retriever who made regular cameos during our video chats. He'd even sent me pictures of Cooper in silly hats, which was probably a little cheesy, but I loved it.

I grabbed my purse, double-checked my phone's charge, and headed out the door, trying to tamp down my nerves. I hadn't felt this kind of excitement in a long time.

The bistro Will picked was perfect—cozy and warm, with checkered tablecloths and twinkling lights strung along the windows. When I walked in, there he was, standing near the hostess desk with that sweet, nervous smile I'd already grown fond of.

"Jessica," he said, stepping forward and giving me a quick hug.

"Will," I replied, smiling back. "It's so good to finally meet you—in person."

Dinner was easy, the conversation flowing naturally like we'd known each other for years. We talked about everything—favorite movies, embarrassing childhood stories, and, eventually, our families.

He shared stories about his 12-year-old son, Max, and his 10-year-old daughter, Sophie. There was such tenderness in his voice when he talked about them. "They've been my world," he admitted, "especially after their mom passed away. It's been five years, but the kids and Cooper? They keep me going."

My heart tugged at his words, and I felt safe enough to share my own story. I told him about Lily and the co-parenting arrangement Lucas and I had worked so hard to maintain. "Lily's my whole world," I said, smiling at the thought of her. "Lucas and I may not have worked out, but we've always tried to put her first. It's not perfect, but it works."

Will tilted his head slightly, studying me. "And Lucas? He sounds like a good guy. Is he okay with you dating?"

I laughed. "Oh, he doesn't care. We've been in such different places for years. Honestly, he's been busy with his own life—well, he was, until he and his girlfriend hit a snag."

"What happened?"

I hesitated for a second, wondering if I should get into it, but I found myself telling him everything about Lucas and Emily—the proposal, Lily's questions, and how everything had unraveled.

Will listened without interrupting, his expression thoughtful. When I finished, he leaned back in his chair and nodded. "Sounds like Emily's scared," he said simply.

I sighed, swirling the last bit of wine in my glass. "Yeah. But scared enough to shut him out completely? It's just... a lot."

"It is," he agreed. "But you know what it sounds like to me?"

"What?"

"It sounds like Emily needs to hear from you that it's okay to move forward—and that Lily will be okay."

I blinked, caught off guard by his insight. "You think so?"

"Absolutely," he said. "You're a huge part of Lily's life. If Emily knows you're on board and that you trust her with your daughter, it might help her feel more confident about her place in all this. When Katie, my wife, got sick, she wrote letters to our kids. I don't know how she found the time or energy to do it. But she had seen something in a movie or somewhere that a dying mother had written letters to their kids for all of the milestones that would come in their lives. Graduating from high school. Going to college. Getting married. Having a child. All of it. And in her first letter to the kids, she talked about how I might want to move on someday and that if and when I did, it was okay with her."

He paused for a moment before moving on. "And she wrote a very similar letter to me. Telling me that if I wanted to move on, it would be okay. That she wanted that for me. And for Max and Sophie."

His words hit me straight in the gut. "Wow," was all I could say at first. "That seems like a lot to take in."

He nodded. "It was, and I won't tell you that reading those first letters wasn't difficult. But it was like she was giving me permission to live my life. Giving kids permission to live their lives and supporting me in mine. It was a gift. And maybe that gift is something Emily could use from you."

I thought for a moment. He was right. I'd been so focused on watching from the sidelines that I hadn't considered how much my voice might matter.

"You're a good guy, Will," I said softly, smiling at him. "Thank you for sharing all of that with me."

"And you're a good mom," he replied with a grin. "Thank you for listening."

The rest of the night flew by, the conversation flowing as easily as it had in our Facetimes. When we parted ways outside the bistro, Will hugged me and kissed my cheek, his warmth lingering as I climbed into my car. We agreed that he would give me a call tomorrow night after we had had time to assess for ourselves how the date had gone.

But I already knew two things. One, I wanted that second date with Will. And two, I needed to talk to Emily.

58

Emily

VALENTINE'S DAY HAD NEVER been a big deal for me, even when I was married to Andrew. It was always just another day, peppered with the occasional box of chocolates, a bouquet of flowers, or a dinner out. But this year, it felt different—almost as if the universe was taunting me with what I had lost, or perhaps, what I had pushed away.

I curled up on the couch with *The Women* by Kristin Hannah, one of my favorite authors. I'd been devouring books lately, seeking solace in the pages and lives of fictional characters. It was easier than facing my own tangled emotions.

I was closer to calling Lucas. I could feel it. I'd picked up my phone a dozen times in the past few days, scrolling through our old texts, staring at his name and pictures we had taken together. But something kept holding me back. It felt like there was something missing, something I needed before I could move forward, before I could even consider salvaging what we had.

And then there was the silence. Lucas had stopped calling. At first, I thought maybe he was just giving me space, but now I wasn't sure what to think. Had he moved on? Did he still want to fix things?

The doorbell rang, pulling me from my thoughts. I glanced at the clock. Late afternoon on a Friday? And on Valentine's Day? I wasn't expecting anyone. I set the book down, marking my place with the cover flipped open.

When I opened the door, I was stunned to see Jessica standing on the front step, her coat pulled tight against the February chill.

"Jessica?" My voice came out uncertain, a question more than a greeting.

"Hi, Emily. Can I come in?"

Her tone was calm but carried an undercurrent of determination that caught me off guard. I hesitated, unsure how to handle a surprise visit from Lucas's ex-wife. What was she to me? The mother of Lily? My almost-stepdaughter's mom?

And Lucas? My boyfriend? My fiancé? My ex? I didn't know what to call him anymore.

"Sure," I said, stepping aside to let her pass.

She walked in without hesitation, her eyes scanning the room. Her gaze landed on the couch, where my book lay. "Funny that you're reading this. I am too," she murmured, a small smile tugging at her lips before she sat down.

I closed the door behind her, still trying to process what was happening.

"Sit down, Emily," she said, her tone gentle but firm, like she wasn't going to take no for an answer.

I crossed the room, lowering myself onto the couch opposite her. My heart pounded as I waited for her to speak.

Jessica leaned forward, resting her elbows on her knees, and let out a deep breath. "I'm not here to cause trouble or point fingers," she began. "I'm here because I care about Lucas. And I care about Lily."

Her words hung in the air, heavy with meaning.

"I know what happened at Christmas," she continued, her voice steady but kind. "And I know why you're scared. I get it, Emily. I really do. Lily is young, and this is a lot for her. But I also know my daughter, and she's resilient. She's been through so much already, and she's come out stronger for it."

I opened my mouth to speak, but she held up a hand.

"Let me finish," she said, her gaze locking on mine and her voice firm. "You're a good person, Emily. I could see that the first time we met. And you've been wonderful with Lily. She adores you. But I think you're holding back because you're afraid of what might happen if things don't work out. And that's fair. It's scary to take that kind of leap."

I swallowed hard, her words cutting straight to the heart of what I'd been wrestling with.

"But here's the thing," Jessica continued. "Life is full of risks. Relationships are messy and complicated, and there are no guarantees. But that doesn't mean you shouldn't try. Lucas loves you, Emily. And he's good for you. I can see it in the way he talks about you and the way he looks at you. And you're good for him, too."

Tears welled in my eyes, but I blinked them back.

Jessica sat back, her expression softening. "Lily and I have talked a lot about what she said at Christmas. And I've explained to her that just because her daddy has you doesn't mean her mommy needs someone, too. She's starting to understand. And she's okay with you being a part of her life."

Her voice dropped slightly, taking on a more personal tone. "I've seen what it's like when Lucas isn't with you. He's not himself. And I think you're not quite yourself without him either."

I let out a shaky breath, letting her words settle over me.

Jessica smiled, a touch of warmth in her eyes. "So, I'm here to tell you that it's okay. It's okay to move forward, Emily. It's okay to take a chance on Lucas and Lily. They need you. And if you're being honest with yourself, I think you need them too."

For a moment, the room was silent except for the faint hum of the heater. I looked at Jessica, this woman who could have seen me as a threat but instead chose to see me as an ally. "Thank you," I whispered, my voice trembling. "I don't know what to say."

"Say you'll call him," she said simply, standing up and buttoning her coat.

I nodded, a small but genuine smile breaking through.

As Jessica walked to the door, she paused and turned back to me. "You're good for each other, Emily. Don't let fear ruin something beautiful."

When the door closed behind her, I sat there for a long time, staring at the book still lying on the couch.

59

Lucas

FEBRUARY 15th, and I was pissed.

Pissed that I'd spent another evening alone, staring at the same damn walls. Pissed that I'd sat through the Super Bowl by myself the weekend before, pretending like it didn't bother me that Emily wasn't there. Cole and Rebecca had invited me over, but I wasn't about to play the third wheel, sitting on their couch while they passed each other chips and laughed at commercials. No thanks.

"Damn it, Emily," I muttered, my voice cutting through the quiet of the house. Or maybe I was talking to her as if she could hear me. "What are you doing to me?"

I hadn't been idle, at least. Work was my salvation these days. The Wilsons' treehouse project was moving ahead, and ground would break on March 1. They wanted a grand opening on July 4, which felt ambitious, but the crew they'd hired was the best in the Twin Cities. I had no doubt they could pull it off.

And then there was the other bed-and-breakfast project. That one felt good—a real challenge. Built in the 1950s, it had charm but zero accessibility. Narrow doorways, no elevator, bathrooms designed for people who'd never imagined a wheelchair might need to get through. The owners were all-in on making it work, throwing money at every solution I proposed. It was rewarding to design something that would give more people the opportunity to enjoy the space.

But even work couldn't fully distract me. I leaned back in my chair, staring at the blueprints scattered across my desk. The quiet was deafening. When the doorbell rang, I sighed, irritated by the interruption. It wasn't like I was doing anything important—just wallowing in my own misery—but the last thing I wanted was someone bothering me right now. I stalked to the door, bare feet padding across the cold wood floor. When I pulled it open, my irritation vanished, replaced by another emotion. I didn't know what.

Emily was standing there, her cheeks pink from the February chill. She looked up at me, her eyes wide.

"Emily," I said, her name catching in my throat.

"I'm sorry," she said, her voice soft but steady.

I didn't move, unsure of what to do or say.

"Lucas," she continued, taking a small step forward. "I love you. I made a mistake. And I want you to forgive me, and—"

But I didn't let her finish. Before she could say another word, I stepped out onto the front step, the icy concrete biting into my bare feet. I didn't care. I pulled her into my arms, holding her tightly against me.

"I love you, too," I whispered, my voice hoarse with emotion.

For a moment, neither of us moved, the cold air swirling around us, but I didn't care, despite the thin protection offered by the short-sleeved Minnesota Vikings t-shirt I was wearing. All that mattered was that she was here, in my arms, saying the words I'd been desperate to hear.

When I finally pulled back, I looked down at her, brushing a strand of hair away from her face.

"You scared the hell out of me," I said quietly, my voice trembling.

"I know," she replied, her eyes glistening with tears. "And I'm so sorry. I let my fears get the better of me, and I hurt you. I hurt us. But I want to fix it, Lucas. I want us to move forward—together."

I nodded, pulling her back into my arms. "Then let's do that. No more running. No more hiding. We'll figure it out."

For the first time in weeks, the pressure that I had been feeling in my chest lifted. We still had a long road ahead, but she was here, and that was all that mattered.

"Come inside," I said, guiding her into the house and closing the door against the cold.

60

Emily

"COME INSIDE," Lucas said, stepping aside to let me in.

I hesitated for just a moment, the warmth of his voice wrapping around me like a blanket. Then I crossed the threshold, and he closed the door behind me.

The room was quiet, the air thick with everything left unsaid. I turned to face him, my heart racing as I stepped closer, wrapping my arms around him. "I am so sorry," I said again, my voice trembling. "I just didn't know what to do. I was scared."

His arms came around me, strong and steady, and he held me close. His voice was a whisper in my ear. "We're supposed to be partners, right? So when we get scared, we can't run away. We need to figure it out together."

I pulled back just enough to look into his eyes, nodding in agreement. His words sank into me, anchoring me in a way I hadn't felt in weeks. But then, because nerves have a way of making me say the most random things, I blurted out, "Aren't you freezing?"

Lucas chuckled, easing the tension in my chest. "Really, that's what you want to talk about? Whether or not I'm cold?"

I couldn't help but laugh, shaking my head. "I guess I just don't know where to start. Do we start over, or do we pick up where we left off? Tell me what to do, what we do."

He looked at me, his expression soft but firm, his eyes searching mine. "I don't want to start over," he said, his voice steady. "I liked round one. I loved round one, except maybe this last month and a half. I haven't felt happiness like this in so long. Let's not start over."

His words hit me like a wave, and all I could do was nod. "Okay," I whispered, my voice thick with emotion.

A smile tugged at the corner of his mouth as he pulled me into his arms again. This time, there was no hesitation, no holding back. His hands slid down to my waist, lifting me off my feet as if I weighed nothing. I wrapped my arms around his neck, burying my face against his shoulder, the familiar scent of him filling my senses.

Before I knew it, we were moving, each step bringing us closer to his bedroom. My heart raced, not with uncertainty but with the kind of anticipation that made me feel alive. One layer at a time, we shed the barriers between us—our clothes, our doubts, our fears—leaving a trail behind us as we stepped into the sanctuary of

his room. The space was dimly lit, the warm glow of a single lamp casting soft shadows across the walls.

Lucas's hands framed my face as he looked at me, his expression a mixture of love and longing. "I missed you," he said, his voice raw.

"I missed you, too," I replied, my voice barely above a whisper.

His lips found mine, and the rest of the world disappeared.

Time seemed to blur as we rediscovered each other, every touch and kiss reigniting the fire that had never really gone out. It wasn't just about the physical connection—it was about coming back to one another, finding our way through the hurt and uncertainty to this moment of absolute clarity.

Later, as we lay tangled in each other's arms, all those worries from the last several weeks began to evaporate—slowly, but evaporating nonetheless. Lucas's hand traced lazy circles on my back, his touch soothing and grounding.

"I love you," he said softly, his voice breaking the quiet.

I looked up at him, my heart swelling. "I love you, too."

For a while, we just lay there, the silence between us comfortable and full of unspoken promises.

Eventually, I shifted, propping myself up on my elbow to look at him. "So, what now?" I asked, my voice light but serious.

He smiled, brushing a strand of hair away from my face. "Now, we move forward. Together."

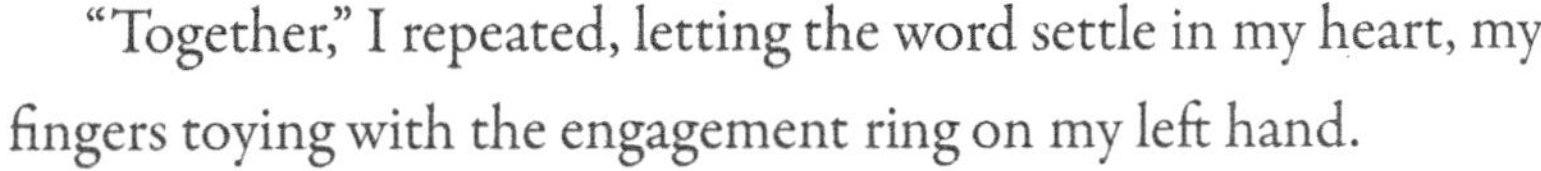

"Together," I repeated, letting the word settle in my heart, my fingers toying with the engagement ring on my left hand.

294

61

Sarah

IN TYPICAL MINNESOTA FASHION, March is proving quite unpredictable. One week it is frigid, the next week there is snow, and the following week is absolutely balmy. But one thing is certain—the warm weather of spring is lurking. And quite frankly, we can all use it.

Mom and I are in her kitchen, packing up her dishes. As I wrap her precious teacups in bubble wrap, I can't help but reflect on the past two weeks. And I certainly can't forget that phone call, first thing on a Sunday morning, telling me that she and Lucas had figured things out and plans to move in together were back on.

The plan was to put the house on the market the first week of April and have Mom fully move out before showings were placed on the calendar. Mom wanted to clear the home of all of her personal things. She was determined to make it as easy as possible for potential buyers to picture their own lives here rather than the one she and Dad had built together.

So here we were—packing up a lifetime of memories. Jake and I had been stopping over every other day or so to help pack or to go through the piles of things she had left for us, convinced we would each want all of the little knickknacks and trinkets from our childhood.

I reached for another teacup, this one adorned with tiny blue flowers. "I remember this one," I said, holding it up.

Mom glanced over, a small smile tugging at her lips. "That's from your Aunt Doris. She gave me that set when I hosted my first book club meeting. I was so nervous everyone would hate my lemon squares."

I laughed. "Those lemon squares were amazing. Jake and I ate half the leftovers before you even woke up the next morning."

"Little thieves," Mom teased.

"Hey, you made them," I said with a grin. "What did you expect? Lemon squares are irresistible."

Mom chuckled, then reached for another dish. "Do you remember the tea set your grandma gave you when you were little? The one with the tiny pink flowers?"

"Of course," I said, smiling at the memory. "I used to make Jake play 'tea party' with me in the living room. He always pretended the teacups were shot glasses and made the stuffed animals drunk."

Mom burst out laughing. "That sounds like Jake. Always had to add his own twist to things."

We worked in comfortable silence for a while, the rhythm of wrapping and packing broken only by the occasional "remember when..."

"Remember when Dad built that treehouse for Jake in the backyard?" I asked, pausing to hold a bubble-wrapped plate. "And I wasn't allowed in because it was a boys-only club?"

Mom's eyes softened. "Oh, I remember. You came stomping into the house, arms crossed, demanding I make Dad build you your own treehouse."

"And he did," I said, grinning. "It wasn't as fancy as Jake's, but it was mine."

"You decorated it with every blanket and pillow you could find," Mom reminisced.

"I practically lived out there all summer," I returned.

Mom nodded, her expression distant for a moment before she reached for another teacup. "It's funny how it all goes by so quickly, isn't it?"

"Yeah," I said softly, placing the wrapped plate in a box.

We continued packing, the conversation ebbing and flowing between lighthearted memories and quiet moments of reflection. As we neared the end of the box, I set down the boxing tape dispenser and turned to her.

"So," I said, leaning against the counter, "what are your plans for the wedding?"

Mom paused, her hands stilling over the stack of plates in front of her. She looked up at me, her cheeks pinkening just slightly.

"Well," she began, "we haven't decided anything yet. Lucas and I have talked about a few ideas, but nothing's set in stone."

"Big or small?" I pressed, raising an eyebrow.

She laughed softly. "Small, I think. Something intimate. Maybe just family and a few close friends. Honestly, I don't need anything fancy—just the people I love and Lucas by my side."

"That sounds perfect," I said, smiling at her.

62

Jake

MY BREATH PUFFED out in white clouds, and I tugged at the edges of my gloves to keep the cold from creeping in. Mom had insisted that we didn't need professional movers. Why spend the money when, in her words, she had a "strapping young son" who could help?

I'd argued—briefly—but one look at her determined face and I knew it was a losing battle. Lucas had reluctantly agreed, though I could tell he wasn't thrilled. He'd tried to suggest a moving company, but Mom waved him off, saying she wanted her things safe and in "capable, familiar hands."

Not wanting to push our luck, I called in reinforcements. Michael was there. And Cole, dependable as always, showed up just after breakfast, and I'd roped in my buddy Travis—one of Mom's favorites among all my friends. He had the kind of polite, easy-going demeanor that could charm anyone, and he and Mom had bonded over his love of old western movies during one of our family's movie

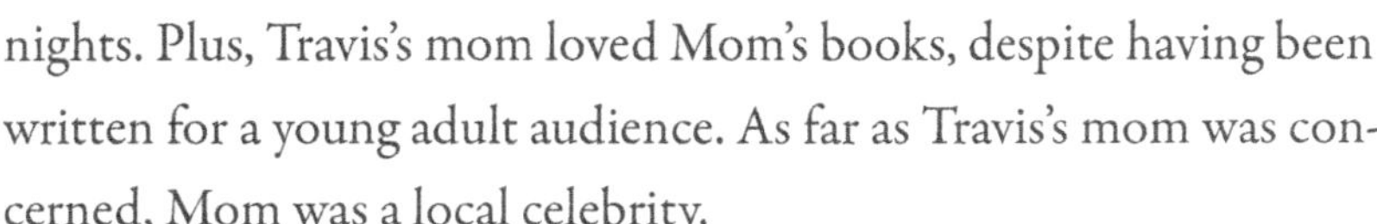

nights. Plus, Travis's mom loved Mom's books, despite having been written for a young adult audience. As far as Travis's mom was concerned, Mom was a local celebrity.

Travis, carrying an armful of neatly packed boxes labeled 'KITCHEN', let out a low whistle. "Your mom's got a lot of dishes, man," he said, his voice tinged with amusement.

"She loves her tea cups," I said, rolling my eyes but smiling. "Every single one of them is apparently precious."

Cole grinned as he passed us on his way back into the house. "She made me bubble-wrap a butter dish for twenty minutes. It's like the crown jewels in there."

I laughed, but I kept a close eye on Lucas as he worked. He'd been cleared by his cardiologist to resume all activities, but the memory of Christmas still took up space in the back of my mind. I wasn't about to let him push himself too hard, no matter what the doctor said.

"Lucas," I called, walking over to him as he bent down to lift an ottoman. "You good?"

He straightened, wiping his hands on his jeans. "I'm fine, Jake," he said with a small smile. "Promise. Not even breaking a sweat."

"Yeah, well, let's keep it that way," I said, nodding toward the van. "Take five. Cole and I can grab the couch."

Lucas chuckled, shaking his head, but he stepped back, letting us take over.

By mid-afternoon, we were nearing the finish line. The estate sale had cleared out most of the larger furniture Mom didn't plan to take to Lucas's house. The few pieces she'd kept—sentimental items she and Dad had picked out early in their marriage—had been carefully loaded. Anything else that hadn't sold or had been claimed by Sarah and me was already in storage near Sarah's house.

Travis walked by with the last box from the dining room. "This the last of it?"

"God, I hope so," I said, stretching my arms over my head. My muscles ached, but the van was nearly full, and the end was in sight.

As Cole secured the final load, Lucas approached me, his hands shoved into his coat pockets. He nodded toward the driveway. "Hey, Jake. Got a minute?"

"Sure," I said, following him away from the others.

He stopped near the edge of the yard, his breath visible in the cold air. "First off, thanks for all your help today. I know it's a pain, but your mom really appreciates it. So do I."

"Of course," I said. "You're family now. Comes with the territory."

Lucas smiled at that, but his eyes quickly grew serious. "Actually, that's what I wanted to talk to you about."

"Oh?"

He hesitated for a moment. "Emily and I have been talking. We've decided we want to have the wedding at Christmas—next winter."

My eyebrows shot up. "Christmas? Like, this Christmas?"

"Yeah," he said, his smile widening slightly. "We figured it was fitting, considering how last Christmas went. We want a do-over with a better ending. Plus, it's a time when everyone we'd want to be there would already be together. Emily's parents can make the trip from Lake Mille Lacs easily, and as for my side... well, I don't expect my dad to show, and Peter..." He trailed off, shrugging. "Let's just say Peter's hard to pin down."

I nodded, understanding. Lucas's brother's missionary work kept him in Ghana, and communication was spotty at best.

Lucas took a deep breath, his gaze steady. "Anyway, I wanted to ask you something."

"Sure," I said.

"Jake," he began, his voice quieter now, "would you be my best man?"

I blinked, caught completely off guard. "Me? I mean—what about Cole? I figured he'd be the obvious choice."

"Cole and Rebecca will have their hands full," Lucas said. "The baby's due in late summer, and they'll be figuring out life as parents of two. And you know how energetic Olivia can be. Emily and I want to keep things simple. And honestly, I can't think of anyone better for the job than you."

I felt a mix of emotions—surprise, gratitude, and maybe, pride.

"I'd be honored," I said finally, still surprised by Lucas's question.

Lucas's smile widened, and he reached out to clasp my shoulder. "Thanks, Jake. It means a lot."

"No problem," I said, grinning. "But just so you know, I expect you to listen to my speech, no matter how embarrassing it is."

Lucas laughed, the sound warm and genuine. "Deal."

63

Lily

I AM SO EXCITED! My new stepmom—okay, Dad says she's not my stepmom yet, but she will be next Christmas—is moving in TODAY!

Last night, me and Daddy had a special night, just the two of us. We watched Wicked in the living room with popcorn, and I stayed up late even though it wasn't a weekend. The flying monkeys were super scary, so I hid my face in Daddy's arm a few times. I didn't want to see it in the theater when it first came out because of those monkeys, but at home, with Daddy, it wasn't so bad.

Now, there's a big truck in the driveway, and Daddy and Jake and Cole and Michael—and Travis? Yeah, Travis is here too—they are all carrying stuff into the house. Everyone's really busy. The driveway is full of boxes and furniture, and it's so much fun to watch everyone go back and forth. I even helped carry a pillow inside!

Inside, Sarah and Emily are telling the guys where to put every-thing. Emily keeps opening up the kitchen cabinets and pulling stuff out. "Need to make room for my stuff, too," she told me with a big smile. I'm not sure where all our things are going, but Emily says we'll figure it out.

And the best part? Emily told me I get to be in the wedding next Christmas! I get to pick out ANY dress I want to wear. I already know what I want—a big skirt that whirls and twirls when I spin. We're going dress shopping in a few weeks, and I can't wait.

It feels kind of weird seeing Emily in Daddy's room. She's taking the blankets off his bed and putting on new ones. They're blue and white and really soft-looking. I stood in the doorway and watched for a bit, and Emily saw me and smiled. "This is my room too now, Lily," she said.

I guess I'm okay with it. Daddy already told me Emily would be sharing his room, and I'd still have my own room, of course. Daddy even said I could get new blankets for my bed if I wanted. But I like the ones I have, with the polar bears and snowflakes, so I told him I wanted to keep them.

When I go back to the kitchen, Emily is unpacking a big box with all these fancy plates in it. "Want to help me?" she asks.

I nod and climb up on the chair next to her. She hands me a stack of little plates with flowers on them, and I help her put them in the cabinet. "You're doing a great job, Lily," she says, giving me a high five.

"Thanks!" I say. I'm glad she's moving in. It feels kind of like when you have a friend over for a sleepover, except she's going to stay forever.

I'm still not totally sure about what it means to have a stepmom, but I think I like it. Daddy and Emily seem really happy, and they've been smiling a lot today. Daddy even stopped to give her a kiss in the hallway, and I yelled, "Eww, gross!" just to make them laugh.

It's going to be different with Emily living here, but I think it's going to be really fun, too. And I can't wait to show her how good my twirl is when I get my new dress for the wedding!

64

Jessica

FLOUR WAS EVERYWHERE. It dusted my scrubs, the countertop, and even a little patch of Lily's cheek. She was giggling as she stirred the bowl of chocolate chip cookie dough with all the enthusiasm of an eight-year-old who had just been promised dessert for dinner.

"Okay, kiddo," I said, wiping my hands on a dish towel. "One grilled ham and cheese sandwich first, then cookies. Deal?"

"Deal!" Lily chirped, licking a bit of cookie dough off her finger before I could stop her.

I arched an eyebrow at her. "And don't fill up on dough, or you'll only get one cookie instead of two."

She gasped, clutching her chest dramatically. "Not one cookie! I promise I'll eat my sandwich. Cross my heart."

It was all about the word choices with kids. Make it seem like a game, a challenge, or a treat, and they'd do whatever you wanted.

And I knew that sandwich would fill her up just enough that two cookies and another glass of milk would be all she'd manage afterward. That counted as a win in my book.

While Lily finished stirring, I prepped the griddle, and the smell of sizzling bread and melted cheese soon filled the kitchen.

"Mom," Lily paused, "did you know Emily sold her house?"

I nodded, flipping the sandwich. "I heard about that. It sold pretty quickly, huh?"

Lily giggled. "Yeah, it only took one offer, and Emily said YES! That's what she told me. Like the house was asking her to marry it or something."

I laughed, shaking my head. Kids had the funniest ways of phrasing things. "Well, it doesn't surprise me. Emily's house is beautiful, and someone probably fell in love with it right away."

"It was really nice," Lily agreed, licking the spoon clean as I slid her sandwich onto a plate and set it in front of her.

While she ate, I leaned against the counter, my mind wandering to the other topic I'd been meaning to bring up tonight. Will.

We'd been dating for two months now, and it was going... unbelievably well. He was kind, funny, and thoughtful, and he made me feel things I hadn't felt in a long time. Things had started off slow, but when we were together, it was like we'd known each other for years. We'd even talked about introducing the kids—his son Max and daughter Sophie, and of course, Lily.

I watched Lily munch on her sandwich, the wheels in my head turning. Will and I had decided that a day trip to the Mall of America would be a perfect way to introduce everyone. Rides at Nickelodeon Universe, lunch at the food court, maybe some ice cream—it felt like a low-pressure, fun environment where the kids could just be kids.

"Hey, Lily," I said, sitting down across from her. "What would you think about going to the Mall of America for a day of rides?"

Her eyes lit up. "Really? Can we go on the SpongeBob ride?"

"Of course," I said, smiling. "But here's the thing—it wouldn't just be you and me. There'd be a couple of other kids, too."

This clearly piqued her curiosity. "Who? Olivia?"

"No, not Olivia," I laughed. "Remember I told you about my friend Will?"

Lily nodded slowly.

"Well, Will has a son and a daughter. Max is 12, and Sophie is 10. They like the rides, too, and we thought it might be fun for all of you to meet and hang out together. What do you think?"

Lily considered this for a moment, her sandwich forgotten. "Do they like cookies?"

I laughed. "I'm pretty sure they do."

"Okay," she said with a shrug, as if that was all she needed to know.

I reached over and ruffled her hair. "Thanks, kiddo. I think it'll be a lot of fun."

As Lily finished her dinner and started shaping the cookie dough into little balls, I let my mind drift back to Will. We didn't see each other as often as we'd liked, but we talked every day, usually after dinner when the kids were doing their own thing.

Those late-night conversations had become the highlight of my evenings, full of laughter, honest confessions, and sometimes... some rather flirty exchanges that left me grinning like a teenager. And physically? Let's just say Will had proven that chemistry didn't have to fade with age. He made me feel alive in a way I hadn't in years.

"Mom, can I eat one cookie while we bake the rest?" Lily asked, breaking into my thoughts.

"Just one," I said, pulling the first tray of cookies out of the oven and confirming she had finished her sandwich.

As she happily munched on her treat, I couldn't help but feel thankful. Maybe it was my turn for happiness now.

65

Lucas

EMILY'S HEAD RESTED on my arm, her warm breath tickling the crook of my elbow. My arm ached, but I didn't dare move. Moments like these—quiet, unhurried—were too precious to disturb. She was here. Finally here. In my house. No, our house. My room. No, our room.

It still felt surreal at times. After everything we'd been through, all the ups and downs, Emily was here, curled into me on a Saturday morning like it was the most natural thing in the world.

Lily was with her mom this weekend, and she'd been brimming with excitement about her trip to Nickelodeon Universe. She couldn't remember her new friends' names, but she had told me she was going to meet some. As she chattered on with excitement about her pending adventure, she kept calling them her "friends," which made me laugh every time. I was okay with that. It made me happy to see Lily so excited.

Emily shifted slightly, snuggling closer, her hair brushing against my cheek. It felt good—better than good—to have her here. We'd spent the last week unpacking her things and trying to figure out how to merge two lives that had been lived independently for so long.

It wasn't without its challenges. I was set in my ways. She was set in hers. And those ways didn't always line up.

Take her showers, for example. Long, hot, nightly showers. At first, I thought it was just something she did after sex, but no—this was her routine. And if I wanted a hot shower, I had to plan ahead and either take one before her or resign myself to a morning rinse. I chose the latter, deciding to get up 15 minutes earlier each morning for my turn at the hot water.

Then there were my socks. Apparently, I have a habit of leaving them on the floor by the bed. I argued that my feet were cold when I walked to bed, and it was easier to toss them on the floor and pick them up in the morning. The problem was that I rarely remembered to pick them up. Since I left for work earlier than Emily most mornings, she was usually the one making the bed—and picking up my socks along with it.

"Lucas," she had said just the other day, holding up a pair of balled-up socks, "I love you, but this? This needs to stop."

We laughed about it, and I promised to do better. So far, I've remembered exactly twice.

Still, I couldn't help but reflect on how different it was to build a life together at this stage. When Jessica and I got married, we were young—not too young, but young enough to grow up together. We figured things out as we went along, learning from our mistakes. And the habits we had built, we built together.

With Emily, it was different. We'd both lived entire lifetimes before finding each other. We'd established routines, quirks, and habits that felt immovable. But as much as there had been a few stumbling blocks, there had also been moments of pure harmony. And I wouldn't trade it for anything.

"Are you awake?" Emily murmured.

"Yeah," I whispered back.

She lifted her head to look at me, her hair a tangled mess, and smiled. "You didn't have to suffer after my shower last night, did you?"

I grinned. "Nope. I'll be taking one this morning. I'm learning."

She laughed, leaning up to kiss me. "Good boy."

I rolled my eyes but pulled her close again, feeling her warmth against me.

Wedding planning, thankfully, had been surprisingly easy. Emily's friend owned a small venue south of the river, and it was perfect for the kind of intimate ceremony we wanted. We'd hired a justice of the peace, a decorator, a photographer, and a caterer. With fewer than 30 people on the guest list, there wasn't much catering to arrange.

Everything about it felt right. Simple, meaningful, and precisely what we both wanted. "This feels good," I said softly.

She smiled up at me, her eyes shining. "It does."

I kissed the top of her head, breathing in the scent of her shampoo—one of those expensive kinds that smell like apples—and let myself believe that, for once, everything was falling into place exactly as it should.

66

Emily

THE LAST SEVERAL MONTHS had been an absolute whirlwind. As I sat at my desk, pen poised over yet another letter, I couldn't help but marvel at how life had changed in such a short amount of time—and in such a good way. Caleb's story, the book that had started as a quiet project during a particularly reflective time in my life, had exploded in ways I never could have imagined.

Sales were through the roof, with the distributor struggling to keep up with demand. Bookstores could barely keep it on the shelves, and the response had been overwhelming. Letters poured in daily—young cancer survivors sharing their stories, parents writing to tell me how the book had brought hope to their families, and even educators praising the story's ability to inspire resilience in their students.

While my publicist handled most of the fan mail responses, I made it a point to sign each one personally. It's not like there were hundreds or thousands flowing in, but a dozen or so each month.

And some of these readers really deserved my time. Sometimes, when a letter particularly moved me, I would sit down and craft a response myself. Like the one I was working on now, from a little boy in Florida who had just finished his final round of chemotherapy. He'd written about how Caleb's journey had given him courage, how he had read certain passages out loud to himself during the hardest nights.

I blinked back tears, finishing the letter and holding it close to my heart before slipping it into the envelope. It felt like the least I could do. I closed my eyes and said a quick prayer, asking God to please spare this little boy from a return of his cancer down the road.

On top of that, I'd just finished Cecelia's story a few weeks ago. It was with the editor now, and I was expecting the first digital layout any day. This book would be a milestone—it was going to be my first title offered as an audiobook. I'd been in talks with the voice artist, an incredibly talented woman who captured Cecelia's voice perfectly. The whole process had been exhilarating, albeit exhausting, if I had to be honest.

And then there was the wedding.

With everything going on—book tours, fan mail, Cecelia's story, and this new life I was building with Lucas—I hadn't had much time to think about the wedding. But every now and then, it would sneak into my thoughts, a little spark of excitement in my day.

This past summer, Lucas and I attended the grand opening of Nature's Love Affair, the treehouse bed and breakfast project he'd designed. It was stunning, and every detail was perfectly thought out. The Wilsons were thrilled with the result and invited us to come back for our honeymoon.

We'd asked if we could bring Lily with us next summer instead—after all, how could we visit a treehouse without her? The Wilsons had agreed, and while we hadn't finalized our honeymoon plans, the idea of spending time there, surrounded by nature, felt like something we would all be able to enjoy when the summer months rolled around.

But that was the thing—we hadn't had time to finalize anything. Between my book tours and Lucas wrapping up his latest architectural project—a massive renovation for a historic bed and breakfast—we'd barely had a moment to breathe. And a rumor from his architectural firm was buzzing that he had been nominated for an award for his work in designing a handicap-accessible space so that more guests could enjoy it.

Despite everything going on, I wouldn't trade any of it for the world. Life with Lucas had been everything I'd hoped it would be. Sure, there had been adjustments—like learning to share space and compromise on habits—but there had also been so much laughter, so much love.

I glanced at the calendar on my desk. Just a few days until Christmas. It would be our first as a blended family, and I wanted it to be special, especially after the cacophony of last year. We'd kept things simple this year—no over-the-top decorations or extravagant plans.

Just us, our families, and the kind of warmth that didn't require anything more than being together. And of course, a wedding.

As I finished another letter, the faint sound of footsteps caught my attention. Lucas appeared in the doorway, his shirt untucked and a mischievous and seductive grin on his face—his attempts at a seductive face were more laughable than anything, but I still found it endearing.

"Hey," he said, leaning against the doorframe. "Still at it?"

I smiled up at him. "Just a few more. These kids—they deserve a response."

He walked over, placing a warm hand on my shoulder. "You've done so much, Em. Don't forget to take a moment for yourself."

I reached up, covering his hand with mine. "I will. But this—it matters."

He nodded, his eyes filled with understanding. "I know. That's one of the reasons I love you." I laughed softly, standing to face him as he said. "Speaking of reasons to love me, I was thinking we could have a bit of fun before lunch? You know, something a little naughty?"

I laughed but launched myself into his arms and let him carry me off into our bedroom.

67

Jessica

THE SOFT GLOW OF CHRISTMAS lights from the Christmas tree in the corner reflected in Lily's wide, excited eyes as she snuggled under her favorite fuzzy blanket. The Netflix movie played on, and the plot was predictable but magical in the way only Christmas movies can be. Lily was completely absorbed, but I was only half-watching. My attention was mostly on my phone as I texted Will.

We were exchanging little jokes and talking about our plans for tomorrow. He'd be bringing Max and Sophie to his parents' place early in the morning before driving down to spend Christmas afternoon with me and Lily before the wedding. I could feel the excitement bubbling up in me, but it wasn't just about seeing Will—it was about how our lives were starting to feel more connected.

The invitation to Lucas and Emily's wedding had arrived a couple of months ago, and I'd been genuinely surprised to see my name on the guest list. Not that I doubted their goodwill—Lucas had always been great about keeping things amicable between us for

Lily's sake. But still, a wedding invitation from your ex-husband isn't something you expect every day.

Lucas had called me to explain that he and Emily had agreed they wanted me there, not just for them but also for Lily. And I had appreciated that—more than I could say. At the time, I'd RSVPd as just one. Things with Will were going well, but it had felt too soon to assume he'd be part of something so personal, especially my ex-husband's nuptials. Now, though? Things were different.

Will had become a steady part of my life—and Lily adored him. And it was clear to me that he adored her right back. Yet I hadn't thought of asking Lucas about bringing him up until now. It felt rude to ask at the last minute, but the idea of attending the wedding without Will didn't feel quite right anymore.

"Be right back," I said to Lily, standing up and stretching.

She barely looked away from the screen, her focus glued to the movie. "Okay, but can you make more popcorn?"

I laughed. "Of course. Gotta get your fill before the braces come, right?"

She grinned, flashing her crooked teeth my way, and I headed into the kitchen. I tossed a bag of popcorn into the microwave. As it started to pop, I pulled out my phone and dialed Lucas.

He answered on the second ring, his voice warm but surprised. "Hey, Jess, is everything okay? Is Lily okay? Are you ready for Santa?"

I cut him off before he could keep going. "Everything's fine. Lily's great, watching her movie, all set for Santa. But I did want to ask you something—and it's totally okay if you say no because I know this is super last minute."

"Okay," he said cautiously.

I hesitated for just a moment. "I was wondering if I could bring Will tomorrow night?"

There was a beat of silence on the other end, and I bit my lip, bracing myself for his response. But before he could say a word, I heard Emily's excited squeal in the background.

"YES! Bring Will! Please bring Will!" she exclaimed.

Lucas laughed, and I could practically hear the smile in his voice. "Well, I guess that settles it."

I let out a breath I hadn't realized I was holding and smiled. "Thank you, Lucas. I know it's last minute, but I think it's important."

"It is," he said, his tone kind. "And Jess... Thank you. For being there for Lily and for everything you've done to help make this work."

His words hit me harder than I expected, and I found myself blinking back a sudden rush of emotion. "Of course," I said softly.

The microwave beeped, breaking the moment, and I turned to grab the popcorn bag. "I'll see you tomorrow," I said.

"See you tomorrow," Lucas replied.

As I walked back into the living room with the freshly popped bag, Lily's eyes lit up.

"Popcorn!" she cheered, holding out her hands eagerly. And I sat beside her, pulling her close and breathing in the smell of those soft curls on her head.

68

Emily

THE MORNING SUNLIGHT filtered through the frosted windows of Sarah's spare bedroom. It was a simple space now—cleared of the usual odds and ends Sarah and Michael kept here. All that remained was a single bed, Sarah's childhood bed, delivered here just for this occasion. The sight of it made my heart swell. Sarah had thought of everything, and this little detail brought memories flooding back, grounding me in a way I hadn't expected.

The night before had been wonderful. Spending the evening with Sarah and Michael was full of laughter and lightness, which was exactly what I needed. Jake and Ainsley had popped by for a short visit, and my parents had, too, and we had exchanged Christmas gifts. Sarah had given me a blue handkerchief that she had worn on her wedding day, a gift from my own mother—my 'something blue'. And my mom had given me a pearl necklace that she had worn on her wedding day—my 'something borrowed'. And Ainsley, of all people, had brought a small tea set that her mom had sent her from England. She had made a point of making all of us tea—this was my 'something old'. And Lucas had coordinated with Sarah for me to open a small jewelry box containing a new pair of diamond earrings—my 'something new'. It had been such an amazing and thoughtful evening, and I was full of blessings.

But now it was just Sarah and me in the room, the quiet anticipation of the day settling around us as we prepared for the wedding.

My gown was simple, a fit-and-flare style with long sleeves to combat the December cold. It wasn't over the top but felt timeless—just like I'd wanted. As Sarah helped me fasten the last button at the nape of my neck, I caught a glimpse of myself in the mirror. My blonde hair, pinned back in soft waves, framed my face. The gray that had started sneaking in years ago was hidden, thanks to my loyal visits to the stylist. I looked... happy.

"Mom, you look beautiful," Sarah said, stepping back to admire me. Her emerald green dress was stunning, the rich color highlighting her fair skin and making her blue eyes pop. She looked absolutely radiant, and I couldn't help but smile.

"You're the one glowing," I said, reaching for her hand. "That dress was made for you."

She laughed softly, shaking her head. "Stop. This is your day."

Across the hall, Michael's quiet expletives filtered into the room, pulling both of our gazes toward the door.

I raised an eyebrow. "I think he's losing the battle with his tie."

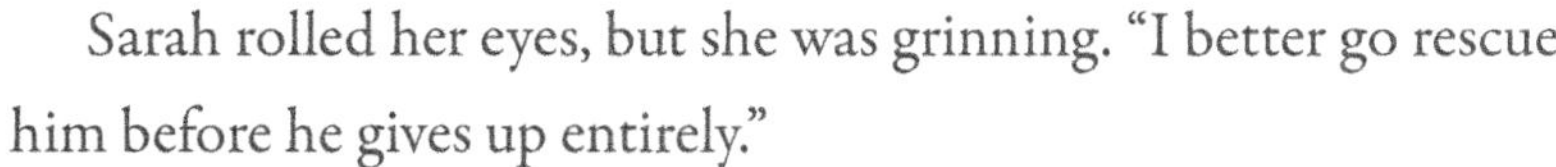

Sarah rolled her eyes, but she was grinning. "I better go rescue him before he gives up entirely."

"No," I said, stepping toward the door. "Let me."

The hardwood in the hallway was filled with the soft sound of my gown brushing the floor as I crossed to their bedroom. Michael stood before the mirror, muttering under his breath as he wrestled with the silk tie.

"Need a hand?" I asked, leaning against the doorframe.

His head whipped around, and his eyes widened as he took me in. "Emily," he said, letting the tie fall from his hands. "You look stunning."

I smiled and stepped forward, picking up the tie. "Let me."

I quickly tied it, my hands moving from muscle memory honed over years of helping Andrew and then Lucas with their ties. When I finished, I smoothed it down against his shirt.

"Better now?" I asked, laughing softly.

Michael grinned, leaning down to press a kiss to the back of my hand. "Much better. Thank you."

"Of course," I said, stepping back. "Now, no more cursing. It's a wedding day, after all."

Sarah joined us a moment later, her arms full of coats and scarves. "Ready?" she asked, looking between us.

I nodded, my heart thudding with a mix of nerves and excitement. "Ready."

The three of us made our way to the car, Michael holding the door open for us before sliding into the driver's seat. The air outside was crisp, our breaths visible in the cold. But inside the car, the warmth of anticipation filled the space.

As we drove to the venue, I watched the snow-dusted streets of this town I'd called home for so long. The familiarity of it all wrapped around me like a favorite blanket. But today wasn't just another day in this town—it was the beginning of something new.

Today, I would be marrying Lucas.

69

Sarah

THE ROOM WAS WARM with the glow of candlelight, and the snow outside cast a soft shimmer through the venue's tall windows. I stood at the front, waiting for my mother to appear at the other end of the aisle.

The music shifted to a lovely tune by Train aptly named Marry Me, and every head turned as she rounded the corner and began her walk down the aisle. Lucas's eyes lit up the moment he saw her, and I felt my throat tighten. His expression said everything—this wasn't just a wedding. This was love, deep and real, the kind that some people never find.

As she reached him, Lucas took her hand, helping her step into place. I saw his thumb brush across hers in a small, tender gesture that nearly undid me.

When it was time for the vows, I stood at my mother's side, her bouquet combined in my hands with my own, trying to absorb every word. Her voice was soft but steady as she spoke to Lucas, telling him how he had brought light and laughter back into her life. She told him she hadn't been looking for love, but he had found her anyway, reminding her that love doesn't follow plans or timetables—it simply arrives.

Lucas,

From the moment we met, you saw me—not just the pieces of my past or the chaos I carried but all of me. You've been my anchor in life's storms and my greatest supporter in life's joys.

You've shown me what it means to trust again, to love fully, and to build something new and beautiful. With you, I've found not just a partner but a teammate, a confidant, and my truest friend.

I promise to stand beside you, to weather whatever comes our way, and to celebrate every victory, big or small. I promise to love you with all that I am, to cherish the life we're building together, and to honor the family we've become.

Today, I take your hand, not just as your wife, but as your partner in all things, for all the days to come. I love you, Lucas, now and always.

And Lucas? His vows left the room silent, save for the occasional sniffle. He spoke about how he'd never thought he'd find someone who understood him, who could walk alongside him as a partner in every sense of the word. He promised to love my mother with all he had, protect her, laugh with her, and hold her hand through every step of their lives together.

Emily,

I never thought I'd find someone who truly understood me, someone who could walk alongside me as a partner in every sense of the word. And then you came into my life, and everything changed. You didn't just see me—you saw the man I wanted to be, the man I could be with you by my side.

You have this incredible way of making life fuller, richer, and more meaningful. You've brought laughter into my days, peace into my nights, and a love into my heart that I didn't think was possible.

I promise to love you with all that I have, to protect you, to support you, and to hold your hand through every step of our journey together. I promise to listen, to laugh, and to never stop growing with you.

And as we build this life together, I promise to cherish the family we're creating—Lily, you, and me—a team that will take on whatever comes our way.

Emily, you are my home, my heart, and my forever. I love you. Today, tomorrow, and always.

I bit my lip, fighting the tears that threatened to spill. These weren't just words—they spoke volumes about everything they'd been through, even before finding each other, and to the love they'd chosen to build despite the challenges.

When the judge pronounced them "wife and husband," the intentional switch in phrasing caught everyone off guard. But quickly, the room erupted in laughter, and even my mom couldn't help but chuckle as Lucas pulled her into his arms and kissed her.

It wasn't a polite, restrained kiss. Oh no, this was a full-on, sweep-you-off-your-feet kind of kiss. I didn't think people their age could kiss like that, but clearly, I was wrong. The whole room cheered, and my mom's face was flushed as they broke apart, laughing together.

Hand in hand, they turned and walked back down the aisle. My mom, ever the playful spirit, tossed her bouquet high behind her as she went. It soared through the air, and of all people, it landed squarely in Jessica's lap.

Jessica looked up, startled, her eyes wide as she clutched the bouquet. Will, sitting beside her, burst out laughing. "Someday," he said with a grin.

Jessica tilted her head toward him, a small smile playing on her lips. "Yes, maybe someday," she whispered back.

The reception was everything my mom and Lucas had hoped for—small, intimate, and full of love. There was laughter and dancing, and Lily's giggles were a constant background melody as she flitted between the guests, Olivia chasing her close behind.

As the night wore on, I caught up in the happiness filling the room. It was infectious, the kind of joy that reminded you how good life could be.

Near the end of the evening, a slow song began to play. My mom stood off to the side, watching Lucas twirl Lily around the dance floor, her face glowing with happiness.

I walked over and took her hand. "Dance with me?"

She smiled and nodded, letting me lead her to the center of the room. We swayed together, the music soft and steady around us.

Leaning in, I whispered in her ear, "Mom, I love you. And… you're going to be a grandma."

She pulled back slightly, her eyes wide as they searched mine. "What?"

I nodded, a smile spreading across my face. "Michael and I are having a baby."

Her hands flew to her mouth, tears immediately brimming in her eyes. "Sarah," she breathed, pulling me into a tight hug. "Oh my God. You've just made this day even more perfect."

We held each other close, and I couldn't help but think how far we'd come—all of us. This was a new beginning, not just for her and Lucas but for our whole family.

70

Jake

I STOOD IN LUCAS'S KITCHEN, sipping a cup of coffee he'd brewed while he fussed with his tie in the mirror above the counter. They had a long day ahead and would need the caffeine boost. "Does this look right?" he asked, glancing at me for reassurance.

"It's fine," I said, stepping closer to straighten it. "You'd think an architect would be better with details like this."

He smirked. "Not when it comes to ties. Never been my strong suit."

Lucas looked sharp in his dark suit, but there was a nervous energy about him that I wasn't used to seeing. It was strange to see him so rattled. I wondered if my mom had the same jittery excitement wherever she was, getting ready with Sarah—at Sarah's house, I think? All I knew was where I needed to be and when.

When I thought back to when my mom and Lucas first started dating, I couldn't help but marvel at how far we'd come. Back then, I'd been guarded, skeptical even. Lucas had seemed like a decent guy, but I wasn't ready to let someone into our lives—not like that. Mom had been through so much with the divorce, and I'd been protective, maybe even a little too much.

Then came Lucas's heart attack, a moment that scared all of us. It had been terrifying to see someone who had become such a steady presence in our lives suddenly so vulnerable. And those seven weeks after Christmas, when Mom had shut him out entirely? I still wasn't sure how they had managed to piece things back together, but they had. And now, here we were, on his wedding day. On Mom's wedding day.

"Ready to go?" Lucas asked.

I snapped myself out of my thoughts. "Yeah, let me grab my coat."

The drive to the venue was quiet. Lucas seemed lost in his thoughts, so I didn't push him to talk. Instead, I used the time to reflect.

These past five or so years had been a whirlwind. Watching Mom rebuild her life after the divorce was something I hadn't fully appreciated until now. Starting over isn't easy. It's painful, messy, and full of lessons you don't think you need—lessons you'd never ask for.

I thought about the pain Mom must have felt when everything with Dad fell apart. The courage it took for her to step into a new relationship. The patience it must have required to blend her life with Lucas's and, by extension, Lily's. It wasn't just about her finding love again—it was about creating a new way of life that worked for everyone involved.

And yet, here she was. Happy. In love. Glowing in a way I hadn't seen in years.

"You're awfully quiet," Lucas said, glancing over at me as we pulled into the venue's lot

"Just thinking," I admitted.

"About?"

"About how far you two have come," I said honestly. "I mean, it's been a lot. For all of us. But seeing her happy... seeing you happy... It's good. It's really good."

Lucas nodded, a small smile tugging at the corners of his mouth. "She's amazing, isn't she?"

"She is," I agreed. "And so are you. But don't let that go to your head."

He laughed, the tension in his shoulders easing slightly. "Noted."

The ceremony was beautiful, simple yet full of meaning. Standing beside Lucas as he vowed to love and protect my mom for the rest of his life was something I hadn't anticipated being so emotional. But it was, and I couldn't help but let a few tears fall from my eyes.

Later that night, as the reception wound down, I stood off to the side, watching Mom and Lucas sway to a slow song. She rested her head on his shoulder, and he held her like she was the most precious thing in the world.

I wasn't a man of faith by any stretch, but I closed my eyes and sent up a small prayer at that moment.

Please, God, watch over her. Keep her safe. Love her. Protect her. Always.

When I opened my eyes, Ainsley was standing beside me, her hand slipping into mine.

"She looks happy," Ainsley said softly, her gaze fixed on my mom and Lucas.

"She is," I replied, squeezing her hand. "And I couldn't ask for anything more."

Everything felt exactly as it should for the first time in a long time.

71

Lucas

THE HOUSE WAS MOSTLY QUIET, just with those typical house noises blending into the background—the day had been long but perfect in ways I hadn't dared to imagine. Emily was asleep beside me, her breathing steady, her hair spread across the pillow like a golden halo. My wife. I still couldn't believe it.

Wife.

The word meant more than I had expected. It wasn't heavy, though. It was grounding, steadying like the roots of a tree digging deep into the soil. It was a promise made and a promise kept. And as I lay there, staring at the ceiling, my heart was full.

Today had been a whirlwind of emotions. Watching Emily walk down the aisle, glowing like she'd just stepped out of one of those cheesy Hallmark Christmas movies she loved so much, had taken my breath away. For a moment, it felt like the world had stopped turning. And when she reached me, her hands trembling slightly in mine, I knew—there was no turning back. Not that I wanted to.

The ceremony had been beautiful, intimate, everything we'd envisioned. Sarah stood by Emily's side, expressive with pride and a glow that I hadn't noticed in her before, and Jake at mine, looking sharp and strong in his suit. Ainsley had caught my eye during the vows, giving me a subtle thumbs-up. And Lily—oh, Lily. She'd twirled her way down the aisle, her flower girl dress billowing around her like a princess in a fairy tale.

But even with all that joy, there had been a slight pang of sadness. My dad wasn't there. Peter wasn't there. It was hard not to feel their absence, but both had found their own ways to reach out.

Peter, always the elusive one, surprised me with a video call earlier in the day. Seeing his face on my phone screen was a shock, but it was a good one. He'd smiled that easy, lopsided grin, congratulating me and telling me how happy he was for Emily and me.

"I'll be back stateside in March," he'd said, his voice crackling slightly over the connection. "Standing in for a pastor on sabbatical at a church in St. Paul for six months. We'll catch up then."

I couldn't remember the last time I'd seen him in person, and the thought of having him close again made my heart ache in the best way.

And then there was Dad. Ever the man of gestures rather than words, he'd sent a card. Inside, a simple note: "Congratulations, son. I'm proud of you. Love, Dad." And tucked alongside it was a check—a generous one.

Emily and I had already decided we'd use it to upgrade our flights to first class whenever we got around to planning that honeymoon. Maybe this summer. Maybe next. It didn't matter, really. I didn't need a fancy trip or tropical beaches. All I needed was her.

Because now she was mine, and I was hers.

Life felt precisely the way it was supposed to be.

I turned to look at Emily, her lips slightly parted in sleep, the faintest hint of a smile still lingering on her face. She looked so peaceful, so content.

And then there was Lily. My sweet, fiery Lily. She'd charmed everyone today, of course. Tossing flower petals with dramatic flair and later stealing the dance floor during the reception. She'd even taken Emily's hand at one point, twirling her around until they were both laughing so hard they could barely stand.

Emily and Lily—the two true loves of my life.

I'd gained an extended family. Sarah and Jake are different, but both are fiercely loyal and loving. Michael, who'd welcomed me into their family with open arms and dry humor.

I was blessed beyond measure.

I closed my eyes, letting the day's events wash over me again. The vows, the laughter, the warmth of everyone we loved gathered in one room.

Tomorrow, life would continue, and the world would keep turning. But tonight, in this quiet moment, everything was exactly as it should be.

Emily stirred beside me, murmuring something unintelligible in her sleep. I brushed a strand of hair from her face, pressing a soft kiss to her temple.

"Goodnight, Mrs. Nicholau," I whispered, smiling to myself.

And for the first time in a long time, I felt whole.

Epilogue

Lily

DADDY'S SUV WAS PACKED with coolers, bags, and baskets, and Emily and Daddy were busy unloading it all. But I wasn't helping. I was too busy staring up—not at the sky. I was looking at the treehouse.

It was huge. Like, really huge. Bigger than any treehouse I'd ever seen and way cooler than the one in that cartoon I watch sometimes. It was my Daddy's treehouse. Well, not his because Daddy said it belonged to Mr. and Mrs. Wilson. But he had built it. Okay, maybe he didn't hammer the nails or stuff like that, but he made the plans and told the builders what to do.

"It's like it floats in the air," I whispered to no one, even though I could see that most of it was held up by the trees and some really big beams underneath. The spiral staircase in the middle was my favorite part. It started at the ground and wound all the way up to this balcony with walkways that went to three front doors.

We were staying in the middle house. Daddy said it was the biggest one, with two bedrooms, a bathroom, and a tiny kitchen. I couldn't wait to see it.

Daddy pulled a basket of my Barbies and some of my stuffies out of the back of the car. He had even packed my Switch in its carrying case. But as I looked around the property, I saw the big swing set in the distance and a swimming pool on the other side. I knew there would be plenty to do, even without my toys.

I should've been running up the spiral stairs by now, but I wasn't ready. Not yet. Instead, I walked over to Emily.

She was standing next to the car, pushing the button to close the back. I tugged on her hand, and when she looked down at me, I pulled her closer so I could whisper.

"I love you, Emily," I said softly. "Will you go to the treehouse with me?"

Her face lit up, the way it always does when I say something she likes. She bent down and kissed the top of my head, then held out her hand.

"Of course I will, Lily," she said, smiling.

And with that, we walked together toward the spiral staircase, ready to explore the treehouse that Daddy built.

Afterword

Emily

Dear Lily,

Today is a very special day for your daddy and me. It's the day we promised to be together forever, as partners and a family. And you, Lily, are one of the biggest reasons today feels so perfect.

You might not remember this when you're older, but there was a time when I wasn't sure I belonged in your life. A time when I let my fears get the better of me. I wrote you a letter back then—one that I never gave you. It was a letter filled with love and apologies, but also with confusion. I didn't understand what you were trying to tell me with your questions, and I didn't trust myself enough to handle things the way I should have.

I thought your questions—like asking who your mommy would marry if I married your daddy—meant that I shouldn't be there. That maybe you needed things to stay the way they were without me. But now I understand your questions weren't meant to keep me away. They came from a place of curiosity, from a little girl trying to figure out her world as it changed around her.

Lily, your world has changed so much in such a short amount of time, and I know that hasn't always been easy. You've had to learn how to live in two homes instead of one, and you've watched your mommy and daddy find their way forward in separate lives. But through it all, you've been surrounded by so much love. Your mommy loves you fiercely, and your daddy does too. And now, I get to love you, as well.

When I first met your daddy, he told me about you. Even before I met you, I could see how much you meant to him. You're the reason his eyes light up when he talks, and he tries so hard to make life fun and full of adventure. I didn't just fall in love with him—I fell in love with the way he loves you.

Being a part of your life has taught me so much, Lily. I've learned that love isn't about replacing anyone or filling a gap. Love is about adding to what's already there, improving the good things. I'm not your mommy, and I never will be. But I am someone who will always cheer for you, always listen to you, and always care about you.

Today, on my wedding day, I'm giving you this letter because I want you to know how important you are to me. I want you to know I'm here for you—not just as your daddy's wife but as someone who loves you for who you are. I hope this letter is something you can keep, something your mommy can read to you whenever you want to hear it.

You've made me laugh more times than I can count, Lily. You've shown me how to see the world through a child's bright, curious eyes. You've taught me patience and joy and reminded me that it's okay to ask questions—even the hard ones.

Thank you for being you, Lily. Thank you for welcoming me into your life in your own way and for letting me be a part of your journey.

With all my love,

Emily

Acknowledgements

I feared writing this book when I planned to sit down and write it. After writing a memoir and my first nonfiction book, writing a fiction book felt a bit out of the ordinary. While I had written many fiction stories in my youth, I had never envisioned myself as a fiction writer.

Yet, as I thought through the characters and mapped out who they were and how they would fit into this story, the pieces started coming together. The story practically told itself. Perhaps most surprising to me is that this story didn't go the way I had planned it to. While I won't divulge the details because I'll save that original storyline for one I may work through in the future, I think this story went in the direction it needed to go.

Though some of this book is based on my own story, it's important to understand that the majority is fictionalized in the way a true story should be. But in its foundation, I hope my readers will see the real struggle for those who experience a divorce and start over, how it affects everyone in its wake, and how all those people need to find a new path forward.

While this story has a happy ending, I know many do not. For those struggling with the aftermath of their own relationships' demise, I feel you. I get you. And I hope this story can give you some hope because a brighter future is always there if you are willing to reach out and grab it.

With that, I have so many people to thank. I have been so fortunate to meet and get to know hundreds of people throughout my life, all of whom have had some type of impact that helped me become who I am. So, I apologize right now if I missed calling you out here. Please know that I am thankful for the role that you played and for being a presence in my life.

To that end, I have to start by thanking my family, especially my husband, Scott, whom I love so very much. You are my future and second chance at happiness, and I am so grateful for this life we are building together.

To my children, Cate and Zach, wow, I continue to be amazed at the two of you each and every day. Watching you become who you are has been the greatest joy of my life.

To my son-in-law, Nathan, thank you for being you and for the love you have brought into our family. I am so fortunate to call you my son-in-law.

To my own stepdaughter, Faith, remember that you are the one I choose to love. You are a choice, and I wouldn't have it any other way. Your infectious giggles and hugs bring so much joy to my life.

To my mom, dad, and sister, thank you for the childhood you provided and all the life experiences you gave me along the way. I am so fortunate to have grown up in our family, with every joy and challenge that came to us along the journey. And thank you for the support you have shown me in these recent years as I have navigated the harsh circumstances that life threw my way.

To my best friend, Kirsten, you continue to be my best person. I love you more than words can ever express, and that's something to say from someone who claims to be a writer.

To the Classy Bs: I've thanked you before, and I thank you again. How can one woman be so lucky to have a dozen or so friends there for her whenever she needs them? I only hope I am as good a friend to all of you as you have been.

To Missy, Shelley, Jackie, Erin, Robin, Karen, and all those other ladies who tolerate me clicking away on my keyboard writing instead of crafting on our weekend getaways: Thank you. I so enjoy our weekends away, gossiping about life and catching up on everyone's families. And I am thankful to each of you for being you and always being there.

To my neighbors, Jennie, Aimee, and Kirsten, thank you for welcoming me into this neighborhood when Scott and I were first creating this life together. Thank you for being there for those walks, those wine nights, and even for a good cry here and there.

To my extended family, the Schreibers, thank you for welcoming me and my children into your lives and supporting Scott and me as we have created this new life together. I love you all and am so grateful.

Last but definitely not least, thank you to the team at Fox Pointe Publishing. Thank you for helping me through this third book, which, who knows, may turn into a fourth and fifth. Kiersten, thank you for your leadership, guidance, and, most importantly, your belief in me and for helping me share my thoughts with the world.

To Scotty, thank you for designing the most amazing book covers that help reflect who I am and the stories I have to tell. Your covers are inspiring, and I am so appreciative of everything you do to bring my stories to life.

About the Author

Ann Schreiber is an accomplished freelance copywriter, blogger, and owner of 'Copywriting For You.' She has been in the marketing and sales business for over 25 years and is passionate about business-focused writing.

She released her first book, *Perseverance. Reinvention.*, in 2024. Her second book, *The Top 10 Mistakes I Made My First Year as a Copywriter*, was released in March 2025 and chronicles the mistakes she made during her first year as a small business owner in copywriting and content writing.

Ann received her bachelor's degree in English communications from the University of Minnesota and her master's degree in business communication from the University of St. Thomas. She has two adult children and remarried in February 2023. She is now blessed with a wonderful husband and young stepdaughter as well.

Ann enjoys reading when she isn't busy typing away on her laptop for her clients or for fun. Her favorite authors include Colleen Hoover, Jodi Picoult, and Kristin Hannah. Ann also enjoys spending time outdoors, working out on the Peloton, and taking her son's Basset Hound for daily walks.